# JIM MORGAN AND THE SEVEN SINS

# JIM MORGAN AND THE SEVEN SINS

BHARAT MADAN

BOOKSWAGON

**Jim Morgan and the Seven Sins**

***Edition 2018***


**Published by**
**Bookswagon**
**www.bookswagon.com**
**An Imprint of**
SR Ecommerce Factory Pvt. Ltd.
2/14, Ground Floor Ansari Road, Daryaganj,
New Delhi–110002, India.

**customerservice@bookswagon.com**
Ph.: 01141521153, 40159253

**Ordering Information :** Visit our website **www.bookswagon.com**

Printed at
*Radha Press, Site 4, Sahibabad (U.P)*

**For you Mom and Dad**

Thank you for believing in me and my work

Thank you Mudrika, Vanshika, Samridhi and Rupal for supporting me in my amazing journey. Nikhil, Shikhar, Naman without you guys I wouldn't be an author. Not to forget Srini. Navneet, Niraj and Rahul, you guys pushed me when I needed it. Sumit special thanks to you.

# Chapter 1

The pages of the novel blew in the usual cool morning breeze. It made my pen roll down the table. I made to my study, but the soporific spell of the morning did not leave me. As I sat down, I began pinching the bridge of my nose but it didn't seem to help me open my eyes.

'Sebastian… Sebastian!' I called out loud. Listening to my agitated voice, he jumped from his seat in the kitchen, stood on tiptoes and swiftly entered the second story of the mansion. He stood at the threshold of my study, looking alarmed. He finally plucked up enough courage to ask, 'Yes sir?'

'I told you not to keep all these bills on my desk. Where is that goddamn pen?' I shouted. 'And why is my coffee not on the table?' My anger made him turn abruptly and walk out briskly. I got out of my seat, throwing my chair backwards. 'Why do all the numbskulls have to land up as my domestic help?' I muttered to myself and went inside the bathroom. I splashed some water on my face. The signs of slumber and inflammation in my eyes faded away in the reflection in the mirror. When I came back to my desk, I found that my freshly brewed black coffee was kept at its designated place.

My pen lay on top of the novel. I sat again, and then lifted my third bestseller. I got fixated on the title again. 'Killed by the Building,' I said. Even though I authored the book, the name still struck me as peculiar.

The morning was real, yet the rarest I had seen. It seemed like things that were about to unfold. A slight feeling of strangeness crept over me. The moment knocked on the doors of my brain, announcing the arrival of someone who said he would come, but in time. It was like déjà vu.

'I have been here before. It is exactly like the morning I encountered twenty years ago: a similar temperature, a cool breeze flowing through the open window, the deadly silence and the stillness of the atmosphere!' I looked out of the window and went on with my life, with the exception of those white birds sitting on the branches of my Eastern Redbug Tree in my veranda. Anxiety and apprehension ran through the fabric of my being. I dashed out of the room, crashing the novel against the coffee mug in my negligence, rendering it to bathe in the liquid darkness. I hastened to the center of the garden where I encountered him the last time. I looked around vigorously: I was all by myself. I ran to every nook and corner of the bungalow to meet my creator. Sebastian saw me rush past but didn't have the guts to ask me after being reprimanded in the morning. I came back to the table. My book wasn't there.

'Is he here again?' I asked myself. 'Are you with me?' my mind asked, loudly.

'I've always been with you Jim, how can you forget that?' A familiar voice reached my ears. I turned around. When I saw him stand before me, I was riveted to the ground. 'I've been watching over you.'

My mouth opened after a struggle, for seconds, to gather my faculties. I finally spoke, 'God!'

It was him! God was back again, in my life. I didn't know how to respond. We exchanged glances silently. He behaved like a spectator, and I, like a witness. Someone banged the door open and came rushing inside.

'Jim, you can't keep missing deadlines like this! I can't stall the publisher forever. If this keeps up, your writing days will be history!' Although my subconscious registered an unexpected visitor's arrival and the dissatisfying words she bawled at me, God had my undivided attention trapped on his figure. So, my ignorance of her entrance, reached her.

'Jim! Look at me. I am talking to you. At least answer me!' She looked at my face. It was still fixated on God's mature but playful face. It seemed impossible to me to hide the effect that witnessing God's image had on my face. The overwhelmed expressions were visible to her but God was visible only to me.

'What's wrong with you?' She tried to break my gaze. But, she couldn't. I felt a vacuum in my ears. Her words reached me, but my mind rejected her words. All I could focus on was the visual in front of me.

'You know what the laughable part is?' She resumed. My peripheral vision continued to subconsciously register her actions. Her hands went into her pockets. She assumed a disapproving expression on her face. 'You don't care, or, you don't show that you care. That leaves us, your friends, to wonder why we even…' She shrugged and sliced her hand in the air. Without saying anything more, she left. God still wasn't giving me the words to end my sensation. My brain was numbed by the fear of facing the ghost of my past again.

'It has been a long time, hasn't it?'

'Twenty years! How can anyone forget God's previous visit?' I thought, and he read it.

'I can read your thoughts, Jim! I'm God. Now, I suggest you break your silence.' He soothed my sensations somehow. 'Would you not like to welcome me?'

'I need time, I need some more time,' I said with some hesitation.

'You weren't prepared, then. You aren't prepared now. I hate to break it to you, Jim. I don't like to be the bearer of bad news. You just ran out of time. You must pay for the sins you committed.'

'What sins are you talking about, God?'

'You've always been acquainted with them, but you still don't accept it. You've felt it throughout your life. Every morning, you have these whispers that revive the terrible nights when you had trouble sleeping. Every morning, your mind returns to these awful nightmares, where you see someone screaming, someone crying and someone dying.' On hearing this, the hair on my hands rose. Goosebumps rose on all parts of my body. 'You know you did something wrong but you don't know what it was and when you did it. What I told you was…' There was a flashback of a young and vibrant twenty-year-old Jim. That was when I saw God for the first time. He told me back then, 'Sins of the past shall haunt your existence. Misdeeds must be paid for and events will unfold not now, but in a while from now. Enjoy while you can. I will accept your request to delay consequences, but remember this. They will reach your life. You shall be delivered.'

God, in the present, said, 'You know what I talk about and you still act like you are unaware. I know as much as you that a life of seclusion was also a result of your…'

I interjected, 'The sins I committed? The ones I am not aware of! How could I be familiar with them anyway? How would I know of the things that I did in my past life?' God's look pointed out that nothing could prevent the misfortunes that were heading my way. I understood that rather unwillingly.

'You look terrified. Are you sure that I'm God and not the devil?' Indeed, I was terrified to the bone. Not because of him, but because it was time for me to pay for my past life sins. Humans are afraid of things that are unknown. In my case, I had committed seven sins. Not one, but seven deadly sins. My intelligence speculated that I could be banished to hell for eternal suffering, but he said something else that surprised me.

'No no! Jim. I'm not here to banish you to the flamed halls of hell. That concept is the brainchild of human beings. I created this world for you to engage in work that delivers you to the path of spirituality. You take birth and suffer hardships in life till you do enough pious deeds to reach me and eternal bliss.'

The former part of the sentences piqued my interest. 'So you mean to say that…'

'Now, don't be hasty. You are not going to hell. But that doesn't mean you are a free bird in this life.'

I was ashamed to be so naïve and less far sighted to imagine in a split second that I didn't have to pay my penalties. More speculations about the nature of my punishment intruded my mind. There were harsh possibilities for me. I said after a brief pause and some grimness in my tone, 'What must I bear?'

'That's what I don't like about authors! Always thinking ahead of time and beyond all reasoning. Come, let's sit. I am old now and I need to relax!' A white sofa configured in U-shape that spanned my large room appeared at one corner of the room. 'I love conversations. I know you don't really like engaging in them, but I guess my being God is something important!' There was a sarcastic edge to his tone. He was in the center, crossing one leg over the other and resting his hands on them. I sat down, relaxed, but I couldn't help leaning forward. I was still nervous.

'You are anxious to know. I can see that, but I am in no mood to cut to the chase. It has been so long. How are you, Jim? How is the new novel coming along?'

He was God. He knew everything. Why was he asking me all this?

'Because I want to talk to you. Doesn't God deserve a chat with the best writer of this time?' he remarked. That made me partake in the dialogue requested.

'I am stuck! Somewhere…'

'You still have a young mind. The youth these days lack the attribute of perseverance.'

'Oh yes, it makes me angry, disturbed and unhappy, too, when I quit work, because my hands don't move my pen like they used to.'

'They paused during your previous work too, but that didn't stop the writer in you!'

'We both know that I wasn't writing alone.' 'Oh! Really?'

'You were there with me, in my thoughts, supporting me, standing by me when I was working on my books. Even with all the doubts and full stops of the world that stood as obstacles to my uninhibited writing flair, I had you to turn to, just not physically.' My voice fell on the last words, as if I was going to end there. But after drawing a short breath, I continued. 'My pen stopped at times. It wasn't receiving any stimulus from my mind because of a dearth of ideas. But it still moved. The ink didn't stop flowing. It was you, wasn't it? You moved my pen even when the ideas stopped emerging.'

'That's the work of God. I will be there with my children when they remember me. Not in the exact manner or form they expect me to come in, but in the aptness which leads them ultimately to me.'

'What do you mean by 'ultimately leading to you?'' 'Everything starts and ends with me. There will come a time when you will reach me too. Now that I have said this, let me reveal why I am here!' His posture changed. His hands were now open. He uncrossed his legs and got up. My reflexes made me get up as I stood erect. The sofa vanished from my vision. 'I made you aware in our last meeting that you committed sins. You felt the consequences of your actions follow you throughout your life and haunt your existence but they haven't manifested in their true skin. No matter what you did, what usual or unconventional means you adopted to obtain relief, even with the fortune and popularity you amassed, you still find yourself abysmal. There is an air of mystery in your life. You withdrew from the city life to live away in isolation. You've been attempting to run away from this fact but to what point?' He paused and looked out of the window. 'You have seven days left. Find out what you did in your last life and pay off the debt that you have accumulated through your sins.'

'Just seven!' I was in great shock. As I took my first step toward him to double check the number of days left with me, I felt the world around me swirl. Before I could understand my position, I collapsed.

*****

I woke up slowly. My head was on the table. The fog in my eyes blurred the vision of the book that was just inches away from my nose. I lifted myself up and rubbed my eyes to rid them of the blurred vision. I was alone in my study. To confirm this, I gazed around and registered the actuality of the room. Things were precisely as they were before the Almighty arrived. My eyes looked up tiredly, to look at the clock that hung above the door. It was 6:30 AM. Looking at it, my brows furrowed and I frequently closed and opened my eyes to see if I was dreaming. The fog had completely lifted and I checked the time again: it was the same.

How in the world?

My surprise took me back requested to the table. My novel didn't have any coffee stains. Everything was unbelievably normal. I got up, but as I turned around, my legs didn't support the weight of my body and I fell to my knees. I felt like I had been woken up after years of slumber. I tried to remember everything. Suddenly, I saw Noah bang the door open and come rushing inside, 'Jim you can't keep missing deadlines like this! I can't stall the publishers forever. If this keeps up, your writing days…' She saw me on the floor and stopped. I was still dazed by the happenings of the morning. 'What happened to you, Jim?' She quickly came to me and pulled me to my feet. They were still shivering. My voice lowered to almost a whisper for myself, 'Back in time!'

'You look like you've been writing for nights without a break. Haven't you been reading the newspaper?' The daily newspaper didn't reach thirty miles away from the city. I had disconnected myself from information. 'They've listed you as the most intriguing yet mysterious author of the current generation. Aren't you forgetting your promotional spree?' I looked at her, my thoughts half with her and half at God's words. 'I've arranged a session at the Prescott University. Do you want me to finalize the schedule for the afternoon? It shouldn't take more than thirty minutes to reach there with your reckless driving.'

I looked at her with marked cynicism. 'You have led a retreated life for too long but I have managed to publicize your next novel! You're a celebrity and you should know how to act like one!' she said.

'Call me a reluctant celeb…' I pulled myself together. 'Whatever, but your image needs you to be present there. They'll honor you with some writer's award!'

I looked at the shelf behind her, containing more awards than I could care to count. 'Yeah, I need an award now,' I joked.

*****

Two hours later, upon my entrance, people began to applaud. The echo was unusually high, which made me look at the audience that I was about to address. I looked across the hall. It was a full house. Talk about overpopulation! I didn't like too much attention. But what could I do? I had to be under the spotlight in an arrangement exclusively designed for me. The recently constructed 20,000 square feet hall captivated my imagination. Fitted with state- of-the-art chairs, lights, it became more vibrant with the passionate students. Chairperson Prescott and other prominent dignitaries sat with me. The announcer didn't waste a single second after the applause muffled.

'Ladies and gentlemen, we are privileged to have a guest with us. He needs no introduction. He successfully led us into a romantic world with A Long Mile with You. Then, we embraced accepting ourselves the way we are through Alone and Happy. We were put through suspense by Killed by the Building. We've been entangled in solving the mystery of The Mute Witness. We were humored by Witty Mitch. Lastly, we were literally taken into The Thrill of Lying and now...' she raised her hand and pointed in my direction, 'our guest will spill the beans about his next and I've heard that it's a thriller!'

How the heck did she know that?

'Do you want to hear the writer speak about his next?' she energized the crowd. The crowd yelled in chorus 'Yes!' She continued, 'Rumor has it that he has been living away from the bustling city in a peaceful and remote location where his imagination stays uninhibited by man or animal.'

I turned to look at Noah, who sat next to me. I couldn't appear clumsy, so I desisted from opening my mouth. Noah, I'll have a word with you about this. She read my mind and flashed an innocent smile at me. I had to force mine.

The announcer continued, 'I'll make sure to get his autograph for all the lovely ladies present here!' The crowd laughed a little. 'Ladies and gentlemen, put your hands together for the most handsome and magical writer of our time!' I stood up prematurely and gave the crowd another reason to laugh. 'Jim Morgan!' she finished. The Chairman got up to save me from embarrassment, followed by the rest of the members on the table. I went to the announcer. She held my hand without warning. She kept shaking it for many awkward seconds, while telling me how big a fan of mine she was.

I said, 'I know! It is a pleasure. Now, may I?' I turned to the audience and looked back at her. She released her grip very slowly. It was a sensual gesture that sent flirtatious vibes to me. Her look was coquettish. I wasn't habituated to this for a long time but I composed myself. I took the podium and the crowd grew silent.

'Thank you, Monica, for that wonderful introduction. I was too eager to speak to the audience, so I got up like an excited ten-year-old. I also thank the Chairman for making me realize that I'm not that young anymore!' Many in the audience laughed. I resumed, 'So yeah, I am here to talk about my next novel and the inspiration that goaded me to…' The sound of someone's phone ringing erupted. It broke my momentum. A guy somewhere in the middle of the third row from the stage took his phone out and silenced it to avoid embarrassing himself. 'You might as well answer it my friend, it could be your girlfriend. Or else, you will end up like me: separated.' The crowd didn't understand the complexity of my reply. I intended it as a pun but my deep baritone didn't support my intention. The Chairman offered a cover, almost immediately. 'Well that's the spirit of a great man! Calming the students by joking about himself!'

I nodded, feeling a sense of security, and then continued. 'I hope the others here are single. Or, should I expect more calls?' This time, my audience got the joke. 'As I was saying, the inspiration that goaded me to write my next,' I paused to offer a very confident impression of my speech. Only, I had no idea what lie I should feed my fans with. Their eyes were riveted on me. Sadly, my extempore skills deserted me at that very moment. The lack of words made me tense and it gave way to nervousness that surfaced on my face. I prolonged my pause. People at the table started to look at me with confusion, but I only looked at Noah. She moved her lips and I read them as, 'Jim speak up!'

The media kept rolling their cameras and it became clear to me. Nothing was going to save me from a blunder that would be highly publicized for months to come. There was unease among the audience. My eyes began to wander around, looking at several faces that now, out of suspicion, started to discuss the reason for my silence. This unsettled me even more. My body had frozen now. After an unreasonable gap, I finally heard a voice speak three words: 'Comes from you!' Everyone was surprised. Their attention was back at me, again. I was surprised the most because it was my mouth that spoke these words, even though I had no intention of saying them.

'Yes you and everyone who is sitting here. My inspiration comes from you, as you are all connected.

When I look back at my work, I realize that my six novels are also connected. I am trying to find out the connecting dots and I am close to discovering them.' Words continued flowing out of me without my control. That brought a chill in me. 'The book is halfway through. The story is so compelling and thought-provoking that I am still not out of its grasp. I am still under the spell! So, I leave you with words that will sow in you the seeds of curiosity. Can you find the common links inside my novels before I do? That's my next!'

Everyone was pleased to hear that. I spoke words that weren't mine and withdrew two steps away from the podium. That gave everyone a signal, a signal that I had said what I came for. Somehow, it generated an unexpected standing ovation. Then, Noah came and took the podium. She furthered the applause by announcing a once-in-a- lifetime opportunity to have lunch with me. Things turned out far more splendid than expected. I stood silent, as the Chairman drew near me with the others on stage. 'I thought you had an enormous influence on people only through your writing. I was wrong. Your confident tone and wise choice of words impressed me today. Congratulations and thank you for your valuable time!' he said.

We shook hands and I barely managed to stay in control. We were directed by a photographer to assemble for a group photograph. We did that in a matter of seconds. The applause reached amazing levels and photographs were clicked. Having attended hundreds of interviews and conferences, I knew what to do next. I waved my hand in a poised manner to the people. The crowd roared with enthusiasm.

The session was over. We were requested by the Chairperson to proceed for lunch. We walked with them, Noah and I. She began to study me. She deduced that I wasn't able to let the triumph of my speech go down my throat.

'What's the matter Jim? Why the quizzical look?' 'Was it I who spoke all that?'

'I can't say for sure. I haven't seen you speak so well in my life!'

I didn't speak those words! It was my mouth and voice, but it wasn't me speaking.

'You've been acting weird since this morning, Jim. Is everything ok?'

'No… I… mean… ah yeah… Everything's okay!' I hesitated. She didn't seem convinced. How could I convince her when I was in doubt myself?

We had lunch and wine. It was that time of the year when autumn was turning into winter. I savored every drop of the wine, but it did not do much to take my feeling of being unsettled. A gentleman with gigantic specs appeared on my face.

'May Ich have the pleasure of introducing myself to the best writer and bestselling author of New York? I am Nathan Conrad from the Daily Bugle.'

'Do I know you?'

'No sir. I assure you that we are meeting for the first time.'

'Are you a critic?' 'I'm an admirer, sir.'

'Well then, Mr. Nathan Admirer, how may I help you?' 'Forgive me for not standing on ceremony. My eagerness for this meeting made me come to you…' He stood silent for two seconds and then said, '…unannounced. It is a rare opportunity to catch the great writer in person. Many of our readers want to know a lot about you, Mr. Morgan. So I must speak with you for our readers!'

I hope this doesn't take long. 'Yes, you may!'

He pulled out a tiny note from his coat's pocket and a pen from his front pocket to make notes. 'For the last couple of years, you have a reputation of being reclusive. What made you come down here?'

'Noah made me come down here. You must be aware that she is my Public Relations Manager and a good friend. She takes care of things with the publishers and readers for me.'

'How does it feel to be back with the masses?'

'I can't exactly say that I am back, but I guess I too am human and need to socialize.'

'The announcer made a startling revelation that your next is going to be a thriller. People were speculating about your current work and nobody had the slightest clue. How did she get to know your secret?'

'That threw me in a state of bafflement. Like you said, I am reclusive. I haven't shared much with Noah, either. Perhaps, she has hidden cameras fitted inside my room.'

'I can't wonder why a single lady would do that against a single man!' We laughed, although cautiously, at this.

I said, 'But it must have been Noah. She must have sneaked past and gotten a gist of what I am working on. It is hard for Noah to keep things to herself. But I guess she decided that it was time that my readers are fed something!'

'So you and she are close?'

I didn't like hearing that I was linked with anybody, especially Noah. 'Don't even think about it!' I made it clear from my tone that he had crossed a line. But that didn't stop him from advancing further.

'Oh I understand Mr. Morgan. You have been single for a long time now. It is okay to let things loosen up and go with the flow. A lady like her can please a man like you!'

'You filthy reporters have the nerve of saying such crap! Security!' I shouted, looking away from him. 'Who let this man enter?' I turned to the reporter. He had vanished. I looked around and didn't find anyone moving. The members of the board came quickly, hearing my voice.

'What happened, Mr. Morgan? Is everything okay?' a senior member asked.

'I told you I don't want to be interviewed. You still let this mad man come here!'

'Sir, the Chairman's order was to arrange for high profile visitors only. To avoid an unfriendly confrontation with the paparazzi, we closed the entrance to the media fraternity.'

'What? Then who was he?' I asked in confusion. As I watched the startled spectators around me, I considered going back home to bed, hoping to sleep and wake up with all my senses intact. But lucky for me, Noah came to my rescue.

'That's our Jim, always catching the organizers off guard with a silly prank!' Just after she said this, the commotion I created was gone. I watched the apprehension leave face of the organizer. A mixture of anxiety, apprehension, nervousness and a lack of understanding of what actually was happening had settled more in me while the world continued to run at its usual pace. This morning, I had an unexpected visitor that I still refrain from accepting as God. Thirty minutes ago, I had spoken the cleverest words of my life, but they were not my own. Now, I had seen a man who was a ghost to everyone else around me. This was too much for one day!

'Jim, something's not right with you today. You just broadcasted a lousy act so openly; you've never done anything like this before. I'll talk to the Chairman and tell him that a great idea just struck you. So, we must head back!' Noah came up with a reasonable explanation for our early departure.

I didn't wait for Noah. I stepped outside to get some air. The frightening event of the morning came to my mind. It confirmed that the happening had indeed taken place. I had discarded it as a nightmare. As I walked, I realized that the campus was breathtakingly vast. It could absorb three football stadiums put end-to-end. The breadth was

even greater. I stood before a very intriguing creation at the center of the campus. Water spouted in a mélange of rainbow colors from the artistically made fountains. The mist of the fountains covered me pleasantly. I ignored the sign prohibiting anyone from crossing the red line. I wanted to feel the breeze that brought dew on my face. This structure elevated the dignity of the place. I had heard that people hailed the structures of this university as a stunning synergy of traditional materials and modern settings. It was a progressive bridge between old moral values and modern beliefs. This structure, in particular, was most talked about and assumed to stay in vogue for a century to come.

My host, the Chairman, came to receive me with his entourage. It reflected the power of wealth and authority that any founder could exercise over his followers. I sensed that he might be a moderate-to-tough man to initiate a conversation with.

'Do you like my creation?' he asked, as though he was the architect of the breathtaking construction. Simply admitting that I liked it would sound plain and disrespectful. Saying that I disliked it was out of question and unacceptable. I should speak in an artistic way, to truly match the grandeur of the structure. 'Your affinity to the finest details of awe-inspiring structures is inspirational! It is a genuine privilege to be in the company of a great visionary like you who, single-handedly gave birth to the most exquisite…'

The Chairman's brows were raised together. 'Your prowess over words is better than you admit, Mr. Morgan.'

You have no idea how long it took me to articulate these lines in my fourth novel. 'I appreciate your compliment, sir. I will also say that this place, in my humble opinion, is a frozen poetry.' I had also used these words smartly from the description of a place in the same chapter of the same novel. After this, the Chairman went into deep thought of admiration. He held his hand out to shake mine, and gave me his name in person, 'Chairman Prescott.' It fit perfectly, and exerted a surprisingly pressing force on my hand. That surprised me, given the fact that a seventy-year-old powerful man doesn't necessarily have this kind of a grip.

'Jim Morgan!' I responded. After that short meeting, Noah appeared and I thanked the Chairman for the opportunity. We left. I was lost in thought in my car, and let Noah do the driving. I asked her to get down first at her place, and that I would leave after that. After reaching her place, I took the wheel and said goodbye to her. She stood there, on the road watching my car's rear lights depart, till I swerved to the left and went out of her sight.

*****

I was in my Jaguar XJL and drove north, past a church. I tried to clear my mind of the thoughts that put me in a state of discomfiture, but my mind kept flashing images of God from the morning, and of the people in the hall. I wish I had company with me in the passenger's seat. After clearing the city and entering a less used freeway, away from the route that would take me home, I stopped the car, turned to my left and looked at the dull bricks of a large

closed ground. The bricks were a reflection of my life: dull. I moved the car and drove with the brick line. After a minute of driving at a reasonable speed, I pulled my car to a stop. The closed ground had an entry. The entrance was through an archway over which the dedication of 'Victoria's Garden' was engraved. I could not see the end of the quadrangular ground through the gate. I got off the car. I had never noticed this place before, and seeing it now, I wanted to check it out. The moon peered from behind dense clouds. It appeared to be a desolated landscape. The gate was not locked. Once I entered the place, to my left, a tower like building rose above a few trees, a good distance away. I could make out that it was a church, given its traditional façade.

I felt the structure pulling me. I reached it after a few minutes of walking. What appeared like a random building now ran staggeringly wide against the face of the garden. There were two floodlights placed in front of the church to light it. It must have housed artistic paintings that were the epitome of man's creative drawings. It had the finest colored glass that was unreasonably shaped into an enormous star. My eyes couldn't fully absorb the marvel of the now abandoned church, abandoned for reasons unknown. I looked up to see a tall tower having a large bell; it held the rope taut by its weight.

The most revered churches could not challenge the opulence of this church when it must have been open for preachers.

The ground with wild grass, many lifeless trees, the abandoned church and withered leaves filled the surroundings with a cold and unpleasant vibe. While I turned around, my gaze went to a park bench straight ahead.

I don't remember it being there when I entered.

As I walked toward it, I saw a man sitting on it. I walked with longer strides. Something told me that the figure resting on the bench was waiting for me. I advanced toward it. The man had loose legs and hunched shoulders. As I got closer, a revealing fear gripped every movement of my body. There he was, dressed in a jet black three buttoned suit, a black tie, black everything - except the fair face that radiated a cheerful smile. He motioned with his head for me to sit beside him. He had rich and silky hair the color of ebony. His eyes had me locked in them. I swear I could see the entire universe in his unblinking calm eyes. There was something very welcoming about them. My climbing trepidation was no longer with me. This time, I had a comforting aura in his presence. Just when I sat next to him, he got up and said, 'Come, let me show you something.'

'Why'd you ask me to sit if you wanted to walk?' He did not turn back or answer. 'Okay,' I said and followed.

As he walked, he instilled life in the plants with every step he took. The beauty of a dreamlike enchantment that I was fortunately a witness to was indescribable. I followed him up the mounting land and then descended again. As we covered some ground, we approached two trees that stood tall like guards. Their branches touched each other,

and together, they made an arch that appeared like a gateway to heaven. In the center, I saw radiant moonlight shine toward me. Like a fascinated child, I wanted to reach it. I imagined a silver road forming from the gateway, advanced with the shadow lines of the evening moon and melted into it. 'I like coming here!' he said. 'Victoria planted every tree, every flower with so much heart!' The moment my eyes went up a little, I realized that beyond the ground, there was a large lake that looked like a sea.

God said, 'Don't you fall in love listening to the sound of waves falling over the shore, the breeze making the leaves rustle?' I could see the faint dew of the waves fading into the atmosphere.

'This place is magnificent, almost like the majestic gardens of fairy tales that I read in my childhood,' I said.

God turned to me, 'Do you remember exactly what you said this evening?' He demanded specifics, but my mind was gripped by fear at that point. Had it been cool in the slightest, I would have generated those exact words before him.

'I don't remember them.' I was uncomfortable, given the stress I had to put on my brain to recollect them. I had an Eidetic memory but only this time, it left me in the lurch. God turned and began walking back to the bench. 'Keep trying, this is important.'

As I stressed harder, I saw that life around us was turning motionless. Things turned as dead as earlier when he went past them. 'Jim, I want you to focus.'

Yes definitely. I ran my hand across my head. After a few steps I said, 'It had to do something with my books.'

'Keep pushing!'

'There, is some relation among them. A connecting link!'

'Um, Hmm.'

'But I don't see how! Each novel has a different plot and setting. Each is based on different characters and emotions.' I kept racking my brain to draw any part of the sentence so I would use my words to make sense. All the while, I had my right hand on my mouth with the index finger supporting my nose with several rubs just below it. I said to myself, 'You know it, Jim, just say it!' I didn't believe my assurance, though. We walked for long now. Everything fell silent. I could hear my own thoughts. 'Common link,' I said. Then I looked up, 'Common link. There is something that connects all my books.' I was just before the bench then and realized that God was no longer beside me. He stood several yards ahead of me, at the entrance of the park. I took brisk strides toward him. 'What should I do now?'

'What you always make others do!' He smiled and paused briefly before finishing. 'Read!' He stopped at that word. Read. He didn't add anything further.

'Read what?'

'The portals are active. Go now, you must find your sins before it is too late for you.'

An hour later, I was at my study. A Long Mile with You, my first novel, was lying on my table. 'I don't remember keeping it here. Sebastian doesn't touch my things. Maybe God wants me to read this!'

On the first night of the last week of my life, I realized what I had to do. But I didn't know what was going to happen. 'He said the portals are active. What does he want to tell me?' I asked. After an hour of reading the book I came to page 200. 'I don't remember writing this in my book. How did this get published?' I caught the page that wasn't written by me. I realized it was written by God. In an instant, my eyes darkened and the feel of the room changed. Fear planted its seed in me. I felt like I was being teleported.

# Chapter 2

It became startlingly dark everywhere. My book wasn't in my hand. My work table was gone.

Suddenly, I felt my shoes sinking into something. I looked down. I was standing on a muddy road. I lifted my right leg first. 'Where the hell am I? Have I teleported somewhere?' Looking around the place didn't give me much of an answer. New York had never looked darker at midnight. So in the initial moment of my bafflement, I figured that this couldn't be the city. I appeared to be standing at a crossroad of some solitary part of a suburban area. There were no pavements or trees lined up beyond the muddy road. I tried looking some distance away from the crossroad. Given the darkness of the surroundings, it was difficult to stretch my vision to far ahead. The wild bushes that spread around everywhere limited my view to a few yards from the road. I was nowhere near civilization. I looked at the starless sky. Only a dull moon appeared behind my head as a tiny speck in the vast expanse. The place was alone and there wasn't a human eye near me to see me advance in any direction.

Glancing down at the road ahead, I asked myself, 'What do I do now?'

The limited radiance of the moon hid behind the clouds and all of a sudden was visible. It gave me a company, that of my shadow. I looked down at it and adjusted my vision to the blackness of my surrounding. For no wise reason, decided to move in its direction. The eerie calmness of the place started to escalate the fear in my mind. I found it difficult to navigate in the direction that my feet took me. I noticed that there weren't any tire tracks on the road that could reflect a sign of human movement. I had walked for some time now. I realized that the road had become narrow and was taking a sharp left turn up ahead. The wild green became dense and terrifying as I walked in the middle of nowhere. A creepy sensation began to take shape in me. I felt that someone was watching me from behind the trees and shrubs. A few glowing eyes of ferocious animals appeared from behind the bushes. I became cautious and slowed down. More eyes emerged from a couple of surprisingly short tree branches from my right. The eyes followed me as I proceeded. The sounds of a few nocturnal animals echoed from right behind the bushes. It felt like a signal was given to the others at the turn, who were taking their position, waiting for their prey to arrive at the perfect hunting spot. I wanted it to be just a feeling, nothing more. I was afraid to turn back and become the midnight meal of jungle predators. I was also afraid to continue moving but it didn't make a difference. Something told me to take a chance and keep moving ahead. I had my gaze fixed dead at the turn. I treaded carefully, the turn came and I took it, going past a creepy tree.

My intuition led me further down the road that had, as it occurred to me, no end. For some time, I kept walking. I didn't have the guts to pause for as much as a glance. But eventually, I looked back. Seeing the glowing eyes vanish into the darkness behind me, I breathed a sigh of relief. What I inhaled surprised me. The air, as it felt when it met my nostrils, had no trace of pollution. Finally, some sense of safety had seeped into my brain and I started to inhale as I normally do. It created a familiar feeling: the feeling that I got from living in the outskirts of a city which was industrial or vehicular pollution free.

This place must be located in the outskirts of a city or somewhere in an underdeveloped village.

For the first time, I exhaled smoke from my mouth. I had sensed a drop in temperature earlier, but didn't care to notice much. And now, as I was walking in a less cautious manner, I wrapped my chest with my hands to generate some warmth. Another cloud of smoke came out as I began to breathe somewhat heavy air. About fifteen minutes had passed since my arrival in this no man's land. I was losing hope to get anywhere. My eyes peered at the last point where my vision extended and I finally saw something other than wild nature and its inhabitants.

Is that a house?

My most valuable sight at that hour of the dreary night was that piece of land where I caught sight of this house.

Thank God. My legs were infused with energy and they began to run, although intermittently. This road was dry which was surprising but I didn't care. I wanted to get to the house as fast as I could without making much noise and waking up the creatures.

Soon, I stood at the face of the dilapidated structure. In the first instance, it appeared abandoned but in another, I saw a dim light illuminating a window in the ground floor. Someone is inside. I hadn't imagined, even in my wildest thoughts, that I would find safety and pleasure in the company of a total stranger. I judged that this person in the building must be living a life of voluntary banishment.

I went to the door and thumped it without much force. No one answered. 'Is there anyone inside?' Again, I got no response. Should I break the door and get in? Almost instantly, I heard a few footsteps approaching the door. I withdrew a little. The door opened and a man emerged. He looked like a strong, youthful man and had a surprisingly mature face, but his hunched shoulders seemed to tell another story. I looked down at his hand and immediately noticed a wine glass. It wasn't empty. He looked at me in the eye. I tried to face the situation bravely but his indifferent stare affected me. I didn't say first and neither did he. The wind whispered and was louder than us. He started to scan me and while he did, I found in him no desire to live, something that I had never before encountered in anyone I met. Though the man seemed under the spell of intoxication, his eyes made out that I was from a different place given my modern attire and I needed shelter.

'What do you want?' he asked in a gruff tone and transferred a foul smell of alcohol while looking sharply at me this time. I didn't think about a satisfying and judicious response.

'Ah, sir…' I didn't know what to say. He relaxed. Somehow my lack of response turned his flush face to a calm shade. He turned and didn't care to gesture toward the inside as a signal for me to get in. Probably a solitary life had made him inhospitable, just like it had made me. I thought that he was going to close the door on my face. Then, as I was about to call him, he said, 'Come in, it is not safe out there.' He went in, leaving the door open for me. I wasn't expecting him to say that. I raised my head in disbelief and my gaze reached the empty sky. Without delay, I dared to go in. But, I stopped short. There were scattered newspapers lying almost everywhere on the floor. It was bright enough inside for me to understand the heading of one of the newspapers with a cursory glance: Stephen goes bankrupt after factory burns down to ashes. He stepped on it, but I had read the line. He kicked some papers to slide them under the sofa. It looked like he didn't want me to read them.

'I'll get you some water. You may sit but do not touch anything!' he said, using both friendly and hostile words in the same sentence. He didn't wait for a reply, I saw him go inside a darkened room. I was not planning to sit and leave my guard down. I looked around at the walls and objects to gather a good idea of the scope of my security at this place. There weren't many heavy objects he could use to sink into my head. The walls were old. The paintings didn't interest me much. Curiosity led me to rethink the man's identity. Looking at the newspapers lying on the floor again, I assumed this guy was Stephen Malcolm. The engraved letter S that I earlier saw on the door knob made it unmistakable. After having looked around, the place seemed safe enough. I can relax a bit now and hopefully, he will tell me where I am. I was about to ease myself on the sofa but I didn't. It shouldn't take him this long to get water. I moved toward the darkened room assuming that it was the kitchen. I could barely see what was inside. The flicker of a candle wasn't illuminating enough. Just a dim light made its way inside the room through the curtains of the only window in that room. It was a bed room. 'Who gets water from the bedroom?' I wondered. I saw a door at the end that was connecting to another room, perhaps the kitchen. I took two steps inside the small room and in the third one I kicked a small object under the bed.

'What on earth was that?'

I dropped down to my knees and started to stare at the broad opening under the bed. I saw a couple of newspapers but something that should not be there caught my interest. I decided to lie on my stomach and slithered underneath it and placed one hand on the dusty floor and stretched the other to reach the object. I exhaled with the effort, making the dust blow ahead of me. Oh God! Why didn't I mind my own business and stay back at the sofa! I pushed my body forward to reach it. That collected a lot of dust on my chest and stomach. Suddenly, loud thumps from the next room startled me and my reflexes kicked in. I tried to get up, cracking my head in the process. 'Ouch!' I said aloud. My head hurt with the collision. I took my hand to the spot and rubbed, forgetting that dust was being rubbed with it. I took the object in my hand. It felt like a pendant with a chain. I put it inside my shirt pocket then pulled myself out.

He watched me as I stood up. He seemed angry. 'I am, I was just…'

'You can have water. After that, leave!' he said. I felt it fit not to argue and instead, do as he said. Forcing a small smile, I went back to the sofa outside the room. He came with me to see that I didn't go elsewhere.

Just when I reached behind the sofa, we heard a heavy fist pounding on the main door. I looked at Stephen if he had a clue as who it could be. The pounding grew heavier making me realize that there wasn't a friendly person on the other side. For a second, it stopped. In the very next second, the door broke. The figure that stood there had kicked it open. It was a man. He came in and drew a revolver from his overcoat, glaring at Stephen, who was almost immobile. I felt a surge in my heartbeat. We were under attack! I gingerly raised my hands in the air without a word, trying not to draw his attention. I turned my eyes to look Stephen. He didn't seem intimidated against the hand that threatened to take away his life from him.

The man brought the gun to Stephen's shoulder level and said, 'My client has a message for you.' The assailant pulled the trigger, the gun roared. I got a jolt from the loud sound but I was frozen. The bullet pierced Stephen's flesh and cracked the shoulder bone. I saw the force take him to the wall. Stephen realized that a bullet was inside him. He felt the searing heat of the bullet and it delivered a strong shock wave. A circle around the bullet hole was framed by his blood he looked at it. Blood gushed out of it. His trembling hand tried reaching his wound. But before it could, he was brought down on his knees and he fell forward on his face. Stephen lay defenseless, on the ground. The man put the gun back inside its place and walked forward. Stephen managed to turn his body up. His breathing slowed dramatically, his face displayed pain but it was peculiar to see his eyes. There was no fear in them. The killer came toward the fallen body and took a dead aim at his head.

'The interest just doubled. We will take what we want with or without you. Next time, my bullet won't miss your head!' The killer had said what he wanted to. He turned. I watched him walk slowly out of the house. There wasn't anything that I could do, he would have shot me. I turned to Stephen and got down on my knees to look at his wound closely and contemplate his chances of survival. I had a weak heart when it came to scenes of blood and violence. I was always repulsed by the sight of blood. It was coming out of his shoulder. It looked like the killer had deliberately shot him there to make him suffer. He was going to be alive, but for not more than an hour.

'This bullet cannot harm me, but the poison will,' he said, still in a bit of shock. 'That was my last drink. It tasted far more bitter than usual,' he said, and smirked. It didn't seem like an expression of regret. 'Anything is better than this life less of respect.'

The man was dying. The uncertainty that lead to this event gripped me. Then and there, I wanted to understand why I had been sent to this time and place. What events had led this man to die like this? How was I connected to all this?

The truth must be passed onto me.

'I may not get you justice but I must know whatever happened to you that resulted in this. Who was that guy?'

Pain was visible on his face and it only increased. I took his hand, placed it on the wound and applied gentle pressure on it. 'Keep the pressure there,' I told him. His eyes began to droop. 'You must focus. Save every ounce of strength you have, to answer me. I must know what happened.' I tried to focus on him more than his wound.

He took a couple of seconds and began to engage in his last conversation. His eyes opened and looked straight up ahead.

'We were four best friends. Mark, Michael, Jason and I. We wanted to do something big in life, live the American dream.' His eyes turned to me. 'The passion for money-making drives a man insane. It consumed the four of us. We started a factory to manufacture tube lights. But, there was no fortune in selling them. Fortune always lay in the road less taken. Our ambitions led us down the wrong one. We began getting involved in some immoral business. I had convinced some very wrong people to issue me heavy loans in cash. Our business began to flourish, but right when things seemed great, something terrible happened. Someone set fire to our factory. Our creditors wanted their money back with interest. We were all bankrupt. It didn't take time for the news to explode everywhere. I spent the last few weeks of my life trying to pay off the debt, but it was too much for me. The value of my property isn't worth even ten percent of what we had borrowed. Initially, they gave me a month's time but then, they grew impatient. I received death threats at home. I had no option but to come to this place, but they found me here as well.'

'You said you were involved in immoral business. Did you do something illegal?'

'Yes, I did. But we had it covered from all sides. There was no way anyone would find where we had our interest.'

'But you attracted enemies. Do you think someone was against you?'

'Not one I can name.'

'Tell me about your partners. Did they ever do something irregular that made you suspicious of them?'

'We worked so rigorously in our working lives. In fact, even after giving my heart and soul to the project, I still feel they were more passionate than I was.' In an instant, he smiled, remembering the hard work he had put in with his partners. That seemed to give him a small reason to forget his pain. 'They came to the premises everyday with renewed zeal. I wondered how they had so much energy.'

'Perhaps they were passionate on the face of it, but had hidden motives.'

'You don't seem to trust people…' I relaxed and leaned back against the wall. 'Men can never be trusted. I think this happened to you since you trusted someone.'

'We shared the same goal of bettering the state by providing cost-effective lights,' he continued.

'But you were the one who had a majority in the business, right?'

He was surprised. 'How do you know that?'

'I read that in one of the headlines in the newspapers out there.'

'What else did you read?'

'Not much. Just that your name is Stephen and that you suffered heavy losses after someone reportedly set fire to your factory. That's what the media has referred to – an unfortunate result of revenge.'

'The media writes anything. They don't have the slightest idea.' His statement reminded me of the nonsense that the media had fabricated about me to make headlines. He was right. The media writes anything. My last correspondence with a reporter, the one invisible to everyone, had been hours ago at the university dinner.

'Do you have the slightest idea who did it?' 'I told you I don't know.'

I took out the pendant from the pocket. 'Does this mean anything to you?' The long chain had the initial 'S' at the end.

His drooping eyes settled on it. His expression turned to one of disgust. It must have brought back the memory of a sour incident. I realized that my question was poor, given his already worsening condition. He pointed at a picture that hung on the wall. Blood gushed from his wound when he did, and he screamed in pain. I saw him suffer slowly, as both, the pain of his wound and the torment of poison, were taking him closer to death. This man had amazing personal strength that kept him engaged with me in the final conversation of his life. I went closer and saw the picture. He was in it, with a lady and two girls. I took it down brought it to him.

'Is this your family?'

He looked down at it. As he saw the picture, I saw peace in his eyes. 'Mia and my kids are safe in Rome now. They cannot be found. Perhaps, that's the only right thing I did in the last couple of years. I knew my end was drawing near but I didn't expect to go like this.'

He was spending the last minutes of his life watching his wife and daughters in the picture he held in his hand. I wanted to know more. I wanted answers, but couldn't ask him more. At the very last minute of his life, his hand lost the strength to lift the picture. It fell out of his grasp. He spoke a couple of silent sentences with his eyes closed. I saw his lips moving before he departed. He must have been praying.

At least he didn't die alone. I straightened his body and walked to the next room to fetch a sheet to cover him. I did what I wanted. I gave him the respect he should have

received but the world hadn't given him. As I covered him, my sight fell on his wound. After his heart had stopped, blood had begun to coagulate. Right before I left his corpse in peace, I put the picture over his heart and sheltered it with his hands- where it truly belonged.

I took a detailed look at the locket. There was a chain and a pendant comprising a blue precious stone. The initial 'S' was carved inside the oval. The shimmer of the piece was spellbinding. I had never seen a stone glitter so brightly. I held it up. Realizing that it was similar to a blue sapphire of the highest quality, I put it in my pocket.

Maybe this will help me find something.

I never wanted to know anyone's secrets. They were too much of a burden to keep. But as I stood over the body and bid farewell to the stranger, I realized that some secrets had been passed onto me and that I had to make use of them for my salvation. I took one last look at him.

'May your soul rest in peace, Mr. Stephen. May your family stay safe and find the courage to live without you, like you intended.' I turned to the exit. My gaze lifted to the broken door. Its hinges were almost out of their places. I proceeded to stand short of the exit. I was defensive and didn't want to take chances with life. I stared out of the door at the darkness covering the road. There was no trace of the hit man, at all.

The coast was clear. I took my first step out when a surprising thought struck me. He didn't even look at me once! It was as if I was not there! Was I visible only to Stephen? How is that even possible?

My intelligence told me that a hit man would not leave evidence behind and definitely not one that could talk. He hadn't looked at me or pointed the gun at me. He didn't even try to intimidate me. Why? My reasoning told me that he should have at least injured me, but he didn't do that, either. I was certain then, that I was present in the time and place only for the victim and not for the killer. But I sought confirmation to strengthen my belief.

I walked out onto the road. I looked in both directions. 'I can't go back where I came from,' I reasoned with myself. 'Perhaps I must keep going ahead.' I turned right and began walking to wherever the road was going to take me. It was still dark. There was no sight of civilization, house or shop, just the usual noises of the nocturnal inhabitants of the jungle. The blackness started growing thicker with every step I took. A sense of fear accompanied with uncertainty of the direction taken now had me in their grip. My steps became smaller. Suddenly, what I saw scared the living daylights out of me. A cloud of blackness began wrapping the road at its mouth. My feet stopped. I took two steps back, but the darkness kept advancing toward me.

'What on earth is happening? I must go back to the house,' I said to myself. I turned around, and was appalled. Darkness was approaching me even from the opposite direction, too. I withdrew again and looked to my right, and then all around me. It was coming from everywhere. I went haywire. Before I could think any further, it was pitch black. Darkness had wrapped me. The gruesome events that I was a witness to were terrible enough. But now, seeing black everywhere with my eyes open was bloodcurdling. I didn't know where to move next. The noise from the forest was now muffled. I felt alone there. I stood there for half-a- minute. Without any comprehension of my surroundings, I began moving blindly through the dark. The Earth under my feet suddenly turned flat. The temperature went up a little. That scared me more.

'What's happening?'

My hands extended forward as I tried to hold onto something. I moved around, without any sense of direction. 'Hello, is there anyone out there?' I called out.

I heard only silence in response. I could hear my breath become heavy and fast. I was scared. I had to do something. Standing was not going to help, so I pushed ahead not knowing whether I would trip over something or hit something. My fingers felt a wall. It was strange, because I had not seen any wall anywhere along the road. I placed my palm flat against it. It is a wall.

It was vaguely familiar. I moved my hand to the left and shifted with my feet to see if there was a door, or if the wall ended somewhere. Three shifts of my feet, and I got hold of an object. It feels like a switch! The pressure of my hand pressed the object. There was light everywhere. The immediate glow dazzled me. I stretched my hands upwards, covering my eyes from the light. As my vision became clear, I saw the wall that I see every day. I turned around to figure out where exactly I was. It looked like my study. I was back!

'Am I really back?' The comfort of my room was not reaching me. I wasn't sure if my eyes were telling me the truth or were telling a big lie. I looked at my hands. There was no blood on them. The table and contents on it were exactly as they were when I was reading. The page that took me to that place was open.

I took the locket out of my pocket and put it on the table. Ruminating over what had happened and how this locket was special, a name struck my head. It was a name that I saw on the gates of the park gate. That's when a familiar voice reached me from behind.

'You're right. It is connected to Victoria Holmes.' I turned.

It was God.

# Chapter 3

It belongs to Victoria Holmes?'

'No Jim, that's not what I meant. S is not Victoria's initial.'

That was common sense and I didn't show any this time. But he said that it was connected to her. 'Am I related to her somehow? Was she connected with Stephen Malcolm?'

'That is something you will have to find out on your own.'

'How do I do that?'

God smiled. 'Now that's something Jonathan will tell you…' he whispered in my ears.

'Jonathan White? My editor? How in the world would he know?' I was confused. Then, it occurred to me that Jonathan was a celebrated reporter before he became my editor. Perhaps he would have written the story of the burnt factory back in his days as a reporter. Maybe he knows something.

'Or maybe he doesn't,' God said and confused me.

'You just said he will tell me something. Now you're saying maybe he doesn't know!'

'Well, there's only one way to find out!'

'I have to meet Jonathan,' I thought. The curious mind of a writer always tries to find alternatives. So did mine. 'Or maybe I can use the book, go back in time and figure this out from Stephen himself, before he died.'

'I am afraid you can't do that Jim. The time portal can only be used once.'

'What?' His answer was a blow to my hope. That meant that I could only use one novel for one round of time travel alone. Five novels remaining translated into five opportunities to travel back in time. The numbers were not in my favor. I became a little demanding now. 'I didn't envision that I'll be sent back in time like this! I don't know where and in which year am I going to be teleported. I don't even know how much time I have to find answers when I am sent back. You are God, you should be helping me.'

'Why do you think I am here? I am giving you a chance. My work is to stand with you when you need me. But you have to fight your battles; I can't win them for you.'

'Just give me something more than what I already know. That'll be really helpful.'

'Make your mind work then, Jim. You will get all that you need to know.'

'What can I think of? Stephen is dead! I don't know his partners, the name of his factory or their whereabouts.

All I know is that he was involved with the wrong people and paid the price with his life. This pendant that I hold, his name, and the date his factory burnt down: that's all I have now.'

'So you know something useful.'

'How will June 2nd, 1976 be useful to me?'

'Youth is always useful, it is up to you how you use it.' 'Stop giving me riddles, you're not helping! I wish this drunken Stephen had put his agility and mind into action.

Ambitious fool that Stephen! He kept drinking and spoiling his youthful days.'

The white sofa appeared again and God relaxed on it. I frowned, unable to understand what he wanted from me. I clenched my teeth, thinking he was having fun at my expense. I moved toward him in anger and then it hit me.

'Wait!' My eyebrows relaxed. I frowned again as I began to ponder on the details. I turned to my table and took a seat. That's where most of my thoughts assembled to form something sensible.

Stephen should have been 25–27 years old when I met him, not more. Young face, strong hair and body all add up. That means, today, on June 2, 2016, he would be 65–67 years old. Assuming that his friends were about the same age as he was, I think that… I got up from the chair and turned to God. 'Bingo!'

'It was about time you started thinking logically,' God said.

'Nothing about the partners was mentioned in the headlines. Well, not that I could read them, but there has to be a possibility that some or all of his partners are alive now. I must find them. Where do I start? They could be anywhere in the world!'

'Perhaps they are still in New York...' he said and disappeared again. His entry and exit had become so unpredictable. It was hard for me to realize whether God was helping me or confusing me with the way he was doing things. At that moment, I felt an immense need for the mystery to unfold. I took my cell phone from the table and started dialing.

*****

'Hello,' he said in an unwelcoming tone.

'The world's quandaries cannot be solved by man alone. Divine grace will show the way,' I said a line he had suggested for my novel, 'The Mute Witness.' It sounded like a password that only White and I knew.

'Jim?' He couldn't believe the identity of the caller. In my entire life, I had never called him myself. I always directed my interactions with him through Noah. Besides, White was still fuzzy from his sleep. At sixty-five, it was natural for his body to take its time to be roused.

'Look son, if you are attempting to play a prank on me, first, it is not the right time, and second, you are messing with the wrong man.'

'John, it really is me!' I realized that my voice was finally familiar to him.

'Jim is that you? It's 3 a.m. Is everything okay?' he asked.

I was momentarily dazed by the sudden illumination.

'You never keep track of time, do you? I need to discuss something very important with you. It is urgent. I'll be there in an hour.'

'Do you want something specific?' White was always to the point. He valued details in everything and asked me a direct question.

'You'll know when I get there. I hope you can make good coffee for the two of us!'

'Is Noah coming along?' 'Nah, just me.'

'Okay, I'll see some….' I hung up before Jonathan could finish.

He put the mobile phone back to its place. Then, he swung his legs off the bed and sat up. He murmured as he frowned, 'He never calls. It must be really important,' and got his body up to look prepared for the unexpected visitor.

Nobody in the world had the nerve to wake him up like this, not even me. Though he did not have a family of his own, and I was not the best son he could ask for, Jonathan had always treated me like I was his own. He learnt to find peace in living alone, and in living without someone to live for. He thought he would have one less thing to worry in life, that way. But he was always fond of Kathryn, my wife. He planned to leave all his wealth to her, for her non- government organization in Los Angeles. A fortune that

would make it run for over a decade without organizing fundraising events or seeking donations.

The modest apartment was located on the twenty-fifth floor of the skyscraper. The three bedroom apartment with minimal furnishings was his formal residence for the last two decades. White preferred a good view of the city from the balcony that gave him the bliss of morning sunshine. Every day, at dawn, the radiance rose from beyond the horizon and entered his room. Since the time when he was a reporter in his young days, he had surrounded his life with a gigantic library containing innumerable books ranging from mythology to science. White's habit of reading five newspapers every morning made him a collector of information. He was widely known for this skill of his. An apartment at Hawthorne Heights, being in the center of New York City, couldn't be afforded by regular city dwellers. The city's rich and intelligent population lived there.

After an hour, his doorbell rang. White slid off his couch and moved toward the door. 'Who is it?' he stood at the door and didn't open it.

'It is Jim.'

The door knob turned and he opened the door for me. 'Jim! Please come in.' The door opened two or three inches, since he had not taken off the security chain from its place.

'Looks like your intelligence is fading with age, John!'

'From where I see it, your sarcasm is increasing with yours,' he replied. I smiled. We always had this habit of teasing each other with our wits. But, he always had the upper hand. I was too good with words; he was too good with responses. Despite my lousy behavior and timing, I went inside. He didn't need to offer me a place to sit. I never stood at ceremony around him. I took the couch and saw a mug of coffee waiting for me on the table. Jonathan was still puzzled. He was eager to know, but let me take my first sip. After that, he asked the first question that was intended to shake off his cobweb of uncertainty. 'So Jim, what brings you here at this lazy hour of the night?'

I was about to bring up the subject. I was troubled, and I saw myself through his eyes. Jonathan would consider me crazy if I told him about God. I preferred the idea of asking him all that I had in mind stating that it was purely for research. I looked down at his feet, uncertain of how to phrase the very first question.

'You clearly look like something's bothering you.'

I looked up at him. 'Yes, you can say that. The thing is, I've been trying to finish my seventh, but for some time now, I haven't been able to write it.'

'Word is that it's a thriller.'

'How did you come to know that? I never told you about it!'

'These days, son, news travels faster than the speed of light.'

'Those journalists at the university must have...' I abused them in my mind.

'Jim, you must not forget that the blood of a journalist courses through my veins. I hoped you would appreciate the efficiency of a journalist's network.'

'I do! I appreciate it. After all, they've helped me market my novels across the border. I don't like it when they say things I don't want them to say.'

'That is something nobody likes. Now, let's not drift away from the reason why you're here.'

'June 2, 1976, a factory was burnt to ashes. Do you remember it?'

Jonathan frowned for a long time. He appeared anxious when he asked, 'What takes you to that date, may I ask?'

'I'm working on a story that may be inspired from incidents that took place around that date, with people related to it. I need details.' Jonathan was silent. He looked at the floor, perhaps trying to remember details from his experience. 'I believe you covered that story. A reporter like you could not have missed it!'

'Nobody could miss it,' he replied in an instant. 'What do you know about it?'

I put my coffee down on the table. 'I was hoping you would tell me about it from the very beginning.'

Jonathan got up and went for a bookshelf behind the couch. '1976,' he murmured as he looked at books and collections of reports on the shelf. 'Are you sure it is a thriller and not a horror?'

I looked back at him. I didn't know what to say. I wanted to say it was both but I kept my silence. He reached for a set of reports with a black cover and brought it to the table. As he put it there and flipped through, I saw a collection of articles that were cut and pasted. He turned the pages. In one of them, I saw the same newspaper heading that I had seen at Stephen's abandoned house: Stephen goes bankrupt after factory burns down to ashes.

Jonathan kept flipping pages, perhaps to remind himself of the details he had covered. He stopped at a page where a picture was pasted. It looked like the outside of the large factory premises at whose center there was a big symbol carved of stone. The gigantic oval and the four vertical lines than ran inside it.

'What's that?' I asked.

Jonathan looked at me. 'When I looked at it for the first time, I didn't realize it was a symbol. When I did, I came to know that the four lines you see inside the oval represent the four partners who ran that big business. God knows how fast they progressed. But more importantly, it is this oval that piqued my interest. Look at the oval, Jim.'

I did, and did not find it attractive. 'So, this oval, did this also symbolize something?'

'No, it didn't. It just meant that at all points of time, the kingpin would have the four members under his fist just like the oval has the four lines inside it.'

'Who kingpin?' Jonathan raised his brow, as a sign of not wanting to be interrupted. But I was curious. 'Go on. I'm listening.'

'I've something that might be useful.' He left me to fetch another report from the same shelf. He picked up a file and opened the front page just to check if it was the right one. 'Ah! Here it is,' he turned to me. There was several newspaper clippings related only to the case. 'Look at this,' he pointed to an article which had four men standing next to each other, posing for a shot. Then, he sat next to me. My eyes focused. I recognized one man clearly, Mr. Stephen.

'These are the four partners of Juber Corporation. The leftmost is Michael Welsh, next to him is Stephen Malcolm, then Mark Hawk and the rightmost is Jason Smith.'

'Tell me more.'

'The four of them were friends since childhood. Studied from the same high school St. Mary's and went on to take up random jobs immediately after school.'

'They didn't go to college?'

'Kids never liked studying then, kids don't like studying now. That was one of the many common things among them- they disliked studying. The four came from not-so- affluent backgrounds. They had ambition, which got them a charm to earn money fast.'

'How did they start this company?'

'They said that one day, Jason got to know how to make the best tube lights from a factory he was working at. He decided to leave his job and share the idea with the others to see who wanted to join him. After hearing his idea, all decided to leave their jobs and start working on his project'

'So this clearly was Jason's brainchild.'

'Yes, the idea came from him. He was the wise one. But idea without men and money has no value!'

'Did they grow fast?'

'Not just fast; theirs was the fastest in the history of new entrepreneurs. They had grown powerful within a year of their venture. A high profile official of the local government sanctioned all of their projects. No organization had patents or approvals as fast as they did. They were growing too fast for anyone to ignore them. Everyone wondered how they did it. Their growth raised many eyebrows and it certainly raised mine. I was told by my chief to start digging.'

'They don't look like they had been up to something bad.'

'That, Jim, is something that doesn't meet the eye.' He looked at the faces of the four partners in the picture. 'My eye on the other hand, saw beyond these constructed smiles.'

'Well, what did you see?'

'Envy, rage, deceit. I saw all the sins that a man could commit.' I shivered when he said the word sins. 'You look awfully uneasy, Jim.'

I took a moment to respond. 'I live my characters, you know.'

'So Iguess you want to make these four your characters.' 'Tell me, what happened to them.'

'Then,' Jonathan paused as he looked sharply at the picture and then at me. 'Tragedy got them.' The expression on his face turned serious and he continued, 'A few people knew about the unfortunate turn of events. Fewer still knew it was all a conspiracy by one of the partners, Michael Welsh, who suspected that his wife Victoria had relations with Stephen Malcolm. Tragically, Stephen was killed by a bullet in his upper shoulder. They found his body in one of his remote houses.'

Stephen had an affair with Victoria?

Jonathan continued, 'It is sad to know that a rich man never approved his daughter's affair. She fell for a jerk who built rags-to-riches stories in a short time and then she falls for his partner. What a shame!'

I looked away. I started questioning whether the man deserved my sympathy or not. Many questions rose in my mind. Why would he drink poison? Was he guilty? Perhaps he had a relation with Victoria and knew that death was circling upon him. It was so convenient to think that the cause of death was a gunshot. His wife and daughters never got to know he was a cheat. He planned it nicely. That jerk cajoled me into giving him sympathy.

'Jim?'

I took a moment with myself before I went back to him. 'How do you explain the death of all the partners?'

'Did I mention all the partners?' he asked, puzzled. 'Yes,' I frowned, 'you did.' Lying wasn't my best suit but I said that without thinking.

'Oh, I don't remember saying that. I must have mistakenly said that.' He knew he hadn't said it, but didn't want me to come out from my world of thoughts.

'You're an editor. Don't go editing facts, please.'

'That was an honest mistake and we're talking about something that happened four decades ago. I'm not a historian, you know.'

'But you were the finest reporter Daily Herald had at that time and correct me if I am wrong. You also covered the details of the story.'

'Since when have I become so important that you started knowing what I used to do?'

'Will you give me the exact details please? I've a novel to finish here!' I raised my voice a little. I was angry to have taken Stephen to be a good person. Jonathan remained polite and cooperative.

'Okay, okay. There's no need to yell. The three partners were killed. Make a note of it,' he looked at me with sarcasm and I looked back at him, frustrated. 'One hasn't been heard of since the murders.'

'Which one?'

'Mark Hawk. It was speculated that he was also murdered, only his body wasn't found but if you ask me, I'd say that he fled to somewhere safe and has kept his identity hidden ever since.'

'Mark Hawk. You have to be alive, else I won't be for long,' I murmured.

'Did you say something?' 'Nothing important. Carry on…'

'It was a fiasco for the young entrepreneurs and the government that had its interests in the project.'

'You mean to say that the government also funded the project?'

'Give me a break! The government's attitude was hostile to these ambitious projects. Michael knew about it. He had some connections with a kingpin from the underworld. He got the permit. It should have been the black money that he brought for the team that got them all killed when they were unable to repay.'

'What's the chance that Stephen got the funds and not Michael?'

'Why is Stephen of much interest to you?' 'I'm a writer, John, I am curious of them all.'

'So far you have sounded more curious about Stephen!'

'Look, I need a central character, he might be the one.' 'You're hiding something, aren't you?'

'I'm hiding the entire story if that's what you mean. And if you want me to continue my research then stop questioning and continue answering!'

'You've always been bossy, Jim!'

'It is better I stay that way. Tell me about the black money and the chances of Stephen's association with it!'

'At least you're frank. Look, logic will tell you that since Michael had underworld connections, he could obtain that huge amount of money.'

'But the underworld wouldn't give him hard cash for nothing. There's bound to be some security at stake and a guarantee of return. You told me earlier that Victoria's father was a rich businessman and he never liked Michael.'

'Yes, in fact, he detested him. Since he was her husband, there wasn't much he could do against him if not in his favor.'

'Was there an equation between Stephen and Victoria's father?' my tone had tinges of impatience in it. It made Jonathan suspect my motive behind the curious questioning. I sensed it and spoke to break his increasing suspicion, 'My book's halfway there. With your help I'll be able to work it off in a month. Now, John, try to remember things the way they were, I don't want you to miss the fine details!'

I noticed him grumbling under his breath. My statement must have hurt his ego. John was known for his keen eye for detail, and he managed to find all kinds of detailed news and information. He was not likely to forget stories, even the ones he had covered in his younger days.

'Not much that I know of,' he said flatly. It wasn't the best response, but it gave me some relief.

I said, 'My best guess would be, Victoria's father had paid Stephen to do the dirty work.'

'I don't get you.'

'What's the father's name?'

'Steve Holmes. He was a real estate tycoon.'

'I'm just saying that maybe, in order to get Michael out of Victoria's life, Mr. Holmes saw Stephen as a tool. He must have made him lure Victoria into romance. And Stephen, being married, was now aiming to get a big amount from Holmes for the service.'

'You really have an imaginative mind. But if I were an investigator, I wouldn't rule out the possibility. In this turmoil, everybody lost something - money, respect, dignity…'

'And Life,' I added. 'Yes, that too!'

'So we have three dead partners: Stephen, Jason, Michael. Mark was nowhere to be found? Hmm, interesting. That reinforces the reasoning I just gave you, John!' Jonathan ran his hand thrice over his hairless scalp. He thought that I was spinning another story from this one. 'Aren't you forgetting Mark Hawk and Jason Smith?'

'Why? You seemed too deeply concerned about Stephen!'

I looked at him with a sense of seriousness.

'I believe that Mark Hawk managed to flee the nation. No one saw his dead body. Michael hung himself in his bungalow. Jason couldn't bear the loss and ate too many sleeping pills. His body was found in one of the burnt chambers of the factory, just days after the tragedy. Poor Jason saw his baby burn down to ashes. He couldn't bear to watch it. He locked himself up in the chamber, spent time looking at the burnt walls and started writing.'

'What did he write?'

'He wrote a note that accused all his friends.' 'What did it say?'

'Oh just the regular, it's all their fault crap. But, there was one very strange thing about that letter. He wrote a strange line at the bottom of the note.'

'And what was that?' I asked, again impatiently.

'Well, first he accused the three. At the bottom, he wrote this,' Jonathan said, and took the copy of the letter from the report. He held it before me and pointed at a sentence highlighted in yellow.

I seek a chance in heaven. I must make amends to the people for the sins I committed.

I dreaded seeing the word sins. It repeated itself over and over again. It made me shake every time it touched my ears or made contact with my eyes. 'I understand that Jason had no involvement in the murders, but I can't understand why he would write something like this.'

'Till I finished writing the report, even I couldn't understand why. The reason why he wrote this escaped the cops and every reporter covering the fiasco.' The alarm buzzed. It was five thirty in the morning. We saw sunlight enter the room through the windows. It was a pleasant sight.

After a momentary break, Jonathan returned to the conversation. 'I had reported deaths at that time, suicides of varying nature, even. But no one had left a note like Jason did. It left many confused.'

'You forgot to tell me about Holmes and his daughter Victoria.'

'I was wondering if you were really into details.' 'Come on, John! Tell me.'

'I felt terrible the first time I came to know about it. I still feel terrible telling you.' I had never seen Jonathan turn as pale as he had, now. I gave him time to respond. 'Poor girl, she was brutally raped and murdered. Poor soul, that young girl! What saddens me most is that her father, Steve Holmes, had vanished just before the incident with his fortune transferred to unidentified account holders. He never returned. Not even when she was given a proper burial.'

Jonathan felt terrible, and so did I. I never expected things to turn this ugly and to know that somehow I was connected with all this saddened me even more. I put my hand on his shoulder. He sighed and looked at the file, contemplating on giving me the report. He shrugged first, as he held it closed in his hand. 'Here, take this. It ought to give you all the details that might help you build the suspense you seek for your seventh piece.'

'I won't need it, John. Facts can be twisted. All that you see in the newspapers isn't reality.'

'I thought writers need to be imaginative. Seeing the analytical side of one, I must say that I am rather surprised. You seem like you have seen it.'

'You have to see it to believe it.'

With peculiar expressions, Jonathan said, 'You talk like you've been there when it happened.'

I wish I could tell you that I was there. I looked at him without saying a word.

'I've a word of advice for you, Jim. A man's last words are as real and honest as his soul is. You may see things from this point of view. It might help you build the story.' I couldn't agree more, but after the intellectual discourse and reasoning, I realized that this wasn't true with Stephen Malcolm. He lied and hid things from me, even at his last moment. But, I decided not to divulge the truth to Jonathan. He tapped the reports and said, 'A reasonable conclusion of my experience is that no matter what you feel, you should always keep the reports safe with you. Time can bring with it a demand for information.'

'Yeah, you're right.'

'I don't want you calling me again at 3:00 AM.'

I took his word of advice and before I left, I looked back and said, 'It was 1:42 AM, you old man.'

Jonathan smiled and wished me, 'Godspeed Jim.'

# Chapter 4

Alone and Happy, the title of my second novel had been made a brand in itself. It appeared on an icon on T-Shirts, mugs and other accessories. The cover that my design consultant Abdur from Abdur Khan Designing Co. made for me was still appealing. My work's intention gained clarity in the form of an image of a man's eternal struggle to stay happy. The book was rejected many times by many publishers. People called it an imitation of various books done by random authors. Only the people close to me knew that I was a genuine writer and never was one for unscrupulous means. The publicity I received pushed the sales of the novel dramatically, and I became a trend setter and a record holder in the writing world.

My readers were surprised by my philosophies of life. They got a treat of reading a never-imagined-before perspective of life. But nobody knew that I had the least knowledge about the subject. This book was a result of unending discussions with my manager Noah. Moreover, my personal experience of an unfulfilled marriage with Kathryn took me the extra mile toward penning the whole story. Although, I must admit that it was an awkward experience writing this one since it was happening at the time Kathryn and I were embroiled in domestic arguments that eventually lead to our separation.

The book furthered my reputation as one who discarded of the institution of marriage. I was thought of as the man who believed marriage to be an institution of hypocrisy. The breathtaking inputs I inscribed in the book were being related all over the world by people unhappy in their marriages. It then became believable when my marriage broke just after a week of the launch. Surprisingly, Kathryn and I never signed the divorce papers. We were simply no longer together.

Publishers threw lavish parties to lure me into contracts with them. Offers from the wealthiest single women came to me. Fame was at my feet, although I was in constant conflict with married people. Amidst the glare of a lavish lifestyle and presence of rich and powerful people, I was alone and unhappy.

For some time, reporters called me a Casanova. No matter how much good or ill they wrote about me, they never had enough of me. I tried to divert my mind, amuse myself in the company of prettiest of women. A supermodel in the swimming pool tonight, another face tomorrow and some other face the day after: all of it was only as a treat for newsmakers. But I never made love with anyone other than Kathryn. Not even a passive kiss. How could I? They were beautiful, they were amazing, but they were not Kathryn. Today, Kathryn and I are mid-aged and still single, although not legally. We were soul mates. Even though we lead individual lives, we still have respect and love for each other. There weren't any misunderstandings or a speck of distrust between us.

She just wanted something from life and I wanted something else from it.

I dedicated my days and nights to writing. The more I wrote, the more she drifted away from me. Or as I believed, I caused her to drift away. She wanted my time and I was obsessed with work. Finally, a point came when she decided to express her disappointment with her marriage and said goodbye.

It was 7:30 AM when I was in my study. I read all the clippings, memorized all the pictures in the file that Jonathan had given me. There was nothing useful. Nothing cleared the doubts in my mind. I had to travel back in time if I needed to know how I was related to these people, and what sins I had committed. Most importantly, I had to know who I was and how I had committed them.

Now, as I held the second novel in my hand and daring to read it, I couldn't hope to start without the most critical element of my reading time: a mug of black coffee. I had already finished one cup when I got home at 6:30. But my system worked only when it was loaded with a lot of coffee. I reached the end of my patience. 'Sebastian, where's my coffee?' I yelled, not knowing whether my high-pitched voice made it to the kitchen downstairs or not, 'How many times do I have to tell you that I want a mug of hot coffee on my table? Whether I drink it or not, I should see a fresh cup after every hour!'

'Here's your coffee!' In an instant, I got what I wanted but from the hand I didn't expect.

I had the prologue section of my novel opened. 'Leave it on the table,' I said to the person, thinking it was Sebastian, with my eyes still at the page. He didn't follow my instruction. My instincts declared that Sebastian could not ignore me, so I turned my head.

'I was hoping you would sit and have it with me!'

I got a jolt. God's way of appearing every time in a flash was scary.

'Oh! It is you again,' I said. He held the cup in one hand and another cup in the other. I looked behind him at the sofa he sat on and said, 'You must love that sofa piece so much.'

'Everyone's got preferences Jim. Can't I have mine?' 'Yes, you can. You are God, you can have anything. But for a change, it would be better to have something else like a chair or a bean bag or something. Why do you carry that same piece with you?'

'There is a lady in France, a trader. She sold her family jewels to start a small furniture business. Can you guess who her first customer was?'

'Judging by the way you're saying it, I'll say that this piece was her first offering and you were her first customer.'

'Partly correct. That's her first sofa set, alright, but she didn't sell it. Her mother always taught her to offer things to God first, before she offered it to anyone else. She presented it to me at a church with much love. Since then, I preferred to sit on it and I take it to many places.'

'Is it comfortable?'

'Comfort is a word that humans value. I value emotions, feeling and love.'

'Why do I sense that you're here to pull my leg?'

'Oh! You hurt me. How do you think this way? Who am I to criticize the great author Jim Morgan? Look at these,' he said, as he gestured at the shelf where my five novels were placed as precious collector's items. Then, he gestured toward Alone and Happy, the one I held in my hand. 'It is works like these that have lifted you to the pinnacle of the writing world.'

'Yet it crippled me in my personal life. Success comes at a cost,' I thought.

'And you paid the price for it,' he said.

I looked down and frowned as the idea had popped inside my head many times. 'Indeed I paid the price.'

'Is that not a sin?' he fired immediately, his look appeared rigid. He had deserted the ever cheerful look on his face. 'Living the life I gave you for work and just work! Not appreciating loved ones and small moments of joy, wasting days for whom? Readers who you don't even know or care about?'

I wasn't in a mood to speak and thought, 'What else am I good at?'

'You want a better life, son. Take care of your dear ones. You committed sins in your previous life. You are not doing anything different in this one!' I had the odd sense of taking the latter part of his sentences more seriously, and was cursing my life. That angered me.

'This guilt always whispers in my ear!'

'Guilt for what?' God's tone became louder. 'You have everything you need: money, fame, respect, friends, success… What's the guilt that you cry about?'

'I don't know, I just don't know!' I said in frustration, holding my head in my hands. I went back to my table and banged my hands on it. I could not imagine anything good about my life at that juncture. The room was silent for the next few seconds. I wished he'd stop criticizing me for my mistakes.

'Karma, Jim,' his tone calmed. 'They follow every being. You made yourself do this to yourself.' He was absolutely right. In hindsight, I felt that I had permitted this to happen. With a draining sentiment of regret I managed to say,

'What can I do? What can…I do?'

God faded away from my study, but an unusual whisper reached my ear. Take this opportunity to get rid of these whispers. Don't waste your life.

I saw Alone and Happy on my table and next to it, the coffee he had brought. I gathered my courage to bring myself to a calmer state, and to achieve the frame of mind to take my next trip to past.

# Chapter 5

I let my eyes scan the maze of words and find out one odd scene that I didn't want to make a part of the story. This one was a very lengthy novel, about one thousand pages. Surprisingly, it had sold millions of copies. At page 490, I started wondering, 'Did people even finish it?' Alone and Happy was a satire on marriage. I had penned many lovely memories that I had shared with Kathryn, in the book. Every passing moment and page brought back flashes of the happiest days of my life. Reading on, I felt the romantic side of me surface again.

As I came to page 567, the satire on the main character's married life bloomed. It struck me that the very moment that I had made a foray into the literary world, my relationship with Kathryn had weakened. The demands of my readers distracted me, made me write more while spending less time with her. Not long after my initial success, passion turned into a dangerous obsession. It was inescapable. The fame that I was about to receive from this novel, drew my eyes away from my marriage responsibilities. I went on reading further.

On October 30, 2008, I was attending a ball after my novel's launch party at the Los Angeles Film City hall 14A. Arguably, one of the most gigantic halls in the entire city was booked by my publishing house, Steve and Jones. It was the first of its kind of party thrown for an author whose second book had bagged ten million dollars in purchase of copyrights for movie production. That amount was huge for any author at that time, making me join the league of authors like J.K. Rowling, Dan Brown and Stephen King.

Sadly, it was on Kathryn's birthday. I had promised I would slip away from the party and reach our favorite private dinner place at the Cicada Restaurant, on Olive Street, in the financial district. At the center of the place, at 10:00 PM, I was in conversation with a few influential members of the Film City when my eyes fell on a very attractive young woman walking directly toward me.

'Isn't that the top contender for this year's Miss America?' I asked the publishing head, Steve, who stood next to me while Jones attended to other invited celebrities. Embellished with expensive makeup, she was strikingly beautiful and her poised walk radiated confidence and opulence.

'Yes, that is her. And Jim,' I looked at him, 'she seems interested in you!'

'What?' I was taken by surprise. Steve didn't waste a second and left me alone. 'Hey Jim, I think that's the chief of the LAPD, I'll catch up!' Three seconds later, I received the company of the sexiest girl I had seen from a very close range.

'Mr. Morgan, I'm…,' she began.

'Kirsten David, it is a pleasure to meet you,' I extended a humble hand.

She placed her hand in mine and said, 'The pleasure is mine.' Immediately, she gloved my hand with her other hand, and I felt a slight rub that triggered a pulse of excitement. I was uncertain as to how to respond. She pulled me a little and brought her cheek next to my right cheek. She touched it and turned to touch my other cheek with hers. I drew a tempting breath of her perfume.

'I'm sorry, Miss. I'm married!'

She smiled a scintillating smile, one that held me completely captive. 'We can all be unmarried for one night!' I didn't know if it was one of the witty answers the models were required to give or was she openly flirting. I couldn't deny that she had something different about her. Her aura had an attractive effect about it.

'Sir, I have an urgent call for you,' my assistant stood behind me and whispered.

I turned my face a little, my eyes still on Kirsten. 'Not now, Neville.' I turned my attention to her again and we exchanged a pleasant smile.

Neville didn't withdraw. 'Sir, I am very sorry but this is urgent.'

I tried playing it cool, and said, 'One moment please.' I turned away from her to talk to my assistant. 'Can't you see I'm busy?'

'But sir…' I cut him short with a silencing glare. It lasted for only an instant and that was enough to convey my intention to him. I turned back to the model, ignoring Neville and the caller.

It turned out that Kathryn had tried to reach me and my phone was with Neville Campbell, my assistant and a student from a prestigious university in Los Angeles. He outperformed a thousand other candidates in a literature test to become my assistant. I liked his peoples' skill more than his merit. But apparently, he was bothering me with it.

'Mr. Morgan, I've…' she began, but I interrupted her. 'Please call me Jim.' She smiled at my frankness. 'Okay, Jim, I'll be Kirsten for you. Let's not disappoint this amazing night! Come, let's go.' The gorgeous lady wrapped my hand from the inside to walk like couples do and took me to the bar. No man could have resisted that, least of all, me, who was under the spell of seduction.

From the corner of my eye, I saw Neville looking at the phone. He seemed unsure of what to say. I watched as he brought it to his ear, and heard him faintly. 'Hello, madam.'

'Is that you Jim?' came from the line.

'I'm sorry but Mr. Morgan is engaged with someone at the moment.'

After a pause of three seconds he heard, 'Is that someone a woman?'

'I'm afraid yes ma'am,' he closed his eyes after speaking the truth. 'Shall, I take a message for…,' she hung up the phone.

'I'm as good as dead if Mr. Morgan finds out,' he said to himself.

At the bar, Kirsten told me about herself, her ambitions, what it was like to be a super model and such. Then, she gave me a chance to show off my word prowess. After three glasses of wine, I started showering her with words from the distant corners of a dictionary that did justice to her magnificence and beauty. She was highly impressed. I didn't even realize when she had pulled me to the dance floor and we had begun making everyone around us jealous. People were staring at us, talking about me and how big a Casanova I was, and how I had scored the best girl for the night. After losing ourselves in each other's eyes and not keeping track of time, we went on dancing in each other's arms. I felt her body become one with mine. The drinks had cast their spell on me wonderfully.

After a while, she pulled my hand, taking me to a place where we would take the experience further. I forgot I was married, partly because of her charm and partly because of alcohol. As I walked past the dancing crowd, I saw a diamond watch on someone's hand. In an instant, my senses came back to me.

'Kirsten, Kirsten!' The loud music didn't let my voice reach her. 'Kirsten!' I stopped in my tracks. She turned and looked back at me, still holding my hand. 'I have to go, it's really urgent.' She shook her head, not letting my hand go. I went very close to her, almost feeling her breath, 'I really have to go!' It was embarrassing, to have to pull my hand away from her. Turning away, I made it to my assistant, who I had instructed to stand near the exit.

'Please don't tell me it was Kathryn!' I said. 'Yes sir, it was her.'

I was gravely disappointed at myself. 'Why didn't you tell me that earlier?'

'I tried to, sir, but…' he paused, looking for words that would not anger me and make me kick him out of his position, '…you were occupied.' He handed me my phone. I immediately checked the call list.

'Kathryn's call was taken at ten. That was three hours ago. Oh God!' I made a run to the valet area. Three valets were at the receiving point.

'Sir, may I?'

'Here's your card, I'm in a hurry, give me my keys, please,' I said without wasting a second. One of them had the key in hand. I snatched it the moment I saw it and ran to my car. My red BMW Z4 convertible that my publisher had gifted me was parked in the VIP area. It didn't take me long to get to it. I sat behind the wheel and rushed to the restaurant with an expression of shame on my face. There was no traffic and I must have jumped more signals than I cared to count. Within fifteen minutes, I made it to the circular driveway of Cicada Restaurant, didn't bother to turn off the ignition, got off immediately and gestured to the valet to park my car. As I ran to the entrance, the midnight breeze rustled my hair, but didn't calm my worry. I knew the table that was reserved in my name. I hastened to it. The only people visible around were the staff, doing their last bit before closing the place.

I got to the table and found that she wasn't there. The table was deserted, just like every other, at this hour.

The manager came up to me. 'Sir,' he said politely. I turned to face the news breaker, 'madam left exactly at midnight.

She gave this to me and asked me to hold onto it. She didn't say anything else and left.'

I took her ring. The previous day, I had asked her to give me one more chance so I could save our marriage. My mind was clear now. I had blown it. It was all over.

At that precise moment, I was on page 701. The memory of that night was haunting my soul. A tear filled with regret rolled down to my cheek. I am sorry, Kathryn, I should have been there on time. The satire of the novel was filled by the regret of my broken marriage. It sold like hot cakes. I couldn't shake myself of the regret through the time I worked on it. But only the trauma had made it possible for me to make such a bestseller possible. My younger days were locked in a prison of fame and money. No wonder, that I had committed sins in the previous life and also in this one, and that I was paying for it as a result of my choices. The force of mistakes dragged my mind and created a dismal feeling, but I had to continue reading. I took the cup and drank the last drop. It was my fourth cup. Just when I finished it, my eyes fell on a line:

Choices make a man commit a sin. Choices make a man suffer. Man makes the choice and choice makes the man.

'Wait a minute, I don't remember writing this!' I said, when suddenly, a glaring beam of light appeared from the window. I brought my hands together to cover my eyes. It was too strong. It wasn't till I turned that I realized that I had been sent back in time again. I found myself inside the entrance gate of a great mansion. The blinding light came from outside, highlighting a mountain just behind the shelter. I looked down. It looked like a track. To my left, there was a big garden that was lined with trees. I had the same view from my right. The track led to a roundabout at the center, where I saw the familiar symbol of Juber Corporation: the big oval with four vertical lines. I took my first step when the howling wind welcomed me. I shivered in the lawn. Luckily, there were no guards to throw me out. I had no idea what to do.

I am here for a reason, perhaps to know something or to find something. I think I must go inside the house.

With my arms covering my body, I moved to the front door. I remembered the inhospitality shown by Stephen when I had knocked on his door. I didn't want to receive it again. I went behind the mansion to get an idea if there were people inside. At the back, there was a large balcony on the first floor, another on the second and then, a terrace. The rooms were lit. I could see it from the windows. The ground floor had a window just near a corner. I decided to go toward it. It seemed to be a window into a room. I pressed my face on the window and peered inside. No sound came from within. It seemed like there was nobody there. I analyzed the make of the window. It was a sliding window that could be opened from the outside. I remembered reading somewhere that because of security concerns, such windows were modified in the 1970s so that no one could trespass. I held the panel from its edge and pulled it up. It was a noisy affair and I hoped it would not catch anyone's attention. I slipped from the window and found myself in an uninhabited room. The lights were on.

I guess the house master must have no care for the electricity bill! I scanned the room and saw expensive items that only a rich and flamboyant man could own.

The room was deserted, as was the hall that came next. I stood in the silence of the place. It was then that I heard the sound of a muffled voice from upstairs. Somebody was singing. The realization that I wasn't alone was both comforting and worrying. I wasn't sure if it was safe for a trespasser to check upstairs, but I didn't have anything else to do but to let curiosity lead my way. From one side, I reached the wide marbled staircase that led to the upper floor. The volume of voice rose as I climbed up. It was evident that it came from a room on the second floor, the door of which I could see from my position on the tenth step.

I ascended up the spiraling staircase cautiously, making sure that I didn't make noise. When I reached, the voice fell a little. I walked up to the door. Hesitant, I put my ear to the door and tried listening to the voice. Not a single sound came from the room. I moved my ear up the door. The door opened inside with my hand's weight. I cautiously peeped through the key hole. Seeing no one inside, I questioned my hearing sense. Was I hearing things? There was no one inside!

I pushed the door in and went inside. 'That's weird! The house is lit, but there's no one inside.' I looked around. The air smelled fruity from the aroma of candles and a bowl of fresh strawberries next to a bottle of wine on a table in front of the bed.

'You finally came to meet me!' A beautiful lady stood at the door of her bathroom, with a half-eaten strawberry in hand, watching me with seductive eyes. She came forward slowly. Her steps were not composed. She threw the piece of strawberry on the table. I watched it land on the bowl full of strawberries.

'Ma'am, I came here by mistake. I should leave,' I didn't know why I said that but I did.

She came to me, tripped and fell on me as if the force of the shaking floor threw her. I caught her by her hands and she supported herself against me. The way she touched me was intense. Her hand moved higher. I shook my head in an awkward position and said, 'Miss, it is not right,' as if that was going to stop her. She smiled and hurled me on the bed. I didn't expect her to do that. I didn't know what was going on with her. She was clearly imagining me to be someone else or maybe she was doing it deliberately. Before I could get up, she mounted the bed like a tigress, ready to jump on its prey. I watched her crawl seductively toward me, ready to make her next move. Afraid and uncertain of her intentions, I leapt out of bed. She caught my hand and heaved me back, on top of her this time. I fell over her. She looked at me with green eyes, paralyzing me. She rolled over on the bed of imaginary roses. She placed her hands on my cheeks and brought her lips close to mine. It was happening so fast that I couldn't decide how to react. Finally, her consciousness was too weak to stay from falling asleep. Her eyes closed, her hands fell from my face and she was on me, asleep. I took a moment to realize that this was actually taking place. I turned her around and put her on the bed.

Voices of some people sounded on the other side of the door. I didn't want to look like I had attacked her. I got up immediately, remembering that in my previous time travel, Stephen could see me and as I had judged, the assassin could not. I wasn't certain who could see me this time. I didn't want to take any risks. With great caution, I hid behind the curtains of the room. The door was open. Two men entered the room. My eyes bulged out. I saw the same ghost, the reporter that I saw at the university dinner. I stood stationary, as if I had suffered a stroke. 'How in the world is he here?' I spoke in a hollow voice. I couldn't believe my eyes. 'Maybe it is someone else!' I assured myself.

This ghost accompanied another man. Looking at the gestures, he appeared to be obeying the second man. They were watching the lady lying in bed. Their words were not louder than a whisper. I couldn't hear. In a while, when I got a closer look, I was blown out of my mind. It was really him.

How is he here? The man before my eyes now was walking and living in the past. How was it possible? I took in a load of saliva, still incomprehensible and confused.

'Excellent. Our plan is in motion. From now on, we shall not meet till it is over.'

'I will not disappoint you,' said the man I thought to be a ghost.

'You haven't and I know you won't. You made me very happy today. Here!' He took out what I could make out was a passport. 'Take this! You have secured a fresh identity for yourself. The world must never come to know that we were connected. Godspeed to you, Mr. Jonathan White,' he started laughing.

I couldn't believe my ears when I heard the name 'Jonathan White.'

'It was nice working with you, Mr. Holmes. I hope that the necessary cash has been arranged.'

'It has already been arranged. Meet Edison tomorrow at the Daily Herald. He will familiarize you with your new identity and job. You will collect your payment from him.'

Wanting to take a closer look, I had moved the curtain a little further. The guy shot a look at the movement of

the curtain, the shifting of my body weight from one leg to the other must have done that. Immediately, I pressed my hand against my mouth, attempting to suppress even the slightest whisper. He sensed that they weren't alone in the room. His professional assessment of the pattern of the curtain movement cleared it for him. He pulled out a gun and said, 'Mr. Holmes, we have company.' Holmes looked at the curtain. Without wasting a second, made his way out of the room.

I was petrified. If I stepped back, I would fall off the balcony and may not survive the fall. If I stepped forward, there was a possibility he would see me and shoot me on the spot. What was I to do?

He positioned the gun at the curtain and warned, 'Come out if you want to live.'

I didn't say a word or braved a step ahead. He began taking menacing steps forward. 'Oh God! Just help me out of this one, please, please!' As he advanced, he stretched his left hand to shift the curtain and had the gun stern in his right hand to shoot the intruder.

Something gallant got into me. I was about to do the most heroic yet suicidal thing I had ever done. He reached the curtain. Within a second, he heaved it to one side and in a fraction of a second I joined both my hands and swung them on his weapon. It fell off his hand. He looked at the fallen weapon and then, his penetrating eyes met mine. It sent a tremor across my body. In reaction, I took another swing, but he dodged it. He caught me by surprise and landed two fast punches, one on my face and the other on my right shoulder. It knocked the wind out of me. I shook my head as I was hazy for a brief moment. He was about to respond with a follow up, but I launched a swift kick. He managed to block it. I was in a defensive position, expecting him to initiate his offense. Instead of looking at his legs, I focused on using my hands as a shield to block his heavy punches. He lifted his hand to punch me, and I lifted mine to block him from smashing my face. But I misjudged his attack. He pounded on my chest and I fell behind.

In a second, I planted both my hands on the ground and pushed myself up before he could take advantage of my condition. His attacks grew faster. I dodged one, blocked a few and got some hits on my body. I retreated a few steps, knowing that I was outmatched. But he kept coming at me. A good kick sent me back a good three steps. The balcony looked small from the outside. I thought there was not much space, but there was enough to make me his punching bag. Despite my brave counter, the fight took me dangerously close to the edge of the railing. He continued advancing with his fists in front of his chest and the look of a focused killer on his face. I felt my back touch the railing. I looked back to see how bad a fall I was likely to have. The height of two floors threw my guard off balance. He saw the opening and attacked me again. I took a punch to my face. The impact of it flipped me over. My reflexes kicked into action as I scrambled for support to save me from the fall. My hand got to his tie and grabbed it. I fell and took him along. I screamed as I saw him and the stars over me.

He didn't join my scream. Suddenly, everything turned black and then lit up again like the last time, but infinitely faster. The stars far away changed into a ceiling just a few feet away from us.

My body slammed on the ground. My feet touched the floor first. Then, my body, and it hurt badly. He was on me. In half a second, my head collided with his nose. I groaned in pain and he did, too. It seemed to hurt him worse than it hurt me. He covered his nose and lifted himself up. I rolled sideward and stood up. We didn't fall in the garden, but on the floor of my study. We were back to my time, mysteriously. I was curious to know if I was alive. This had happened so quickly that our minds didn't register the possibility of the sudden change in place. Mine absorbed it soon enough, though. I am alive. He looked around in shock. I looked at him, a little relieved, but still defensive.

I thought it was the right moment to attack him. I decided to go on the offensive and shot a punch at him, but he tactfully jerked to my left and swung around me. I didn't see that coming. Next, he hurled me down with my collar. That made me fall on the ground. Knowing that I was not in a good spot, I rolled to get up but he didn't give me a chance to recover. Almost immediately, he jumped on me. With the force of his body, he pressed down on me hard. I felt his legs curl around my body. Before I could do anything, he angled to wrap his shoulders around my neck. He started choking me. I hadn't recovered properly and now he was taking me to death. I couldn't breathe. He tightened his grip. My hands tried opening his arms but I wasn't strong enough to open the lock around my neck. I saw no way out of the lock. I felt my life reaching the brink of death as he kept choking me. My lungs were half-dead now. My eyes were closing as my senses were leaving me. I don't know how, but the desire to live made me try everything to survive. Somehow, I managed to bite his arm through his shirt. He screamed loudly from the pain. I heard the rasp of material ripping as he released me from his clutch.

We got up and faced each other. He opted for a defensive stance. I coughed. Simultaneously, I prepared my right arm for him and kept my left arm at my neck as I tried breathing in. For a few moments we didn't change our stance, waiting for each other to make the next move. Luckily, the adrenaline rush made my senses sharper. I was extremely cautious. After a moment, he fired his hand through the air, the punch was meant for my jaw. I sidestepped reflexively, feeling the force of his knuckles ruffle my hair and charge with a strong fist. He wasn't expecting a sharp maneuver and got jabbed on his face and midsection. The surprise punch stunned him and pushed him back. This time he felt the pressure.

White raged after taking those two hits. I saw him explode when he clenched his teeth and lashed out at me. Against his speed, force and skill, I was ineffective. He punched and pushed me on the table. I punched aimlessly and wasn't able to deflect his hands from reaching my throat. He had my neck in both his hands. His strength was crushing as he went for the kill. I first pierced through the opening and then punched him on the face over and over again. It opened a cut on his forehead but he kept pressing. I was seconds away from death. My right hand went on the table and caught a heavy coffee mug. I don't know how, but I swung it so hard on his face that the cracking sound of the mug sounded out loud. It crushed his nose, deepened and widened the cut on his forehead.

White backed off after the blow on his face, it was wet with blood. He was weakened and insensible. He screamed loudly and charged at me. My heart pounded and my head thrust me sideward. I used his momentum against him. Pushing him forward violently, I jerked him off balance. He tumbled over the chair. The force sent him crashing through the window with his face and he went through it. I managed to throw him out of the window from the second floor of my house. If he survived, he would be in terrible shape. I staggered back and fell on my hips. I was in shock and couldn't open my eyes. Pain began to settle all over my body. I panted. My body was uncontrollably flattened on the floor and my eyes looked up at the ceiling. I was still breathing.

I never expected to end up with a black eye and half a swollen face. I was losing consciousness. I thought about the assassin that went for Stephen and compared the situation with this. 'One thing's for sure, this guy can see me and hurt me.' That was my last thought before my eyes shut and mind went to sleep. I felt the pain slowly fading away. I wanted to get up and see if that guy was dead or alive. I tried opening my eyes, my eyelids felt heavy and a harsh glaring light obscured my view. Then, a face appeared above me.

Kathryn! Is that you?

She had the same old silver streak: it ran till the tip of her hair, accentuating her sophistication and amplifying her beauty. Her black eyes were darker than the heart of an ocean. At the center, I saw my reflection. Her dimpled left cheek was lovely as usual. I felt a familiar longing, one that my decisions had denied me from indulging in, for eight years now.

'Is this what heaven feels like?' I wondered as she moved her hands through my dense hair. Then, my nostrils began to give me discomfort. The air smelled of antiseptic solution. I heard someone trying to wake me up. My ears were slowly gaining their sharpness back. 'Wake up Jim, it is time.' A hand toweled off some of my bruises and my skin became as good as new. I felt the revival of my strength, breath and body.

Only an hour ago, I had been fighting a highly trained hit man in the past and then in present. Although badly injured, I had survived the fight. Then I saw a pleasing dream of a heavenly time I shared with Kathryn and now, I was in the care of the greatest physician of creation: God. He saw the bewilderment flash in my eyes as I saw him holding me in his arms.

'You were unconscious,' I heard him say, clearly. 'I wanted to warn you, Jim,' he was still looking at me. 'That reporter you confronted back at the university was an image I sent as a hint for you. You should have stayed away from him. Now, you have brought him into your timeline!'

'I tried not to mess up.' I looked at him earnestly, 'You knew that this would happen, I didn't!'

'Sometimes a man cannot look beyond the choices he makes. It was your choice to search that room. You decided to hide behind the dusty curtain and not under the bed. You are responsible for the things that happened to you.' I had no idea how to respond to this and I knew that he just gave me an explanation that I couldn't deny. I sat up on the floor with one leg folded and the other stretched out. I looked at my arms. There were no bruises there. Then I looked at my shirt. There were no signs of cuts or bruises there, either.

'I… I got nervous and brought him here mistakenly. I didn't know people can time travel with me.'

'I'm afraid that is a mistake you will have to deal with!' he said, spinning around to face me.

I got up and stepped toward him, 'I don't understand, God.'

'The universe works on the principle of balance. It was bound to happen anyway. I allowed you to go to past so you could understand what wrong you did and take the path of atonement.' I didn't see God's favorite white sofa appear. He didn't seem in a mood to relax or have fun. He was serious and perhaps, worried. 'In order to restore the balance, someone must come from the past to your time.'

'I understand. If that's the law of universe, then it is justified.'

'You also want to ask something else? Go ahead.' 'What is the implication of all this?'

God went up the window and said, 'If you can go to the past, then that means he can come to present.'

I knew the answer before it came from him but I still wanted to hear it. 'Am I in danger now?'

He turned. 'You and the entire fabric of the future timeline are in danger.'

Immediately it struck me. If I did anything to anyone in the past, it would alter the present. Similarly, if he did anything in my timeline, the future would change its course.

'That little confrontation, did that change anything in various timelines?'

'No, that's the good news.' 'And what's the bad one?'

'Unlike you, he can come here and go back anytime. He doesn't have a limitation of time, no restriction of a portal on a book like you do. Your confrontation gave him the power that nobody should have.' My apprehension rose and I felt terrible at bringing him along with me in that fall.

But he should be dead, down on the ground. How's a dead person supposed to use the power of time?

'Tell me God, why are you really here?' I demanded. 'You always show a way. What must I know now?' I thought of calling myself insane for asking such a question. But now, I was no longer convinced that he was here for me. God had braced himself for my sharp words. He stood unaffected and smiled as if he was waiting for it and had an answer prepared.

'Come here, have a look,' he gestured at the ground. I walked up to the window and stretched myself out to take a look at the guy's body.

'What the...?' The shock of the view pulled me back in. I turned to God.

'The only reason he hasn't fallen on the ground is that!'

'He has fallen back somewhere in his time, just like I did, an hour earlier!' I didn't let him finish answering as I had to say it. I felt a hard object under my right foot. I shifted my leg to see what it was. I bent and pinched it between my fingers and brought it close to myself. It appeared like a simple tie-pin, one that must have fallen from the assassin's tie while he was in combat with me. I turned it and what I saw, astonished me. There was a name written over it: Jason Smith. The more I looked at it, the more I sensed that poor Jason was a victim of that sinner. This guy must have taken it as a souvenir after sending him to death.

'But Jonathan told me that…'

'That Jason Smith ate too many sleeping pills.'

'I don't understand. Either he lied to me or he doesn't know or maybe he reported false things. Why the heck was that man calling this guy Jonathan White?' This question left me extremely confused. 'Is this guy in my timeline Jonathan White? It can't be possible. The Jonathan White I know has been a great man, a kind man. This guy is an assassin, a killing machine, one that only has anger and impulse in him. What's happening?'

'I know at this point you are more confused than ever.

You must compose yourself.'

'How can I? I don't understand anything. How am I related to these people? Who is who? I am so confused. This tie-pin, I wished it never came here!' I threw it away, but God grabbed my hand and stopped me from trashing it.

'Every object in the universe has a purpose,' he took it from my palm and slid it into my shirt's pocket. 'This object too has a purpose. Let the time come for it to show you why it is with you and not in the trash can.'

I could only stare at him while he said it. The cheerful smile was back and it had me convinced enough not to object. 'What do I do now? Continue reading and time traveling?'

'I'd say you have a plane to catch!' I couldn't imagine why I had a plane to catch. There wasn't any meeting I could think of. 'You still have to figure out the nature of your past sins.' I sensed that he did not want me to know about things now. There was a time and place for it. Somebody knocked the door thrice. I looked back. 'Who is it?'

'Sir, it is me, Sebastian!'

God disappeared again. I had hoped that he would tell me something and not leave everything to me to figure out. Sebastian came inside with a cup of coffee on a tray. 'Sir, you left your phone in your bedroom. I heard three rings and thought I would tell you!' Where were you numbskull when a beast was pounding me an hour earlier? I took the phone from him. He saw me grin as I looked at him. He thought it wise to get out of the room.

I looked at the screen of my cell phone. It had three missed calls from Noah and one message. I opened it.

Flying off to Los Angeles. Meeting with Steve and Jones. Flight departs at 20:50 hrs.

'I better make a run for it,' I said to myself.

I had to do exactly as advised by God. Uncover the truth behind the killing of Jason Smith. I assumed that if he was killed by this assassin, Michael Welsh was, too. I had to somehow find if Mark Hawk was alive or not. Not to forget Victoria's and her father's case! Finally, how I was related to all of them and in what form had I committed sins? I also had a feeling that I was going to face the assassin soon, hopefully not on the flight. It was difficult to disagree with what I had seen with my own eyes. My time travel told me that my editor, Jonathan White, was the assassin. He was responsible for the murders. I left for the airport. The unexpected surge of feelings that made me long for Kathryn when I dreamt about her were still intact in my veins.

# Chapter 6

For several seconds, the receiving lady at check-in counter number three of John F. Kennedy International Airport stared in wonder at me.

'Hello! Miss,' I looked at her name badge, 'Betty.' 'Are you really Jim Morgan?'

I gave her a quick nod. 'I need a ticket Miss. Will you please get me a specific seat?'

She kept staring at me for long, as if to say: I would do anything you say. The delay gave way to some frustration in me. 'I've read all your books, I am a huge fan, would you please…' she began to pull a drawer to take something out. I could tell that she wanted an autograph.

'Miss, I appreciate that you read and love my work but I need your help immediately!' She didn't listen in her ecstatic mood. She pulled out a pen from her pocket and a notepad from her drawer and laid it on her palm for me. I gave her my signature in a fluid style and went on. 'I'm in a hurry. Could you please have my seat arranged next to Miss. Noah Hawthorne?'

She opened her mouth but I didn't hear a word. She was still under a spell. I had to break it. I raised my tone, 'Betty?' She snapped and quickly responded to avoid embarrassment. 'I really need a seat next to Miss. Noah Hawthorne. Can you please arrange it for me?'

'Sure, sir! Let me check!' She quickly typed some letters on her desktop. Her eyes scanned the screen. 'I'm sorry, sir, she's in economy and we don't have one vacant.' I knew Noah always preferred economy and I always traveled first class. I didn't anticipate a full economy class.

'But I have two seats in the business class. Would you like that?' Money did bring a big difference in my life and I had loads of it. Giving her my credit card and waiting for three more minutes wasn't bothersome. I had secured a seat in time. 'You have to be quick. Most passengers are already boarding the flight, sir.'

'Yeah, I'll make a run for it. Thanks.'

'Enjoy your flight Mr. Morgan! It was a pleasure meeting you.' She extended her hand to feel mine, something that was not the protocol of an airlines employee. I quickly shook her hand and went through a couple of security checks to board the flight. I was the last one on board. I guess it was destiny, as otherwise, God wouldn't bother telling me to catch this flight. The air hostess greeted me with a smile. Any lady who loved to read novels would recognize me anywhere. She didn't. 'Sir, may I please assist you to your seat?'

'No, I'll be fine. Thank you!' I went on from first class to business to economy to find her. Searching for a familiar face was something I hadn't done, ever. At window seat number 7E, I found her looking outside.

'Noah,' I said. She turned. It took her a brief moment to believe that I was there.

'Jim? What are you doing here?'

'You have to come down to business class if you want to know.'

'Well, now you want to talk? What if I ignore you this time?'

'I'm sorry for that, I didn't mean to. Now please, come.

The air hostess is already coming here.'

'Okay, just hang on a second. Excuse me, I would like to go!' she requested the next two passengers to make way for her. 'You've been acting strange lately, Jim.'

'A lot of strange things are happening around me, Noah. Come, I'll tell you.'

'Sir, I have to request you to take your seat, we are taking off!' the hostess instructed us.

'Yes, we're going there, thanks.' We finally took our seats at the business class. I didn't wait for the plane to take off and engaged her in me. 'Noah, I need your knowledge.'

'You need my what?'

'I'm working on a series of murders that took place in 1976 at Juber Corporation. Does the name ring a bell?'

'Not really, you should ask Jonathan, he would know.' 'I did, but I am trying to understand the concept of sins so I can give life to my characters.' She had a look of disbelief. I had never spoken about God to her in life and never dived into the concept of good or bad deeds.

'Are you lying to me, Jim? Because I can tell that when you do.'

I immediately shook my head. 'No, no. The story is exceptional and compelling. In order to make it more connecting to the soul, I have to understand this.' She was still in disbelief. Her eyes were telling me that she was still not convinced. I grabbed her hand. 'I am finally able to write something for my seventh, I can't afford to break the momentum now.'

That gesture combined with the statement had her convinced. 'So what do you specifically want to know?'

'Everything,' I said. It wasn't remotely specific, but it got her started. She looked outside the window first and then started speaking.

'I remember that during my days at Cambridge, I researched on the sins as mentioned in different literatures and holy books of the world. Some sins given in the texts of one religion seemed to overlap others, while a few others appeared entirely distinct. My study says that sins are viewed differently by members of different societies. It will be really difficult for me to familiarize you with them all.'

'I think it will be helpful to you and me if you give me your take on your entire study. There would be a number of sins common among all, right?'

'Yes there are. You're probably right. It would be better if I just tell you what I know.'

'I'm listening.'

'You must have read in various Indian texts about the Kali Yuga, an era.'

'I have. We all agree that the way we live, we are only moving toward our end.'

'So you got the basic understanding that whatever bad deeds we do, they can create a sin. Now, the thing to be highlighted is the action that one performs is either good or bad.'

'Who judges what's good or bad?'

'Well, in Kali Yuga, every living being's mind generates a plethora of sinful thoughts that runs throughout the lifetime. But unless they translate into action, they do not qualify as a sin although it can be argued that it corrupts man to a varying extent.'

'But thoughts cannot be easily controlled by the will of a man; it has to be regulated after years of meditation, yoga and sacrifice!'

'You're right. So when these thoughts are left unchecked or uncontrolled, they can make a man commit a crime. Say, a murder.'

'So murder becomes a sin, right?'

'Not exactly. The thought or emotion that leads to the performance of the action is the sin. The choice that one makes based on that thought or emotion is a sin. Murder is simply the result.'

'What choice do we have? It is all written in destiny!' Some frustration emerged in the form of words as a result of things not going my way lately.

'We can always make a choice. That's what we have been doing: making choices, paying the penalties for them and putting the blame on God and destiny.'

'Is that so?'

'You must understand it like this. Let this energy or whatever you call it…'

'God,' I added.

'Yes, God, is formless and at the same time takes several forms in everything around us. He is nothing and at the same time absolutely everything.'

'You're confusing me more than helping me here, Noah.'

'Why do I always have to spoon feed you? Okay, tell me what's inside our flesh.'

'Our mind, we have a heart.'

'What else? Something that is not in the flesh!' 'You want me to say soul, right?'

'Bull's eye! So think of God as a very big soul. You can call it a super soul,' she started forming a cluster with her hands to simplify things for me. 'God is limitless energy in the form of the soul. He gives birth to living organisms by giving us a very tiny fraction of his soul.' She began to pull an imaginary speck from her hand and placed it over her heart. 'When this tiny soul reaches an organism, it gives it life.'

'Where's the sin part in all this?' 'You want answers?'

'Okay, I won't interrupt again. Carry on.'

'These souls in organisms are supposed to go back to the super soul, which is God. For that, these organisms must do a great deal of good. When they do, they start making progress from the body of an organism to, say, a plant or an animal. After taking several births in various forms, one's soul reaches the body of a human being.'

'But why a human being?'

'Because only we have a brain that can understand God. Our purpose is to accumulate enough good in our account that can get us a pass to leave this material world and go to the spiritual world where our tiny soul becomes one with the super soul.' Seeing that I had started accepting her words completely, she stopped making gestures to animate her points. 'Jim, the most important thing that I've learnt is that anything you do that takes you away from reaching the super soul becomes a sin. Killing may seem to be a murder but if it is done to serve the higher purpose and restore the balance of universe, it is a pious act and not a sin.'

'So you mean to say that if we do bad deeds, or say commit crimes, then we are stuck in the life of a human being?'

'Yes and if you commit sins, you become an animal or organism again. Which means you have to suffer for several coming births!'

'I get that much. What I don't quite get is, how can a murder be good?'

'See, certain members of a society are given the status of a security guard, a cop, an army person. If violence is required, they must exhibit it and they have been authorized for it right.'

'What about an ordinary man? He isn't authorized.' 'He isn't. The societal rules apply to him. But in case

of no other option, God will not consider murder a sin. An example of a murder in self-defense should explain.' 'Okay, this I can digest.'

'Furthermore, one must try to excuse minor offenses and in certain conditions show forgiveness. A murderous act executed under the influence of say anger, false prestige takes one to the regal road to hell. But if you consider both the pros and cons before involving yourself in a fight and are not under the influence of demoniac qualities, then you may say that God wants you to fight.'

'But the law doesn't see that, right?' 'Law is blind and everyone knows that.'

'Oh God! So many innocent people have been wrongly convicted and sent to prison. Where's God when they were doing only self-defense?'

'They had accumulated bad deeds and only through suffering in jail were they able to pay off their debt. The accident or murder was just the triggering point.'

'Okay, so now I can say that I understand your version of Karma.'

'Well, it isn't my version. It is what my studies revealed to me. Oh look, here comes the service. I was thinking it was about time we had something to eat and drink.'

'Yeah, I didn't even notice that it has been some time since we took off.' The air hostess approached our seat and offered us packaged drinking water.

'The drinks and snacks are on their way. What would you like sir?' she asked me first.

'Oh, I'll just have juice before the mini meal. Noah, you?'

'Make that two apple juices, no hard drinks for us.' 'Okay, ma'am!' She went to the seats ahead of us. 'Noah, I understand what we should do and what not. I certainly want to understand what qualifies as a sin.'

'You must relate things with time Jim. These texts were written centuries ago. Now many things that qualified as a sin in earlier times are normal today. Take for example the first sin – Lust. They say that a man commits adultery in his mind when he looks at a woman lustfully. But I argue that since the wheel of time has changed, mere lustful thinking doesn't make a man sinful. Everyone is lustful in mind, and if we go by the old thought, it would make us all sinners. My understanding from one of the Indian texts is that we must not engage in sex life when we are working toward developing spiritual consciousness. If we wish to create offspring, then we must do it when we aim for our kids to follow the similar consciousness.'

'So these texts mean that we can't even have a sex life.' 'According to literature, a sex life is not condemned provided it is used for a higher consciousness.'

'How can our physical pleasures be used for higher thinking? We engage in gratification because of our desire to seek pleasure. That is something highly material and keeps us from going the road to spirituality.'

'You understand things very fast Jim. I didn't expect you to be this quick.'

'I told you I'm serious about this book. I will respect views even if I don't like them. I have a book to complete.'

'Okay, so I was saying that some people can choose to engage in sex life to create offspring that go on the path of spirituality and understanding of God. Body pleasure that creates children for any other motive isn't suggested. A person can choose a path to do material things for spiritual benefits. The status of people differs this way. One can be a student of spirituality when one desert lust and engages in intercourse to walk this path. One can also choose the life of celibacy and study literatures to develop spiritual knowledge. Household people should not indulge in sense pleasure if…'

'It is not used for higher consciousness to spread spiritual awareness. I get it. Tell me about the other sins.'

'There's Greed. Everything material in this world lures us into indulgence. People tend to give themselves over to sensuality and indulge in all kinds of impurities with a continual lust for more. I argued that if a person bears greed in heart while thinking about others, it cannot amount to be a sin. Once a man has lost all sensitivity toward others, and desires material things for himself alone, then it becomes greed.'

'And that's a sin if you greed for yourself. Now the third sin please!'

'You're trying to go too fast. I hope you catch up!' 'Try me.'

'The next one is Gluttony: Excessive drinking and eating. It becomes a sin because the glutton destroys one's body and the body is a gift by God. A person must use his body and mind to do good deeds and reach the super soul. If you don't care for the body, it will not care for you. Next sin is Sloth-disinclination to activities that one ought to perform with dedication. If one doesn't exert energy in performing the deeds that God desires, it becomes a sin.'

'In other words we should understand and fulfill our purpose on this Earth and if we are sleeping the whole day, wasting our time in laziness, we are committing a sin. I must say that I never looked at laziness this way. But there's one question I would like to ask.'

'Sure.'

'How do you know that these things about spirituality haven't been propagated by show-bottle spiritualists who attempt to gather many followers? A lot of people get taken in the wrong direction under false, so called spiritualists.' She looked at me with a raised eyebrow. I shouldn't have doubted her research. 'Please carry on, I trust you.'

'Next, the fifth major sin is wrath, or anger. Not just a regular one but the one that is backed up by a strong desire for vengeance or indignation. We can choose either polite words that can calm someone's anger or harsh ones to aggravate it. The sixth sin that a man commits is envy, a desire to possess something or have an advantage that someone else possesses. The only thing that a man must desire is spirituality and to attain ultimate wisdom to become one with God. In the path of spirituality, one must desert all material desires, evaporate lust and longing for relations and faithfully follow God.'

'What's the seventh and the final deadly sin?'

'Pride. The state of being proud for material achievements, having a prolonged self-esteem that makes you feel superior to others. We must stay humble as all men and women of God are equal.'

I was clearly overwhelmed with her knowledge on the matter. 'I am amazed at your knowledge about all this, Noah.'

'I was ignorant Jim. When I learnt things from holy books, my perspective changed. The purification of one's existence can be done in this birth. A person has to cultivate spiritual knowledge and that comes after self-control. Various activities are considered auspicious for progress on the path of liberation from the material world. The slightest propensity for sense gratification and material possession takes a person away from this path. People acting in the modes of ignorance and passion will always commit one sin or the other.'

'What happens to them?'

'As I mentioned earlier, they will have to remain in this material world either as human beings or descend to lower life forms like that of animals.'

'What about someone who has committed all deadly sins? That person gets eternally banished to hell?'

'No, silly. According to my understanding, that person will degrade his life form to the most primitive and will stay that way till spiritual progress is made.'

'And that can only happen in the human form!'

'Yes. That can only happen when you are guided by a spiritual master, when you become wise enough. There are also transcendental qualities which are meant for making a follower progress in spiritual understanding.'

'Quality like charity!'

'Yes, that is one. It has bifurcations like charity in the mode of goodness, passion and ignorance. The mode of goodness is recommended in scriptures whereas the other two are considered a waste of money.'

We can't even do charity now.

'There are other qualities like performance of material sacrifice, simplicity, forgiveness, freedom from envy and passion for pride, freedom from covetousness and anger; staying gentle, modest and clean, having compassion for other living entities and that also extends to animals and insects, non-violence.'

'I don't think one man can have so many.'

'Jim, that in literature is referred to as a godly man endowed with divine nature. I wish you weren't ignorant like the others but I can't make you think about the world like I do.'

'Is there anything that a lonely man can do in this front?'

'A lonely man is at an advantage.'

I frowned in disbelief. 'Advantage, you say?'

'Yes. A person, who depends on the mercy of God when he or she doesn't get support from anyone, is not alone. He may think he is lonely but he is with the best friend in the universe.'

'God.' She nodded. 'But this isn't practical way of life.' 'Yes it isn't. It is spiritual. God will take care of the one who has surrendered to him. He isn't alone and must not feel lonely for God is accompanying him in his every action. God gives him protection even in the darkest forests of the world.'

I recollected my walk at the dark forest. I was being protected by God. That fall from the balcony with the assassin, God protected me again and I fell in my study.

The air hostess was surprisingly late. A passenger had her engaged in a silly argument. She began serving us our meal along with the drinks.

'I guess we can take a break now,' said Noah.

'Yeah, I think we do.' For the next fifteen minutes while we were busy eating and drinking, my thoughts went on focusing on the seven sins she had mentioned: Lust, Gluttony, Sloth, Greed, Envy, Wrath and Pride. I made them all in my previous birth. Knowing that God was with me, I felt some hope that I will be able to pay for my crimes.

God is guiding me for a reason. I know my purpose now, and I will try to do what I must.

After the hostess cleaned our trays, it was time for me to tell Noah something. God had told me that the assassin I fought, who I was thinking to be Jonathan my editor in his youth, could time travel. He was likely enraged after an unexpected defeat in my hands. He was probably looking for the next opportunity to take his revenge. That meant he would come to my time and harm the persons who are close to me. I could not risk dragging Noah into this.

'Noah, I have to tell you something.'

'You committed sins?' That was meant as a joke but I was serious.

'I tried taking out some details of the Juber Corporation I told you about. Someone tried to kill me for it.'

'Jim,' she was shocked to hear it.

'I have taken care of him for now but this man will come back again to settle the score. I'm afraid that he will target the people closest to me.'

'Are you okay?' she became worried.

'Yes, I am and I will take care of myself. It is you who I am worried about.'

'Have you warned Jonathan?'

'As best as I know, Jonathan can't be trusted. I have more than enough reason to suspect his involvement with the murders.'

She needed some time to process that, 'Jonathan! It can't be.'

'I can understand. It came to me too as a shock the first time I...'

'The first time you...?'

'Never mind. It is a long story but he won't get away with all that he has done.' I told her so much in such a hurry that I didn't think about how she would take it.

'But what is it that he did?' She was puzzled and I thought that if I explained it to her, she would be terrified.

'Something terrible. But I can't tell you exactly what he did. Noah, you must stay away from him. He is not the good guy he shows himself to be. If he tries to contact you, try to avoid it. It is for your own good.'

'Why are you telling me this?' Her voice was startlingly low.

'Because...' my voice cracked and I paused. 'You and I are in grave danger.' Noah felt a chill hearing this. 'I fear that I have dragged you into this mess and I don't want you to get hurt cause of me.' She looked at me in an unfathomable expression. It made me feel guilty; I looked away for some time.

'Jim,' she called me and after some fight with my inner self, I managed to look back in her eyes. She saw sincere regret on my face and in order to reassure me, she placed her soft palm on my cheek. 'It's okay. I'll take care of myself,' she said.

'You must stay low. Try not to call me or meet me till I tell you it is over. Can you do that?'

'I've an arrangement at…' I put my hand over her mouth and stopped her from speaking further.

'It is better that I don't know about it.' I lifted my hand from her. She nodded.

'How do I get to know that everything's settled and safe?'

'I don't know how and when things will become safe for us, but I promise you that I'll take care of things.' She seemed to believe my whisper. That was all I could say to her. The next hour was difficult for her. She didn't eat properly. It was more difficult for me to convince her to go to sleep after a half-eaten meal. But somehow, I managed it. She looked so innocent while sleeping. With all the sensibility I had in me, I thought I did the right thing by warning her. But I had also given a space to guilt inside my heart now and it wasn't going to leave me till I sort everything out.

I looked outside the window. I wanted to see the landscape but it was dark and the flight's motion didn't make it possible for me to see the lights on the landscape below. Watching the expansive darkness through the mirror, suddenly, Icaught the reflection of a man with a hat, specs and coat that frightfully reminded me of the assassin. I turned around. There was a man moving to the first class.

The image dragged the violent memory of a near-to-death fight I survived about half a day ago, again. Suddenly, my fear surfaced and I could hear my own heartbeat.

I just hope this is my wild imagination. It can't be him.

I turned and looked at Noah and then back again at the curtain that separated the two classes. I got up, fought an urge to go and check if it was him. Then, sense struck me. 'If it really is him, he knows I am here and is probably luring me to come there!' I thought. A contrary thought occurred, 'He can't have weapons on board and won't stand a chance in a fist fight with so many people around to help me.'

After speaking to myself, a dash of courage got my feet moving. I paced to the first class. At the separating curtain, I stood and didn't move further while I examined the area. Everyone in the six seats was fast asleep. Only two had no one on them. Maybe someone had gone to economy or business class. But no one gives away a first class ticket! I went ahead carefully, to check the toilets. Both had the vacant sign on their doors. I opened one, it really was empty. I turned around and opened the other. It was also vacant. I looked to my left. Right ahead of me was the cockpit, locked from the inside.

There's no way he could be inside. Perhaps it was just my imagination. I sighed. Moving back to Noah, my eyes caught the comfort of the first class seat that could have been booked in my name. Luckily, it had no one. I had plenty of time to reach Los Angeles, so I thought that it wouldn't hurt to take a short nap on it. Being Jim Morgan had its perks. The staff wouldn't allow anyone to use it but it would make the exception for me. So I didn't bother taking permission and made a bed out of my seat. I looked at the seat beside mine. There was no passenger. It was like watching my very good friend, loneliness, giving me company. I looked up again, took a deep breath and closed my eyes. In the darkness of my closed eyes, I thought about what I would do once I would get off at Los Angeles. I realized that I had no answer. Only time would tell what was awaiting me.

The images of unpleasant dreams finished the journey with me.

# Chapter 7

I got off the plane, but I didn't say goodbye to Noah. I didn't want to derive the slightest clue of her destination. That would mean putting her life at risk. As I was walked out, I saw a small kiosk with books placed at a distance from the escalator, on the first floor. I went to the person at the counter. He seemed to have noticed me from a distance and instantly realized who I was.

'Sir, is it really you?'

'Yes it is me. Good to meet you. Do you have 'Killed by the Building?''

'Yes, sir. I do. Just a second!' he turned and pulled a book off a shelf with the label 'Jim Morgan Books.' 'Here you go sir.'

I took the book from him and pulled out my card to pay. 'Here.'

'I can't take money from you, sir!' 'Why not?'

'Not that I am your fan. But because of your books, my small bookstore runs well here. This is the least I can do to thank you.' That brought a smile on my face. I thanked him and turned toward the escalator, not knowing where to go therefrom. Some pride settled in me. My publishers and distributors, and bookstore owners were thankful to my writing for making their business run well. I had a copy of my third novel in hand. I was about to take the first step when I saw three men dressed in LAPD uniforms march toward me. One of them lead the other two. They stopped right in front of me. Looking directly at me, the leader with the badge name Marshal said, 'Mr. Jim Morgan?'

'Yes, that would be me. How may I help you officer?' 'We have orders to take you directly to the police department.'

'For what? What have I done?'

'Mr. Jonathan White was murdered in his apartment. We have orders to take you into custody for interrogation.'

'What?' I said that loud. Jonathan is dead?

'Sir, you must cooperate. Follow me, please.' The man turned around. The other two came behind me to ensure that I didn't run away. My legs began moving, but they felt heavy. It was extremely difficult for me to digest this news. Jonathan's dead.

The man leading me started to speak on a handheld device. 'Tell Captain Nash that we have him.' Then, he said, 'NYPD wired images of the crime scene to our department hours ago. Officers were told by the security guard that you were the last one he met. We had information of your travel. My team and I have been expecting you for some time, now. We tried communicating with you but your phone's been off.' The man demanded no explanation. It was more like a commentary with information to be given to a criminal. I was distressed the moment he told me that Jonathan was murdered. My mind said, 'Electronics are not allowed to be operated onboard!' But I couldn't bring myself to say it. There was only one understandable scenario for me. Jonathan White, the assassin killed his old self, my editor, Jonathan White.

'Have you contacted Miss Hawthorn?' he asked me.

Oh my God! What kind of an unexpected development is this? I asked her to stay low somewhere till an uncertain time. Now, she might be under suspicion for hiding after the murder! Or, they will think that I killed her, too. I didn't know what to say. I walked silently with them. It was a big airport. Even after covering a long distance the hallway still seemed never ending. Finally, the first set of words came out of my mouth, and they weren't the best choice of words.

'Guys, I didn't do anything.' They heard my plea, but given the orders they had to follow, nothing favorable could have been done from their end. The officer in front of me kept moving. We went past the initial security checkpoint. My sight fell on a man with the familiar black attire, sitting with a cup of coffee, at a table. It was God, watching me gather publicity as the cops took me into their custody. I kept walking with them to the exit, cursing my luck with every step. 'How could you just watch me end up this way?' I tried to talk to God in my mind. Our sights locked.

Right infront of the exit, were two cop cars. 'We will take the second one, Mr. Morgan,' said the officer. One officer took the wheel. The other took the other car. Their leader sat next to me in the back seat. No cop leaves a potential criminal alone in the back seat. The other car was about to lead us.

The cop behind the wheel turned on the overhead siren and it generated ear-splitting noise. I had to shout for my voice to reach the front seat, 'Is that necessary, officer?' The officer turned around and confirmed in a raised voice, 'I'm afraid so, Mr. Morgan.' I couldn't imagine how these cops operated every day with such high noise levels, and even deal with gunfire in some cases.

The car picked up speed. After ten minutes of sitting silently inside the car, trying to connect the dots that led to the murder of White, I finally looked up. At the St. Lauren roundabout, the first car took the third exit and we followed. I knew the city well. My experience with Smith and Jones had led me to attend parties and several book signing events. All that experience had familiarized me with the roads of this big place. In the next signal, cars stopped ahead of us, waiting for the signal to turn green. The cop driving the front vehicle steered into the oncoming lane. Every other car on the road stopped with due respect to the noise of the LAPD siren. I never had been at the receiving end of such treatment, and I didn't like it. After crossing a bridge, we took a left from Mariott Hotel, where I had spent a couple of disappointing nights owing to the poor service. The station was just around the corner now.

The man took out a walkie-talkie from the dashboard. His voice was barely audible to me as the noisy siren swallowed most of the verbal communication. There was one more surprising thing. He spoke informally, in a way that was not expected from an official sent to take a high profile author into custody. Then, as I looked out, I saw God standing on a pavement, looking at me. My eyes were locked on his figure as we went past him. I lost sight of him and his voice sounded in my left ear.

'He should not be in this timeline. You can see that he has started to create turmoil.' He appeared in the navigator's seat.

'These people think I did it. How can I say that someone from the past came to kill himself in the present? It will make me sound insane.'

'Well, then, what would you say?'

'I don't know if I should say anything till I call my lawyer. I have the right to remain silent under the law.'

'Well, then, you should think of a way to escape.'

'I'm not brave enough to risk an escape. That'll confirm to them that I have a hand in the murder.'

'Mr. Morgan, who are you talking to?' The main officer asked me. I looked at him first then to the front seat. There was no one next to the driving cop.

'Nobody, officer. It is just me and my imagination.'

He didn't argue or comment in response. We reached the police quarters. The boom barrier was open for us. The siren was finally silenced. But now, it didn't matter as it had effectively given me a headache in the initial five minutes. Their voices were audible, but it hurt my ears when words reached them. He got off and opened the door for me. I got off the car and saw a huge board atop the building. LAPD. Right in front of the building was a decent garden and big poles with the US flag on them. The wind was dead at that moment, just like my editor.

'Come, we must hurry.' I didn't breathe properly till he took me to the large hall on the first floor. Many eyes fell on me. Many knew me well, but now, my name had entered their list of "Most Wanted Criminals."

'Please sit down, Mr. Morgan. I will be back.' I took the seat at a table that faced a window and a large wall. He left. I was alone inside. I thought it was the cabin for one of the top officials who would handle a high profile case like mine. I looked behind me. There was a large glass.

Outside, I noticed a man being pressed against a wall as he was being frisked by two cops. One had drawn a gun and stowed it after the convict was frisked. I wonder why they kept me in a senior official's room. So far, they've been cordial. Maybe, it is the calm before the storm. I had no way of knowing what was going on in their minds. In just a couple of minutes, I heard a mix of the sirens tearing the silence of the room from what I thought were two-three police cars.

I turned to look at the hall through the window. I felt my apprehension rise when I saw the men sprinting up and down the hall, organizing things. The Captain must be here, I told myself. I heard someone burst inside the hall. That must be him. What a terrifying entry it was. He was a small man with a poker face. He must have been in his late forties. He entered the hall to a standing welcome from every officer. I observed his poised demeanor. He entered the room straight away.

'Mr. Morgan, I am Captain Nash from NYPD. Before you question my authority to handle this case, let me tell you, I do have jurisdiction here. Mr. White has been murdered. The department called for me and as you can see, I am here with you. Just like us, you would have many questions. You will get all your answers soon. So…' He was a hell lot smarter than his looks presented him to be. I realized that I had to be very careful during the interrogation. It would be easy for him to know when I was lying. 'Mr. Morgan, please follow me.' As I followed him, I felt the eyes of many police officers judge me. I never liked the eyes of fans on me, and this made me all the more apprehensive. We went to one end of the hall where an officer opened the door to a stairwell that led a basement. We descended the stairs when I started to size him up. He stopped walking when we reached our destination. The long corridor from the end of the staircase turned left. He brought me to the door of a room. Beyond the door, I knew that I was going to be interrogated. This must be it. The interrogation cell.

He turned around and said, 'Mr. Morgan, I'll see you inside in a while.'

'Will anyone else be joining us?'

'That you will get to know in some time. Now please,' he said, and motioned toward the door. For courtesy's sake, he opened it up for me. I went in without asking him anything, and he didn't take long to shut me in. The interior of the cell was nothing more than what I had expected it to be. There was a table with two chairs, and a regular expansive rectangular glass through which every action, expression and word of a suspect was recorded and scrutinized from the other side. I moved a couple of steps ahead and looked at myself in the mirror. The signs of lack of sleep were clearly visible in my partially swollen eyes. My nightmares hadn't let me sleep properly in the flight.

I thought I was supposed to sit, so I took the chair that faced the door. The air inside was eerily cold and dry. Many convicts must have been proved guilty of crime and sent to jail after grueling questioning. Anyone in my place would feel abandoned and cornered. A sense of being overpowered in a cage could easily make the man with the toughest wits break and give in. Besides, when someone was going to be interrogated by a professional and seasoned interrogator like the Captain, there is no scope to hide things. It's only a matter of time till everything would be revealed.

I looked around to capture the isolation that the walls had created for me. But the first thought that came to my mind did not fit the situation I was in. It was paradise, for a writer. An exceptionally quiet and secluded room was a haven for any writer to sit in and take as long as the mind would want to travel through its thoughts and return to write. I waited. It must have been two minutes. I started tapping my fingers on the table subconsciously, and it broke the silence. There was nothing to do. I looked at the mirror to my right. The image of my eyes looked back at me. I wondered how many eyes were watching me from the other side.

The door opened and pulled my gaze away. He entered the cell with a cup in hand. The air from the outside pushed the aroma to my nostrils. It was easy to identify that it was black coffee. I wasn't sure if he had brought it for me.

'I apologize for being late, Mr. Morgan. The machine takes its time to pour out a decent coffee. This is for you!' I didn't expect hospitality at a place where answers were squeezed out of a person in my place. I was grateful to him for his offering. My addiction to coffee became clear when I didn't take too long to accept it.

'Thank you Captain.' 'I figure you'd need it.'

I was about to take a sip but his comment got to my mind first. I stopped my hand from bringing the cup to my lips. I hesitated to take it, but after what he said, it seemed sensible to drink it.

'It appears like you haven't slept for a day or two.' 'How do you know?' I asked him. He was standing. The question was stupid, as it challenged his efficiency in doing his job. As a master of crime solving intelligence, he had arranged every detail of my time with Jonathan and after Jonathan. He would know the answer even before I would tell him. He scanned my expressions.

'Nobody can sleep after killing someone.' Coffee hadn't reached my stomach yet, and his piercing opening woke up my senses. The sudden dread he sent to my heart made it hard for me to drink. I put the cup back on the table. But his eyes stayed fixed on me. 'I hope you give us specific answers to my questions. That will save us both our time and effort.'

I felt his eyes arresting mine. There was an overwhelming power in the way they looked at me. The eyes that were so plain on the surface that they sent a chill to my bones. I wondered where I would start.

'What brings you here, Mr. Morgan?' 'Research.'

He sensed my unease. 'Oh yes, why else would an author waste time traveling when he could have been writing!'

Given his expressionless face, it was impossible to see what was going inside his brain. 'Would you care to elaborate?'

'Yes, definitely.' This time, I hoped he sensed my sincerity.

'Mr. Morgan,' I raised my eyes. 'My wife is a fan. Care to sign the copy? This is off the record. I would appreciate it if you help me keep it that way.' He took my own copy of Killed by the Building and asked me to sign it for his wife? I didn't understand. Was he being sarcastic? Or, was he toying with me? I couldn't understand. For a brief moment, he had slowed down with the questions. I didn't respond to his request and returned to his purpose being here.

'God knows I am innocent.' 'Every sinner has to say that.' 'I am not a murderer.'

He took the seat and gave silence a moment before piercing me with following words. 'I understand that a writer has the skill to enjoy living alone. What you don't understand, Mr. Morgan, is that when you are thrown behind bars, and hear the screams of killers like yourself night and day through the wall next to your cell, you beg to reverse things, but you can't.'

'Listen, why don't you do your job and find the real killer and interrogate him?'

'That is exactly what I am doing!' He banged the table with fury. The echo lingered for a second.

I got up and turned away. I shook my head four times and got back to my chair. 'I didn't kill Jonathan, okay? Your interrogation, tricks and techniques won't change that!' I paused to take a breath. He peered at me through his piercing eyes. 'If you're an honest cop and you're as good as they say you are, you would find the real killer.'

'If you're not the killer, why don't you help me understand who is?' He spoke like a cop would when he had evidence against the one he was interrogating. I failed to reason with him. He just wouldn't listen. So I spoke no further. I just looked away.

'Mr. Morgan. I will give you some time before you plead guilty. You can take this book and read it. Because if you killed Jonathan White, I promise you that you will only read behind bars next time.' He left me, determined to prove me guilty. I was all alone again. Fifteen minutes later, he entered the room next to mine from where they scanned all the expressions and words. Only the main officer Marshal who brought me here was there, scanning me.

The officer said to the Captain, 'He obviously has powerful connections. What surprises me is that nobody is here to bail him out.'

'Did he ask for a phone call?' 'No sir he didn't'

'That's all the more peculiar.'

'A man of his profile could hire the most expensive and efficient lawyer and you won't even get a single second inside there with him.'

Captain Nash knew that Marshal was right on this. 'Did he do something strange?'

'Nothing,' he recollected if there was anything that I did which would qualify as strange. 'Except, that when we were bringing him here, in the car, he was acting like he was talking to someone?'

'Talking to whom?'

'I don't know sir. It might be an imaginative person or a ghost. God knows what runs in the mind of authors,' he shrugged his shoulders as he spoke.

'Hmm, keep an eye on him. If he's the one, then he'll break soon enough.'

'Yes sir.'

'And if he as much as sneezes, you inform me.' Captain's instructions were clear.

Marshal grabbed his seat again and peered silently through the see-through glass. He saw me sitting with my arms rested on the table. His eyes kept on watching like a predator waiting for its prey to make a wrong move. He saw me get up after a while. He took the radio device immediately from his table. I went off to one corner of the room with the book inside my coat's large pocket. I fell to my hips and then for reasons I couldn't tell myself, I took out the book from my coat.

'Should I report this to the Captain?' Marshal was in a dilemma so he waited for a minute more to make up his mind. The way I was reading my own book looked harmless. He had his hand pressed on the remote radio device that connected him directly to the Captain's office upstairs.

'Yes Marshal, do you have a message for the Captain?' Someone on the other side said. What he was seeing occurred as nothing important to be reported immediately. In one of his former instances he had taken the instruction literally. When the suspect sneezed inside the cell, he informed the Captain after which he got yelled at. He didn't like being yelled at.

'No nothing, Marshal off.' He decided to stay in the parallel cell and just observe my every move.

# Chapter 8

Four hours straight into reading, I finished the book. I was still inside the interrogation room. I wondered where the portal was. I turned the pages of my book again. Nothing happened. 'What do I do now?' I asked aloud. Not getting an answer, I tossed the book to the side. The cover reeked of murderous intentions. It was far deadlier than I had intended it to be. I took the book and scanned the cover. A dark brown-colored haunted building at the center, a shadow looming next to it, broken slabs of rubble and sandstone scattered around the place, a purple sky, a black background and scorched trees around filled the cover. I looked at the shadow. As I moved deeper, my senses stopped working for a second. In an instant, I found myself standing in the place of the shadow, facing the building. I was inside the horrifying picture and it sent shivers through my body, again. My soul had deserted hope for good a moment earlier, had now found change. My gut feeling told me to go into the place and find connections to the victims. I wasn't sure which year or place I was in, but I was sure that I was in the past.

I entered the abandoned building through a large door. Somehow, it felt familiar, but I couldn't frame where I had seen this door before. The darkness and the aroma in the space around me gave me a sense that something wrong was going to follow. The emptiness that filled my surroundings made me look for someone. Several questions filled my head. My inner voice said, 'Walk further, Jim, walk!'

As I walked into the gigantic hall, a sense of unease held me in its grip. The hall ended with a cream colored wall. Just before it, was another wall that created a narrow passage in the space that remained. I wondered what its purpose was. I went to the passage. There was nothing special about it. Then, I looked at the wall. Large slabs were cut into squares to make up the wall. It appeared to be artificial wood. There were letters engraved on seven of them:

S M V M M J S

I could not make out if they were an abbreviation or a code. I pressed my ear against the wall to feel something. The space beyond this wall felt hollow. Knocking confirmed it. I remembered in my book, that I had mentioned a hidden chamber in the building that took lives. Perhaps there was a switch that led into another hall or room. A rigorous look at the wall to find a hidden lever proved futile. I wondered where it was, as I tried pressing my hand at various points. I didn't stop pressing the squares, hoping it would get me entry beyond. After several presses, nothing happened.

Then, the letters got my attention. They were nine feet above. I was six feet tall. I jumped to press the squares with the letter S. Nothing happened. Then, I jumped and pressed M and got the same result. 'God, what am I doing here? Why am I even doing this?' My hand landed on one square, three feet above my head at V. Then, I tried all the letters except the last. I gave up hope, but realized that it wouldn't hurt to try the last. The last one went in a little when I touched it. The S glowed blue and the locket that I held shone. A wide part of the wall swung. I was kicked inside. It closed right after I got in.

There was some light in the place I stood at. I turned around and started pressing different parts of the wall. After fifteen minutes of futile work, I realized I was trapped. There was a way in but no way out through the same door. Maybe there was a way out at the end of this area. I turned to observe the place.

At first, I felt I was standing at an astronomical observatory. This place was different. It was unlike any place I had ever seen in my life. The inside of the star filled room had no boundary and no floor. It was as if I was floating in outer space. There were stars under my feet and there was no bottom. There were stars above me. Straight ahead, I had a jaw-dropping view. Planets rotated around the Sun. I couldn't believe my eyes. I was not sure to check or not, but without any intention, my feet moved. I descended a couple of feet. Reaching the center, I felt a little warmth. I held my breath and looked up, absorbing the magnificence of the planets. 'What kind of a room is this? It looks so real!' I thought I was in a room that was painted and crafted to imitate the solar system. But my soul told me I was in outer space. I still believed my limited thoughts. Watching the exquisitely crafted planets, I was amazed. I couldn't imagine how someone had managed to create this intricate technology in forty years!

That was when I noticed something strange. There wasn't Uranus, Neptune, Pluto and Earth: just the Moon of the Earth and five other planets, Mercury, Venus, Mars, Jupiter,

Saturn and the Sun. I tried finding some reasoning in my memory.

'The planets were considered devtas in the Indian context and heavenly bodies in the western astrology.' These were the words I heard from an Indian astrologer once. I should have taken the astrology class from Kapiel Raaj. That would help me understand why someone created this room and only placed planets that are used in astrology. I remembered that my publishers had advised me to meet the world's number one online Vedic astrologer for research purpose when I was working on my seventh novel. The meeting could have been arranged easily given my profile but I discarded the notion that astrology will interest millions. Not believing that millions around the world have stern belief in the concept that their life is actually run by a mixture of karmas and heavenly planets that exerted divine influence.

The magnificence of the planets had me completely amazed. I went further to absorb the beauty of these big objects when I heard the same wall piece turn throwing two men inside. 'Who could that be,' I said to myself. Not wanting to be seen, I went up to the last planet revolving- Saturn and hid behind its slow movement. I observed the two men coming close to the Sun.

'I can't believe it!' One of the men was Mr. Holmes. I was able to clearly see his face, still hiding myself behind Saturn. 'What's he doing here?' I wondered. I tried to see who the other was. He seemed familiar, and I wondered where I had seen him. He looked very, very familiar. I started rummaging in my memories. It wasn't easy. I had met many people in my life, both important and ordinary. Diving into the vast ocean of faces that I had in mind was easy. Finding the one face that stood twenty feet away from me was like searching for a lost bottle in the ocean. A photograph appeared in a flash before my eyes.

'Oh my God! It is Mark Hawk, one of the partners of Juber Corporation! Could it be that Holmes is the kingpin behind these four partners? But what's he doing here with Hawk?' A sound that I didn't recognize, cracked and I returned from my faraway thoughts.

Holmes spread his arms wide before the view. 'Witness my creation!' he said, as his voice reverberated with excitement. 'I give you the seven astronomical planets!' The second person was surprised. He couldn't believe how real these objects looked. Holmes gave him a moment. 'Do you have your locket?' Hawk nodded proudly. He plunged his hand into his shirt and pulled out his oval locket with the initial M. Both, Holmes and Hawk eyed the glitter of the green locket in his hand. It wasn't possible for me to see it clearly from where I stood. Yet, watching them gave me a sense that the lockets meant something to these powerful people. Hawk glanced up to look at the planets but his gaze met mine mid-way.

'Who's there?'

The illumination of Saturn wasn't much, but when I glanced down; watching my shadow speak for my presence paralyzed me. 'Goddammit!' My ignorance landed me in trouble again. Hawk advanced toward me to have a look. I reasoned with myself that I should withdraw and try to hide somewhere in the shadows of the hall. But my instinct told me to stay where I was. Swallowing my apprehension, I stood at my place. I hoped he couldn't see me just like the assassin of Stephen couldn't see me. He stood two steps before me. I looked at him and he looked back at me. I stopped breathing and didn't move a muscle. Hawk looked at a man whose eyes were begging for mercy. 'There's no one here, sir.' He turned and went back to Holmes.

I could have sworn that he had seen me. I watched him leave me in confusion. I also knew that the people who were connected with me in any timeline could see me. I safely assumed that only Jonathan the assassin could see me and that Hawk wasn't on my timeline, so I was invisible to him.

'A few people realize that these planets are there to govern the everyday life and everything in and around us,' Holmes spoke to Hawk who wasn't ready for this statement.

With the little inputs I got from two astrology papers I read a year ago, I agreed with his knowledge of astrology.

Mr. Holmes saw the skepticism on Hawk's face and understood it. He continued, 'Ancient civilizations have been using the movement of the planets to predict rainfall, famine. Modern civilization being ridiculously selfish uses this science for amusement. You can see those losers flock at astrologers to know about career and marriage prospects.' Hawk went on listening. I also felt at that moment that western astrology had gained steps on the popularity index.

They moved further toward the planet Mercury. 'I had never been fond of the mystics of ancient India. But when I went on a trip to the land that had been a slave of the British for two centuries, I met a mystic sage. Just by looking at my face, he told me things that only I knew about myself. My past was accurately revealed in front of me and my future....' He stopped. Holmes paused briefly and then said, 'The sage said something that he shouldn't have and that cost him his life.' His fist became tighter as a memory reminded him of rage that ran through him. Perhaps the sage had predicted a bad future for him and so Holmes killed him. 'Since then I have admired the science of astrology and the marvel of these planets. That is why I built this planetarium.'

Not finding Hawk interested in his story he came to the point. 'Mercury is my favorite and that is you. It represents intelligence, communication, business, writing, speaking ability and media. Why'd you think that I only allowed you to handle the journalists and not the other partners?'

'Because I can speak,' responded Hawk.

'No. It is because you know when not to speak,' he corrected. 'Your expertise in handling complex questions by the media made me see your talent. It was only a matter of time that I had you working for me.' For an instant, I forgot the trash that Jonathan fed me and focused on his words to understand what these guys were really up to. He looked up directly at Hawk now, and locked eyes with him. 'The locket, please!'

'I'm curious. Why are our lockets made of the gem stones that a planet signifies?'

'These lockets are not merely ornaments to wear. They are keys.'

'Keys to what?'

'Keys to my hoarded treasure! Let me tell you where I stored my treasure. Look at Venus, the Goddess of beauty. All that appeals to you as luxury, convenience, comfort, dress, art, romance and a spouse are signified by Venus. The kind of girls you attract in life is represented by Venus.' I didn't understand why he was giving Hawk a lecture on astrology. But I had the feeling that he would store his precious items related to planets in the balls of each planet. He had Hawk mesmerized with his words. They moved together to Mars now. 'Mars is a soldier, he only takes commands from the king and is always ready to spurt into action. Sun is the king of all planets. Mars represents anger,

competition, sports and will power. Cuts, burns, bruises, blood. Mars also represents land.'

'He has stacked papers of his properties in the giant ball of Mars!' I thought.

'Jupiter is the king's minister. It represents wisdom and expansion. It is also a teacher and gives opportunities to increase wisdom.' Even with his six foot height and good build, Hawk felt small standing close to the enormous Saturn Globe beyond which I was hiding. The rings around it were as captivating as looking at the real ones. Holmes paused and motioned toward the next planet. 'Saturn is the general of the army. It also shows deeds of past and present. This general is the hardest worker of them all. It also represents the limitations, boundary, restriction, order and law, discipline and it delays things.'

As much as Saturn had been talked about in the world because of its beautiful rings, it appeared spectacular in a model too. I scanned the planet and my eyes stopped at the most attractive ring where the heart of its beauty lied. I kept staring it in silence, stupidly waiting for the ring to start revolving. From the discussion that was taking place, I clearly made out that Holmes had done everything in his power to gather his amassed fortune and placed it inside the planets. Whether drugs, cash or papers, I wasn't sure, but I had a feeling that the planets were not empty and had these in them.

'Moon is the mind and it is the emotion. It is the queen of all planets and it represents water. It is the fastest in movement as it clears one zodiac sign in just two and a half days. Our mood changes quickly just like the Moon flies quickly.'

'Hmm,' uttered Hawk.

'So what do you think of it' Holmes asked Hawk. 'Beautiful, aren't they all?'

'Yes,' he said while looking at them. 'But I'd like to know what's hidden inside them.' Of the four partners, Hawk was the sharpest, most detail oriented- a trait that resembled the planet Mercury. He knew that Holmes wouldn't waste a fortune on pump and show planetarium meant for nobody. There had to be a secret behind it. I wondered the same thing. Why blow up a fortune in creating such a magnificent creation of art and not show it to anyone except Hawk?

'Interesting. You are much faster than the others!' said Holmes. His expressions were of amazement.

'Others?' Hawk asked. Holmes smiled at his question and proceeded toward the Sun again.

This meant that he had brought Michael Welsh, Jason Smith and Stephen too, previously. I wonder what he had done with them.

Holmes now stood at the center of the system, under the glow of the Sun. He spread his arms, embracing the warmth that spread from it.

'Behold, the king of all planets!' he said, glancing up at the Sun. Pride was visible in his eyes. 'Sun is the power, the authority, leadership and brightness that shines on others.'

'The only thing that you shone on others is grief,' I commented in mind. Despite my disinterest in astrology and planets, I wanted to know more. After hearing many people of my time dive into the science, I had least interest. I never understood why people made such a fuss about astrology. Somehow, Holmes's knowledge intrigued me.

'So, Mark, it's always no holds barred with you, isn't it?

No limits to what you will do!"

'Well, not entirely. There is a line I will not cross.'

Holmes smiled. 'I trust you with your locket and expect you to give it to me when I need it.' Hawk didn't say a word. His face showed disapproval. He handed the locket over to Holmes. The moment Holmes felt the locket in his palm he quickly turned to the Sun and spread his arms wide as if he had received magical powers. Controlling his reaction, he put the locket in his pocket, felt the warmth under the sun for a long time, turned to Hawk and said, 'I am eternally grateful to you. You will always receive my best!' Hawk faked a smile. He turned and the two slowly moved toward the wall that gave them entry. I didn't look at them. My eyes were locked onto Saturn's rings. But my ears were active. The silent closing of the secret door told me that I was sealed inside. I wondered how they got out of the same door. What was I to do? I waited for a couple of minutes to make sure they had left for good. After a while, my ears got used to the silence that prevailed inside the space. I assured myself I was alone. I stepped out of my cover and stood before the seven planets. From where I stood, I absorbed the grandeur of the gigantic balls. My trips to the past only had sour experiences and pain to offer so far, but this trip was different.

Was I sent back in time just to listen to a conversation or to watch these planets before my eyes? My curiosity to find an answer was about to override my carefulness. I moved closer to Saturn. The letter S was engraved on the huge ball. I drew closer to it. It looked like the engraving on Stephen's locket. Why was it here? I reached for it, but it was beyond my reach. I stood on tiptoes and tried to touch it. My hand managed to touch the ring.

In an instant, the planets became more active and their rotational speeds increased. There was a very strange, high-pitched sound that generated from the movement. The jolt that the movement gave me and the ear-splitting volume it was in startled me. I covered my ears with my hands and pressed them hard, but the noise was killing. The Moon caught speed, as it had the fastest time clearing a zodiac. The Sun, Mercury and Venus had relatively lesser speed, but they were coming in fast, too. I was at the center of their movement. I had to dodge them, but the constant rotation had trapped me in their orbits.

'What the heck? Aah…' I cried loudly as the ear-splitting noise gave me severe pain that reached my brain and stopped me from focusing. I got down on my knees and got up again. My eyes caught the Moon coming at me like a bullet. Everything went still for a moment. I could hear myself swallowing my saliva. I could hear my heartbeats. All of a sudden, the Moon hit me. The sheer force tossed me many feet back, and I fell immediately, thanks to its sheer mass.

My vision blurred before I lost consciousness.

# Chapter 9

Before I opened my eyes, my ears picked up on the sound of distress. It was continuous, sounding like an active ambulance. I woke up with a start. I was on a stretcher. I was being moved inside an ambulance, or at least it felt like that. The alarm hurt my ears. 'My God!' I said, as I struggled to gain sense of my position. Straightening my body wasn't painless. The collision with the Moon had left a lasting impact. I wished that my bones were still in place.

It took me a few seconds to acknowledge that I had arrived back in my timeline. The nurse next to me was examining me. I couldn't move as I was strapped to the stretcher. She looked at me. I must have looked like I had a shock and I was still not out of it. A police officer sat opposite me. It wasn't pleasant to see them both. I closed my eyes and blocked them from my vision. Ironically, I had a few hours to sleep, but not the way I wanted it to be. The door of the ambulance yawned open. The view wasn't friendly. Three armed cops stood outside to assure that I wasn't going to attempt an escape. The nurse and another medical assistant along with the cops helped me come down. I was still on the stretcher.

'Can you get up, Mr. Morgan?' one of the cops asked me. I looked closely. My vision was still blurred. It was Marshal. At the cold question, the nurse rebuffed the officer with an angry glare. He didn't ask anything further. I tried standing. After a short while, I got up. My body was in pain but I could move. I lifted my shoulder to see if it was working.

'Mr. Morgan you must take it easy,' said the nurse.

'I'm okay, I think. Just that my body is in pain,' I replied. I got up without permission. The nurse came to me and the police surrounded me from all sides. They were successful in making me appear like a fugitive.

'Sir, you must lie down. We'll take you for examination,' the nurse said. The nurse and Marshal helped me get on the stretcher again. They began to move me. I reluctantly gazed up at the gigantic building. I dreaded hospitals most. Two cops were stationed at the gate. Marshal and another went to the admission department to finish all the paperwork. I was taken to the first floor in the elevator. I saw lights pass as I was taken into room number 101. It seemed like the last room on the floor, from the elevator.

What was I going to tell them when they ask me what happened? I got up, again without permission. The nurse didn't complain and began examining me again. She took some blood from my left shoulder, and from her expression, it seemed like she had recognized me. Perhaps she knew who Jim Morgan was.

I tried to start a conversation to make myself feel better. 'The blood report and blood pressure would not reveal anything out of the ordinary. I think I am just fine.'

'You will be okay. You are in good hands!' Her eyes twinkled and she turned away with the blood sample. Suddenly, a huge blast shook the entire building. The nurse fell and I got a strong jolt. The sound was not only ear-splitting, but also shook us from our feet. I was scared and ran to the door to find an escape. I opened the door and heavy smoke blew inside. The blast must have taken place at the other end of the floor.

I extended myself from the room. The smoke limited my line of sight. I looked up at the ceiling. There were sprinklers, but they didn't seem to work. The floor badly needed them to work. There was fire at the elevator that I could see, and in the area adjoining it. Smoke started to spread and became less dense. I couldn't see much. I looked back at the nurse, she was still shaken from the blast. I turned my face back at the corridor. What I saw next stunned me to my core.

My nemesis stood at the far end of the corridor, with his hand stretched outwards, holding a gun as he took aim at the head of an inspector. In an instant, he pulled the trigger. A loud sound roared. The poor inspector's body heaved back as the bullet went through his brain. I moved back into my room. The tremors were still alive in my mind and heart. I heard more gun shots after the first. He must have been eliminating everyone who dared to come in his line of sight.

'What the hell?' My heart pounded. I dared to look outside again. I stared down the corridor cautiously. There he was, advancing like a pro hunter. How did he know I was here? My darkest fears had surfaced. My thoughts shifted from taking the nurse with me to finding a way to stay alive myself. I mustered enough courage to sneak past his gaze and hide in the next room. I thought that all I had to do was to stay alive for a few more minutes and that policemen and fire-fighters would flock to the floor. I explained the risk to myself. I saw him look into a room. My heart raced as it realized that it was my moment. I broke into a sprint and with muffled steps, entered the room next to mine. Unfortunately, my dash got his attention. I stood with my back pressed tight against a wall. My heart was constantly pumping.

Within seconds, he reached near my room. I heard his heavy footsteps. Now that he was at the door, he took a step inside. I didn't want to make the slightest noise. I was unarmed, weak and scared. Pressing my lips tight, I prayed. 'God, just don't let him come inside!' The next moment, a loud clang came from the room I was previously in. The nurse must have dropped something. I noticed him. Cautious, he spun and dashed after the sound, going inside with the gun, ready to hunt his next target.

As he went in, I got out and prepared myself for another sprint across the corridor. There was no way I was going to engage in a fist fight with him. I took two steps and heard a shriek from the nurse, followed by the sound of two bullet shots. Enduring the pang of the loss of this woman, I hastened and quickly got inside a room that was two rooms away from mine. When I hid behind the door, a troubled breath came out of me.

Not finding me in room number 101, he got out quickly and started searching the next. 'That was too close,' I said to myself. I looked out again, carefully, and peered to my right. I realized that he was in the next room, about to come out any second. I looked to my left. The adjoining space to the corridor was my way out. I hoped he wouldn't spot me running. I ran, without looking back. A large door next to my door opened. An old man emerged from inside and pulled me toward himself. Behind him, I saw a staircase.

'Come with me if you want to live!' His hoarse voice cut the smoke and reached me. My eyes went wide as I saw him. He had a ghostly appearance. He spun around and ran up the stairs. I followed him. We reached the ground floor. At the top of the stairs, there was another blast from the floor above that shook us completely.

'He's going to bring the whole hospital down,' I thought.

People rushed out onto the foyer. The floor's security system was working perfectly. We heard the alarms. We got out, and it turned out that he had a car parked right opposite the gates. He ran to it and I followed. He took out an electronic key and opened the door. Just when I was about to sit, another blast took care of the windows of the first three floors.

'My God!' I said, as I looked at the black smoke. Fire and shards of mirror flew out.

'Get in quickly, it is not safe in here!' the old man shouted. I got in. Without wasting a second, he put his foot on the accelerator and raced outside.

Afraid that things weren't safe at the police station, I had to ask him to pull over to a hidden place. 'If you have a place where we can lie low for a while, let us go there!' I said. He nodded with his eyes on the road. With the help of this stranger, I managed to escape. The speed of events and the questions growing in my mind didn't let me sit and taste relief, even momentarily. This stranger was definitely someone I had seen forty years ago.

# Chapter 10

We didn't need to search for a safe place to hide. He pulled the car to a house located in the south of the city. The locality was peaceful. It was miles away from the noise of the city. I thought it was his house, or a property of his. 'Come, we are safe here!' he said.

I got off after him. As he unlocked the front door, he said, 'Don't be worried, you're safe with me.' I was a little apprehensive seeing him, again. I didn't know his true intentions. But if he wanted me dead, he would not risk his life trying to save mine at the hospital. I felt my optimism yanking me into the house. I followed him into the living room. Still in fear, I went to the window and glanced around the street to double check that my nemesis wasn't following us. I drew the curtains back so that nobody could see us. I was still afraid.

'Who's the terminator back there?' he asked.

I turned and saw him on his feet. My voice was low. 'You won't believe it even if I tell you.'

'I have seen a lot, son. Nothing surprises me now!' I believed him. He had seen me four decades ago in the chamber of planets. Now that he was looking at the same person in the same attire, and one hadn't aged one bit, he was not likely to be surprised.

'You can relax, now. I doubt he'll follow us here. I have all the time in the world to know what's been happening.'

I agreed and decided to sit. After a slight rub of my lips, I began, 'My name's Jim Morgan.'

'I know who you are, Jim. I read all about you since your first book hit the market. I was surprised to see the same face I saw hiding behind Saturn. Still as fresh as it was, decades ago. What surprised me was how it was possible.'

'Where do I start from? It is too complicated.'

'For others it may be. But I understand that there's only one plausible reason that tells me why you haven't aged. I know that you can time travel.' My eyes grew wide open. He clearly had the intelligence that Mercury epitomized.

'You may start wherever you feel comfortable, Jim.'

I relaxed a bit, gathered my thoughts and then began telling him all that was happening. 'I have written six bestselling novels. But these novels aren't ordinary books. There are certain pages, or lines, that I don't remember having written, but they're there. They're time portals that take me back to your time, when you were young and involved with Steve Holmes. Once I'm able to figure out that point, I am taken to the past.' My claim didn't go down well with him right away. It might have sounded utterly absurd to an ordinary man, but he was trying to process it. Even though the lines on his face showed signs of skepticism, he couldn't dismiss my explanation, seeing me now, looking exactly as I did, forty years ago.

'How do you come back from the past?'

'I can't explain how. I don't know how long I am in the past. When, how and through what medium I'll return, are also unclear. So far, these portals have only taken me to 1976. I don't know what date, time and place they will take me to. I just know that I am in the past when I can figure out lines or things I haven't written.'

'Who wrote those lines?'

'I don't know how to put this. You'll find it unreal. I will still say it, though. God.' He didn't speak for a moment and kept looking at me with curiosity in his eyes.

'Okay. But why are you going only to 1976?'

'Somehow, I was connected to all of you and I did some horrible things.'

'What horrible things?' he asked, looking a little lost.

At first, the question seemed normal. But a second later, I wondered the very same thing. That was exactly what I was not able to find out! Had I even done something wrong? Whatever I had seen so far had not revealed anything on how I had committed sins. It was all these people who had done wrong things - Stephen Malcolm, Victoria and Steve Holmes, the nameless mad man who was chasing me, Mark Hawk and the other two partners Jason Smith and Michael Welsh.

'Sir,' I said, leaning toward him and joining my hands. 'I am still trying to find that out.'

He was even more lost, now. I looked at him sincerely as I empathized with him for his confusion. He seemed uncertain. It was possible that he might not have believed me because I was an author. He was likely to wonder if I was sharing fiction or truth. Yet his expressions reflected patience. Deep down, he knew I was telling him the truth.

He scanned my face and then whispered, 'That's a miracle. You haven't aged one bit.'

Somehow I had seen this coming. I wanted to tell him that I was visited by the creator of the universe but something told me that it would be too much for him.

'I met the mad assassin who blew up the hospital in your timeline.' He frowned listening to this. 'I would like to say he is nameless since that's convenient for me. I got him in my time and almost killed him, but for reasons I can't explain, he has the power of time.'

'What do you mean by 'he has the power of time?''

'He can come and go back from and to your time as he wishes.'

'That's serious. How do we get rid of him?'

'For the time being, I think by staying low and hidden.

Not letting him know where we are.' 'I guess you're right.'

'I want to know about you and Steve Holmes. I need to know everything about the factory, the partners and whatever happened that year.'

'Hmm…' His eyes were down. He recollected from his memory. 'How much do you know about us?'

'I've traveled only thrice. I met Stephen at his house where he was killed. I saw Victoria at her house and you in the chamber of planets. So far, I can only make guesses as I don't know much. But I do get the general picture.'

'Okay. Do you know that Holmes has been supplying Pinatina, a white color powdered drug that was banned in the States but was smuggled through Mexico?'

'He was a smuggler?'

'He was far more brutal than that. Smuggling was only one part of his business in which we were connected. We were making tubes lights, but you don't make a fortune with that. You make a fortune when you transfer Pinatina in the tube light, across border.'

'So he made you a part of it and made money for the partners involved.'

'I hadn't known it till my partners got me involved in Juber Corporation. I had my suspicions, but it was confirmed later. I was naïve, but not a complete fool. We wanted to become rich soon. It was compelling.'

'Tell me where it started from. That will be good for me!' I prepared to listen. The story was definitely likely to be astonishing.

'Stephen, Michael, Jason and I were good friends. We were young and eager to make money. But people at our respective workplaces were hostile toward us. We were engaged in jobs where they devalued our existence and contribution.' I was silent, listening keenly. His words revived an old ordeal. I had felt that in my life too, being devalued. Many publishers had devalued my first book. After eighteen rejections, I found Smith and Jones, who believed me.

'After a month's gap, Michael came out of nowhere. He married Victoria Holmes, the only daughter of Steve Holmes. Everyone knew that Holmes was involved with the underworld and had powerful connections in the political world. His connections and power gave him space to run his illegitimate business without being taken to court. He had vested interests in many businesses: fuel, power, steel, all in the names of which he ran his drug trade. Then, there was education.'

'Education?' I interrupted.

'Yes. He was smart and picked up sectors where he could easily hide his true business. He made people work for him at gunpoint. His only purpose was to make money. He would do anything and everything that would give him money and power. In troubled times, Michael gave us a great opportunity to serve Holmes and live the lives of millionaires. It was evident that he had conned Victoria somehow and made her marry him. Holmes wouldn't do anything to hurt Victoria. That meant that he would not go against his son-in-law, so the game was in Michael's bag. At first, we were shocked with all that had happened and what was coming to us. We didn't know exactly what we were getting into. But, we knew that we would be working in a disguised occupation that would ultimately serve Holmes' motives. Anyone who dared cross Holmes was easily located, tortured and eliminated. But then the dread of our lives surfaced, compelling us to take up the offer. We were humble and simple with a spotless history. But do you know what?'

I looked at him intently. 'The lure of money and appreciation was immense. It led us to create a deceitful history for ourselves.'

'How did you join him?'

'Michael told us that Holmes had a powdered drug that he had to transfer to various cities in the country.'

'I read that it was Jason who came up with the idea of manufacturing tube lights.'

'Yes, you read correct. Jason was the wisest among us. In addition to the idea, Stephen's hard work and discipline paved way to stacking small quantities of the drug in each piece. I was good with numbers and accounts, so I handled that. Michael was exceptional at playing with emotions. He didn't do much work but he got the government officials involved in the project. He lured them to get things done for us. The officials didn't want their names associated with crimes and began working for us.'

I analyzed the qualities of each partner as he told me things about them. Jason had Jupiter's quality of wisdom and expansion. Stephen was disciplined and hard-working, which Saturn represents. Mark's number prowess is the strength of Mercury. Michael represented emotions like the Moon, although he used them for wrong reasons. How could this be a coincidence? It all seemed like a plan of God's. These four people would not come together with these traits in a timeline just to open a treasure. There was more to these lockets and planets that I can think now! He stared at me as I was long gone in a world of questions and thoughts.

'Jim. What are you thinking?'

'It cannot be a coincidence, Mark, that only the four of you came together in that project. Why was it only the four of you? Only because you were friends? I don't think it was a coincidence.'

'I agree with you. After some time, I spent some time each night, thinking about this. I realized that it wasn't Michael who had gotten us into this vicious circle. At first, I didn't want to credit it to faith. But after ruminating over it for some time, I discovered that we were chosen. Each of us had a locket that was made with very special gemstones. The lockets bore our initials. They were passed onto us by someone, and it wasn't a coincidence. I believe it was destiny. My grandfather passed it onto me. Jason and Michael bought them from a second hand store, the owner of which didn't find the oval of much value or relevance. Stephen's first girlfriend got it especially for him.'

'But how did Holmes get to know that you were the locket bearers?'

'My best guess is that somehow, Michael revealed his locket to him and Holmes must have figured that we each have our own.'

'Steve could have taken these with brutal force. Why didn't he do that?'

'I guess we were lucky!' I couldn't help the sarcastic expression that formed on my face. 'To be honest, I feel that these lockets have to be have been passed on willingly by the bearer. Else, they won't open the planets up.'

It seemed a reasonable explanation. 'I have the same feeling. Please continue.'

'Holmes' entire purpose was to make us give our lockets to him with our consent. He devised an ingenious plan to first have Michael in his favor, and then, the rest of us. We were given money, power, business and reputation. Who would resist giving him a locket?'

'That makes four. What about the rest?'

'Didn't you notice? He liked to be as powerful and rule like the Sun. His daughter's name was Victoria. The Venus' oval should have had the initial V. It cannot be another coincidence, right?'

My first and only thought was that it couldn't be a coincidence. Holmes had three lockets with him: the Sun locket which was his own, the Venus locket which was his daughter's and Michael's locket too, of the Moon. 'I understand now. Victoria would have a locket with her initial and a daughter could give it to her father without questioning. If I assume that Holmes has an oval with his initial, he had three with him.'

'He must have convinced Jason too. Maybe he had four.

That leaves us with the locket of Mars.'

'I was going to ask you about it. You should know who has the last one.' He shook his head. He had no idea. Frozen in his body, he thought for some time. He seemed to be collecting all his memories from every corner of his mind to search for a clue that would lead him to the last locket. Only, he couldn't find any.

'I don't know anything about the bearer of that locket.' 'It is okay. Let me know more about you and the others.'

'We thought everything would be alright. With Holmes' power and money, Michael's government connection, my knack to manipulate accounts, Stephen's public relations and Jason's wisdom, nothing could go wrong. Stephen was given maximum ownership since he was good with people and knew how to present things.'

'Who burnt your factory to the ground?'

'Beats me! They speculated that Victoria had an affair with Stephen and Michael destroyed everything in anger.'

'Did he?'

'No, he didn't. It was someone else for sure. It cannot be Michael. When it happened, I was out of the country on a leisure trip. When I came back, I met Holmes directly before finding out about this. He took me to the chamber of planets. The next night, when I got to know about all this, I escaped the country.'

'I wish you knew more,' I was disappointed and he must have heard it in my voice. 'Do you know what happened to Holmes later?'

'I read that a few days after our factory was destroyed, some cops found a dead body in his mansion. They said it was his. The tormentor didn't leave a single sign on the body to help forensics identify if it was Holmes.'

So everyone was killed except him and nameless! The thought reminded me to ask him about Jonathan. 'Do you know Jonathan White? He covered the incident.'

'The incident was covered by many reporters. That name doesn't ring a bell.' I wanted to know more about Jonathan. My mind was still grappling with the thought that the young White who I referred to as nameless killed the present White. But why?

'You look like you have many unanswered questions, Jim.'

'Yeah, one leads to another. I want to know what was inside those planets. Were these lockets keys to them? These planets in the chamber, do you think that he would hide his Pinatina inside them? Maybe he had gold or other illegal stuff inside them and that was why he kept the chamber hidden somewhere.'

'I don't know what was inside the planets. It definitely didn't have Pinatina or Gold. I sensed something magical about them, though. I do know that if there is something inside those planets, it makes him immeasurably powerful. These lockets might be the keys to open them. I can't explain how they made him powerful since he kept it extremely secretive. I guess it had to do with power or life.'

'I don't quite get you.'

'What do people with power and money want?'

'More power and money!' It didn't take me long to answer.

'Precisely. But these people know that they can't live forever. I've studied planets in Vedic, Jaimini, Eastern astrology books. Although immortality isn't mentioned in any text, I have a feeling that Holmes believes that by unlocking the mystery of the planets, he would gain eternal life.'

I realized that those planets meant more than what I had previously imagined. I asked him, 'What about the murder?' Before I could finish the question, I saw him delve into the memory lane.

'For many years, I've tried to forget what I was involved in. But I was a part of something unforgiveable. It followed me wherever I went.'

Despite the normal tone, I noticed the regret in his voice. He reached for his jacket pocket and pulled out his locket: the oval with his initial M. I was confused. 'How'd you get it?' I asked. 'I am certain that I saw you give it to him.'

'You're right. That night, I gave my locket to him. His pride was at its peak, his face was up at the Sun and arms spread wide. I knew that this object was precious to him and that it shouldn't be with him. Not wanting him to have his hands on something that would give life to his sinister plans, I acted immediately, taking it out from his pocket without him noticing it.'

I found some humor in his presence of mind that he showed back then. The smuggler got smuggled! He stretched his hand out to me. 'Here!' his eyes were locked on the locket while turning it around twice. 'I don't know what to say. I feel that it should be with you.' I held the precious item in my hands. At that moment, eyeing the locket that he had just given me, I was aware that a lot of answers were in the palm of my hand. Maybe God wanted me to open up those planets through these lockets. Seeing complete conviction in his eyes, my gut told me that this was all I would gather from him.

'You must take care of your family. They must be in New York.'

'No, I live alone!' In an instant, I was reminded of Kathryn. 'If that madman is after me, he might get to Kathryn too. I must tell her about this!' I thought. 'Mark, I need to make a call right away.'

'Yeah, sure!' He pulled out his phone from his pocket and handed it over to me.

I called Kathryn. She was in the city. I remembered her number perfectly, and waited as the line began ringing. She didn't answer the call. Before the line got cut, the automated answering machine began speaking, 'Hi! This is Kathryn Morgan. I am busy right now. Please leave a message after the beep!' The beep sounded, but the name Morgan resonated in my ears. My heart trembled. Morgan, Kathryn Morgan. She still had my name. My love for her rose again from the deep sea of long lost emotions.

'Is she there?' he asked. His whisper yanked me back to the present. I looked at him in surprise. Not knowing what to say to the voice message, I disconnected.

'She's not there!' The marked expression of a baffled man must have still covered my face, because he asked me, 'Is something wrong?' He watched me. The urge to meet her in an instant overwhelmed me and took control over my senses. In an instant, the amazement on my face evaporated.

'I must leave.' 'What's the hurry?'

'She's not safe with him around. I must warn her!' Having made it clear that I was leaving for my wife, I dashed to the door when his voice stopped me. 'Jim!' I turned around. He had a gun in hand. 'Pray that you don't need this.'

Seeing the gun reminded me of the Ruger Blackhawk I had seen in Stephen's killer's hand. I felt that the call of time may require me to part with humanity and pull the trigger at nameless. Though I wasn't sure I could commit a crime again, protection was necessary. He was around somewhere. I had to prepare myself for him! Anticipating a confrontation with my nemesis, I advanced to him and grabbed the gun. Strain filled my hand as I held the heavy Ruger. The weapon was old and big enough to cover most of my palm.

'No more sins!' I said to myself. Somehow, I didn't want to risk adding another sin to my share. Moreover, the cops would have declared me a fugitive by now. If they spotted me with a gun, it would only strengthen their case. My gut told me to return it to him. It was a risk I preferred not to take. My pious idea led me to hand the gun over to him. He was not in a mood to argue.

'Are you sure you won't need it?'

'I am sure that I would need it!' There was humor in the irony. 'But I must not add another sin to my list!' At that moment, it occurred to me that I had never asked him how he got to know I was at the hospital.

'Jonathan White told me you fled to Rome!' I said.

'Yes. One night, Stephen, through a telegram, asked me to take care of his wife and daughter. That night, I ascertained I would not see him anymore. Through the years, the memory only communicated misery to me, reminding me of all that I had done wrong, starting with the decision to join Holmes. Stephen and the others were like family to me. I decided to take care of his family and we fled to Rome where no one could track us. I did whatever I could to honor his last wish.'

'How'd you get here and follow me?'

'Intelligence can get you places. There's an officer called Marshal in the LAPD. He's my nephew.'

'Oh! Him! You picked someone smart for a nephew!' 'That wasn't in my hand, you know? Though he's not a hot shot in his department, he's very useful. I have wanted to meet you for years now but didn't know where you lived.

It is a coincidence that I was here and he told me about you. He gave me this gun for security. Imagine how much trouble he has to go through to get an old gun out for his uncle!'

That was called corruption. 'I hope I am in his good books now!'

'He won't say it!' 'Say what?'

'That he's a fan of your work. He felt terrible for making you go through hell back at the station.'

I gasped. 'What else did he say?'

'Not much. Just that you need to be afraid of the Captain. If he has his eyes on you, you can't get rid of him till you end up behind bars.'

'I know that. He's a scary fellow!' I marveled at my luck. There was so much power in human connection. With Noah having gone underground and Jonathan dead, I had no one who was smart or powerful enough to look up to in this time of crisis. But his bond with Marshal could prove beneficial for me in the near future. 'I better get going now!' I said.

'But how? You don't have a vehicle with you. Taking a cab isn't safe!'

'I'm not sure. Maybe I will walk to her place and clear things.'

'Here, take my keys,' he said as he tossed his car keys to me. 'It isn't a Jaguar, but drives well.' His sarcasm made me smile. 'Good luck my friend and take care of her.' The thought of Kathryn's answering machine struck me after his words. 'I am busy right now.' Then in an instant, it struck me. Nameless knew I was at the hospital. He would have gathered everything about me by now. This meant that he would know about the people in my life. Somewhere in the distant plane of my mind, a sense of danger registered. 'Oh no!' I whispered, my instinct telling me that something wasn't right. Kathryn was in danger.

'But if nameless was after her,' before the crushing thought emanated in my mind, I felt a cold sweat breaking down my forehead. 'She'd already be dead!' 'No!' I yelled instantly. I spun around and ran for the door. Behind me, Mark called my name but I didn't stop. I left without saying thanks or goodbye.

# Chapter 11

I started the car and revved the engine. The sound of the skidding rear tires distorted the calm of the neighborhood as the car left a plume of dense smoke behind.

Mark came out to see me rush away. My thoughts didn't let me check on him. 'Please be safe, Kathryn,' a deep voice from within kept saying the same to me over and over again.

My car didn't do anything under sixty miles an hour. There wasn't a red light to stop me. In haste, I mounted the car over a footpath. I almost crushed a pedestrian under the car but was able to maneuver right at the nick of time and steered the car right back onto the road. It bounded down the road, sending waves of terror to drivers around me. Through the corner of my eye, I saw people cursing and yelling at me.

I knew most of the conventional routes to Morgan's Home for Gifted Children. It was going to take me time to get there. I was in the southern part of the city, and it was in the West. I decided to take a shorter route.

Watching the right lane stop under a red light at St. Lew's, I swung into the opposite lane and scared the hell out of oncoming traffic. My hand hadn't stopped pressing the horn for some time now. The LAPD must have been really busy at the city hospital, or else, I would have easily drawn its attention by now. I jammed the car when an old lady driving in front of me jammed hers in terror. My adrenaline had been spiking all this time. My intention wasn't to stop. I maneuvered my car away from her and then through the sea of oncoming cars. I cleared the light and cut to my right into Weldon Avenue. The famous avenue of the city at the end of which spread the famous city garden with no walls to let people on the road get a glimpse of the greenery in the concrete jungle. Luckily, the road didn't have much traffic and it let me accelerate my car further. Within a minute, I left the avenue to reach an open ground.

I was so consumed with the fear of losing Kathryn that I was nearly blind to the people around me. My eyes were fixed on a series of lines that my mind had created as the shortest route to the house. I rammed down on the accelerator in a lower gear and the engine moaned in objection. My ears didn't seem to hear it, but as I felt the car pace at a constant speed, my hand and foot automatically shifted to a higher gear, thereby giving the engine some relief and increasing my miles per hour.

Clearing the city garden wasn't going to be easy. But once I would make it over to the other side, all I would need to do would be to keep accelerating for a few more minutes, and then take a sharp right at the T-point of St. Lucia. Tearing through the grass, I constantly pressed the horn and coupled it with dimming and brightening the headlights, to scare joggers away. A young jogger with earphones on jumped into a bush at the nick of time, only narrowly avoiding being run down. Snaking my way out of the garden, I felt my adrenaline hit an all-time high.

'Kathryn, just be okay. I am coming!' When I made it past the garden, for a change, my car stopped drifting and straightened out. The home was only a mile away. A strange view on the road gave me a troubling sensation. Seeing the tree-lined street with few moving cars gave me a tremor. It made me feel like an unfortunate event had happened nearby. Otherwise, this street would have normal to a high level of congestion at this time of the day. At the end, I took a sharp right, and went past Starbucks, where Kathryn and I used to spend our lovely evenings.

The view that followed forced me to brake. I slammed on the brakes and the car skidded to a halt. An ocean of red and blue lights covered the road in an unorganized fashion. Officials, the media and the neighborhood had surrounded the place. Yellow tapes were used to prevent unauthorized people from crossing into the crime scene. The garden in front of the building had the media continuously reporting something terrible that had taken place inside the home. All this noise sent the pigeons scattering all over the place. It struck me when I saw people crying behind the police cars. Many were dragged into several ambulances. Evening birds cried at the sight of all the gore. Under a grey sky, at least fifty media and LAPD cars had assembled around the large home.

Los Angeles trembled that morning. First, a mass bombing at the city hospital, followed by murders at a shelter for special children, and then a madman drove an old Chevrolet through the sidewalks and the city garden. The media had everything they needed to run high on their ratings for another week, given the explosive events and the disturbing details they were going to cover. I clenched the steering wheel tightly. Releasing my grip, I felt the blood circulate in my palm. My muscles began to relax. My nerves were still tight. I hadn't imagined that I would be witnessing such a scene. Forcing myself to exhale, I got off. Watching the corpses of the working women frightened me. I felt helpless. If I went there, the cops would heave me behind bars.

One of the cops was examining a body lying outside. I couldn't make out who it was. He looked at the doctor and gestured with his head. The look confirmed that there was no life left in the body. The sight of the deaths around had gripped people in deep sorrow. It was sudden and deep. I saw people falling to their knees. 'No… No!' loud screams came out of relatives' mouths. Many were outraged. Many couldn't believe the loss of loved one. Some ran from one cop to the other in an attempt to inquire if it was someone else. The voices of these media personnel weren't clear from a distance. I had to take a chance to go near the one who had been standing far from the crowd and reporting the scene. I wanted to know if Kathryn was alive or not.

Amidst the noises of crying, grieving and shouting, I overheard a journalist reporting. 'We've made contact with the founder of the NGO, Kathryn Morgan and she's on her way.'

I felt my breath become normal again. She was alive. The little relief that came to me put my body in good posture, exposing me to a couple of people. Clearly, they weren't into books. I understood since they didn't approach me like fans or crazy people did.

I started talking to myself. "But if I can see this, so can nameless. He would know that Kathryn would come here. She isn't safe yet. I have to do something." I didn't sense someone walking toward me as I was worrying about Kathryn.

'Thank God you're alive.' I turned around and saw that it was Marshal. 'I looked all over the place for you. We have news about this. I figured you would be here.'

'Marshal, you're the only one I can trust, now.

Someone's after me. I need your help.'

'I know. Everything that has happened from last night leads to you. We must work and catch that guy before he kills more innocent people.' He grabbed my hand tight and locked his gun on my chest. 'Do you think I am crazy to let you go? You're the one behind this mess.'

'Please man, I need to tell Kathryn this before she arrives. Her life's in danger.'

'The only place you are going to Mr. Morgan, is jail. The Captain will happily interrogate you before he sends you to jail!' I was in shock at his statement. I tried to reason with him.

'Your uncle, Mark Hawk! He knows that I'm innocent!' The statement got his attention immediately. 'We both want to save the lives of the innocent and you can't do that if you focus on me now. Just give me this one chance. Your uncle believes in me and so must you if we are going to stop this killer.'

Marshal didn't like the sound of it. He let go of his grip on my hand reluctantly. He went back a few steps and looked confused. 'Damn it!' he shouted. 'I shouldn't be doing this!' He came forward with the gun pointed at me again. 'If you are lying then you are in deep trouble.' I nodded immediately. 'Where's my uncle?'

'He's at home, the one in the silent neighborhood!'

'Oh man, that's like forty minutes from here. I don't have much time!' I didn't speak. He stepped back. 'I don't like this one bit but I am giving you a chance.'

'We need a car.'

'Mine's stuck before the ambulances. Can't take that! Wait!' he looked around and saw a cop nearby, with another car. 'You walk first,' he instructed. I followed. After reaching the cop, he came forward.

'Hey, I am borrowing your car!' The cop turned to him with a poker face then to me and stared for a moment before he said, 'No way! Is that Jim Morgan?' the poker face was surprised.

'I don't have time for your fan talk. Now give me the keys!'

'Last time, Marshal, I gave you my car and you ended up getting a big dent above the rear light. I got...'

Marshal had half expected his answer. 'Okay so you drive and take me where I tell you!'

'No way am I going to take you anywhere. We are needed here. You will cost me my job, you know?'

'Look around, man! The team's taking care of things here. Look, call it a personal favor if you want. I need to go right now.'

The man thought for a brief moment. Seeing that Marshal was pressing him, he said, 'You owe me one. Now get in, you two,' he motioned with his head. I climbed into the backseat and settled in for a drive that was going to take thrice as long as it took me to get here. As we passed buildings, I felt the control of my life blowing away from my grasp. Yet I was hopeful that Mark would clear my name from Marshal's head. He was far less cordial to me than I expected he would be, given his liking for my work. Guess it was an officer's job under the uniform that was at work.

The two officers were busy talking about the day's misfortune. I was silent, lost in thought. In just over thirty minutes, we arrived at Mark's house. Eager to get my name cleared, I got off the car and hurried to the front door. Marshal came with me while the cop stood at his car. When I got there, I pressed the doorbell. Marshal came and stood next to me. About five to six seconds passed and we got no answer.

'That's odd. He should be inside!' I said.

Marshal frowned. His uncle was never late to answer the door. He pressed the bell this time, but there was still no answer. 'Maybe he's in the bathroom. Why don't we move inside rather than stand here for ten more minutes? Do you have a duplicate key?'

He looked at me, confused. 'Yes I do but I don't carry it with me every time!' He turned his attention to the door and started knocking. We stood at the door and waited, listening to the silence of the peaceful neighborhood. Still, there was no answer from inside.

'Hey, is there a problem?' the man from the car called out.

'No. The old man's just taking his time,' Marshal responded.

I looked at the knob. My image in the gold paint on the knob drew my hand to it.

'Hey, what're you doing?'

I turned the knob without answering him. Shockingly, it opened. Leaving the door unlocked in a city like this one wasn't the kind of mistake expected from an intelligent man like Mark.

'Uncle?' he called out loud. He went in and I followed. It seemed like there was no one. An elderly person with no contact with the world except Marshal would probably stay indoors. 'Where could he have gone?'

We got to the hall where I had my conversation with him an hour ago. We found him, lying on the same chair he sat last. His eyes were closed. The bullet wound at his head made it clear. His eyes were closed permanently.

# Chapter 12

Marshal fell on his knees with his palms flat on the floor, trying to stand. Mark's head was level with Marshal's. His mouth opened and closed intermittently.

I heard whispers that carried just one word: uncle. My mind was thoughtless, as I was unable to understand what had just happened. This man had saved me two hours ago. An hour ago, I was talking to him. Now, he was no more.

Witnessing another murder made me curse myself. Death follows whoever I meet, wherever I go! It was nameless, for sure. It made me sad and angry at the same time. I didn't know what to do. I went to Marshal, thinking of putting my hand on his shoulder to give him some support. A loud thump sounded. I turned. The cop who drove us here had his gun pointed at my chest. My hands shot up instinctively.

'Both hands behind the head!' he shouted. My luck couldn't have gotten worse. I guess my sins were reaching me now, making my life miserable. He went on ordering, 'Now turn around. On your knees, lie down!' I followed his instructions to the letter. I faced the floor when he grabbed my hands tight, brought them over my back and handcuffed me. 'Marshal, get up man!' he tried reaching him. The shock had left Marshal in psychological turmoil. He didn't seem to understand what was happening behind him. I thought it was all over for me. The Captain and the entire department were going to frame me for this murder. But just when all hope seemed to be lost, I heard a loud yell.

'Put that down!' I tried to look up. Marshal, standing near the body, aimed at the cop. He screamed again, 'Put it down now!' The cop had absolutely no idea what was going inside his head. 'Hands up in the air or I'll shoot.'

The cop couldn't comprehend Marshal's sudden outburst. 'You don't know what you're doing man!' he said.

Marshal came forward, held him by his collar and pressed the gun to his chest. 'Do as I say or I'll pull the trigger.' He pushed him next to me. 'Lie down just like Morgan!' The trembling cop obeyed without a word. In two seconds, he was lying next to me. 'Morgan, get up and put him in handcuffs!' I wasn't going to risk my life and disobey him. I took the handcuffs from his utility belt and locked the cop's hands up.

'Now hand me the key from inside his pocket!' His gun still aimed at me. I stuck my hand into his left pocket and pulled out a key. I looked at him, getting up and stretching my hand forward with the key. He took it and threw it into a corner of the room. He looked at the cop and said, 'I'm sorry, Frank, for this. But he's mine.' His eyes turned to me in an instant. 'Turn around murderer. Get ready for the last drive of your life.'

I turned, my hands were up and I walked toward the door. The door was half-closed, so I pushed it open and saw that Frank had left the driver's door open in haste.

Marshal heaved me inside the car with a push with the tip of the pistol. 'Take the wheel. You're driving!' Surprisingly, Frank had left the keys in place. I jumped in behind the wheel and he took the backseat, keeping the pistol pointed to the back of my head. 'Drive straight till Fifth Avenue!' he said, settled in the back seat. The car's controls were unfamiliar. Being habituated to automatic vehicles, I had trouble with the clutch and manual gear transmission like I did with Mark's Chevrolet. 'Drive now!' he yelled.

'Okay, okay!' I responded. With initial jerks, the car came into life. I looked at him from the rearview mirror. He plunged his hand into his right pocket and tossed his cellphone on the seat. It appeared that he was not going to be using it anymore. 'Eyes on the road, Morgan!' he said as he caught my gaze. As I drove, he put his hand in my collar and pulled something out. He rolled down the window and threw it out.

'That was a high end GPS dot and transmitter I just threw out of the window. So far, every word you or someone close to you has uttered, every movement you have made has been recorded, heard and analyzed by the Captain.'

Back at Mark's house, the cop was able to drag his body to the corner where Marshal had thrown the key. He turned his body and with good estimation got hold of the key. It didn't take him long to unlock the cuffs. He got up quickly and without wasting much time starting searching for a wireless radio. Unfortunately for him, he realized that it was left in the car.

'Damn it, damn you Marshal. What were you thinking? Revenge will only take you to jail.' He looked around and engaged in inspection of the place starting with Mark himself. He scrutinized the body and scanned the area to check for anything that was going to become evidence against me. In a while, he crouched down to look if something was under the chair. His vision caught sight of a gun- the one which Mark gave me for protection and I gave him back before I left his house. It had my fingerprints. With handkerchief in his hand, he carefully lifted the evidence that will go against me. My luck had given up on me.

Back in the car, Marshal held out my novel Witty Mitch from the rear seat. Frank was reading it and so he had it in the car. I heard the book drop. With his gun still at my head, he leaned to grab it. While down and trying to grab the book, he quickly said, 'There's a camera installed at the corner, near your head.' I was going to look at it when he yelled. 'Don't look at it. It's recording everything. I had to play that game back there so that the department and Captain believe I'm possessed with the thought of vengeance and ready to commit a crime in impulse. Don't worry, you're safe with me. Just play along!' He deliberately took time to get the book so that he could finish saying what he wanted.

Just play along? Having heard this, I wasn't sure if he really wanted to kill me or save me. All I could do was to follow him. He had a gun in hand and I wanted to stay alive. He got the book and came back to his position. 'Stop the car near McKinsey's car accessory store. I'll torture you there.'

I pretended to swallow, as if to make fear look natural on my face. I sensed he might have a plan up his sleeve. I couldn't ask him yet, I had to wait for the right time. I pulled the car to the side, a street before McKinsey's.

'The keys stay inside!' he said. I listened and quickly got off. This car's going to get a parking ticket! I saw him grab my book, get off and close both doors.

'Turn around and walk normally,' he ordered and quickly drew near me to ensure that the gun wasn't exposed. I walked several steps and turned left to enter the wide street that had McKinsey's store after three apparel showrooms. The moment we went past the car camera's eye, he attached the gun to his utility belt and came next to me. 'Take this and follow me, Mr. Morgan!' He handed the book and started to lead me somewhere. 'You are safe for the moment.' He sounded like he meant it, but I was still apprehensive. Yet, these words brought the much needed relief in me, although little. After a minute I was able to gather my thoughts and asked the first question. 'How did you know that they had a tracker in my collar?'

'Right from the moment you came out of the airport, you were under surveillance. When we brought you inside the LAPD, we had it inserted there. This device not only locates your position but also transmits whatever you say. The department has been spending much on hi-tech devices these days.'

'Are you really helping me or I am going to die?' 'Inside the interrogation room, I saw you vanish into thin air when you were reading your book. The systems, cameras and everything electronic crashed for reasons unknown and that moment was not recorded. When I got into the room, you emerged from thin air, right before my eyes as if you teleported from some place. But you were unconscious. I felt that there was a force in motion beyond what we could imagine. I couldn't tell the Captain. He doesn't believe in the supernatural. I told people that you had collapsed. Inside the car, the camera records video but it isn't equipped to record audio. When the cops check the tape they'll call for a lip reader who will tell them about the conversation that took place inside and then they'll be misled.'

Following his lead, I realized that living the life of a cop had made him practical and strong. The grief of his uncle's loss was no longer visible on his face but a firm sense of resolve was.

'Why're you helping me?'

He didn't speak and I didn't anticipate an answer so I went back looking at Witty Mitch while walking.

'My uncle was a perfect reader of character. If he trusted you, then I must trust you too,' he said thoughtfully. Trusting me had brought his uncle to his demise. The deadly chain of events that were set in motion would easily devour him, too. I thought of stopping him and going my way. I didn't want an honest cop to go through an ordeal. 'You've to help me find his killer because I'll make him pay for what he has done!' The remorse in his voice overwhelmed me and changed my mind.

'I am sorry for your loss. Mark was a good man and saved me from the man who killed him. I'll do whatever I must, Marshal, to get you justice.'

I looked at my novel, again, feeling that I would be reading it in a while to return to the past. Witty Mitch was the story of an eighteen-year-old struggling student who turned into a great businessman with his wit and contact- building skills. The storm in my head and the situation I was in wasn't conducive to read a humorous satire, but I had to.

'Do you have a place to go to?' he asked, walking toward the setting sun.

'I don't, but there is someone I must find. Kathryn!

We've got to find her. She might be in danger.' 'She's safe with the Captain.'

'What? She's with the Captain now?'

'The Captain has his eyes on you. He instructed the officers to get her at the office when you were being interrogated.' I was quiet on hearing this. There was satisfaction in knowing that Kathryn was alive and safe with the department. 'You should know that I am aiding a fugitive now. I can't help you much without wheels. We might need a car.'

I wondered about taking Mark's Chevrolet instead of a policeman's car. I said, 'Your uncle's car is over!' and he interrupted.

'Don't even think about it. There is an army of cops there. They'll spot us in no time if we go there for a car. Let me think for something.' After a brief moment he asked, 'Do you like doughnuts?'

'Well yes, I do.'

'That makes the two of us. But you should know that you're paying for them'

'I carry only credit cards in my wallet. If the Captain is as smart as you say he is, then he would have informed the credit card agencies to keep track on my purchases.'

'Authors are so imaginative,' he commented. 'What?'

'The Captain's exceedingly efficient but for the moment I have to trust your imagination. How much cash do you have?'

'I told you. No cash, just the cards.'

I heard him groan. Guess no cop likes to pay for his doughnuts! 'I'll find you a place to read. We won't last an hour if we travel by foot. LAPD has eyes everywhere. All the electric poles are rigged with cameras. Only this neighborhood has no cameras due to funding issues!' He saw me become slower. I was tired. 'Can you walk further Mr. Morgan?'

'What kind of a question is that? Of course I can!'

'I assumed that the rich and the famous only commute in expensive cars.'

'Watch me. Where are we going anyway?'

'To the chain that spoilt every cop and citizen in the country: Dunkin Doughnuts. Come on Mr. Morgan we're almost there.'

'Can we dispense with the formalities? You can call me Jim.'

'Marshal,' was the quick reply. He was already heading to our destination. On the way, he folded his sleeves. A mile's walk and we were there. We arrived at Dunkin Doughnuts but he didn't stop there and went past it.

'Aren't we supposed to go there?' I was in no position to demand an answer so I asked politely.

'Our cars are not only rigged with GPS tracking device but also recorders. Our conversation was taped. There's a possibility that the intelligence team will think we will stop here. I don't want to give them the slightest clue about our stops.'

'Oh God! Why didn't I think of it? Does this mean trouble for you?'

'It means that you should welcome me to the fugitive club. Even the cops have cops above them. It is a security measure.'

'In case something like this happens?'

'You're right. Now they think I have become a psycho in the company of an author.'

'Are you not to risk your life?'

'I deliberately mentioned Dunkin' Doughnuts. LAPD officials have a history of understanding the criminal mind. An inexperienced fugitive is predictable. He will look for cash to travel and hide. All ATMs in this zone have cameras installed inside. A fugitive might not risk exposing himself to the camera. So he will use cash and is likely to enter a food joint or grocery store to grab something to eat, thereby exposing himself to the camera. If the fugitive takes a cab from near the deserted cop car, the travel authorities or the driver can be questioned to reveal the identity of the commuter. When we do not have a place to hide or run, we will panic and our chances of making a mistake become high. That's what the department wants us to do. It will only be a matter of time till they pin if we panic. Stealing a car would be the worst mistake. There were alert people waiting for us to make a mistake. LA locals loved to report something to the department. Moreover, a popular figure like you would not make it far on foot and not get spotted. So it is important for us to stay away from eyes. We'll go to Starbucks where my friend Castiel works. Nobody in the department knows that he's my informer. So we'll be safe with him.'

'Starbucks? That's a crowded place!'

'Not in this part of the city!' Starbucks had become an integral part of the city. After a few miles from one outlet, one could easily spot another outlet of the coffee chain. I remember reading about Starbucks' expansion plan in the news which included opening up stores after every mile to kill competition. The plan worked. Competition couldn't thrive and sales increased. But ironically, it killed the sales of individual stores. I had seen that with my own eyes. One wouldn't find readers there who can identify you. No reader goes to that particular outlet as far as I know!'

'Aren't you forgetting the cameras?'

'What camera?' Castiel ensures that cameras don't work when I pay him a visit. That's why he's an informer. Nobody can prove that we are connected in any way.'

'I hope you're not underestimating the department's brain.'

'I won't make that mistake. I know how every nerve in the department's brain sends a signal to another and makes it take a step. My estimate is that Frank would use my uncle's phone to inform the department as he forgot his radio transmitter in the car. He will also check phone history.'

'That means that they will know that I tried contacting Kathryn.'

'Precisely, that is why they will keep Kathryn safe with them. By now, they would have made someone run my employment file to check my list of friends, family, contacts, places I visited and suspected hiding places. Anyone in our shoes would turn to somebody for help. But if they don't know who we would turn to, they can't pin us down!' I had no choice but to follow him. I was impressed by his quick thinking. Any officer of his rank wouldn't be this intuitive or intelligent. Perhaps Mark taught him to be this sharp. I decided to let him do the thinking.

I said, 'I hope we'll be safe there!' I exchanged a glance with him. 'We won't even have to pay him!' I was able to break his stern expressions for two seconds when a smile flitted across his face and ended slowly.

We reached the place. I looked up to see the enormous Starbucks board that hung overhead. My craving for dark coffee could draw me to anything and everything that had coffee in it. I thanked Marshal in my mind for having an informer and friend here and for choosing this location. A video camera adjacent to the board aimed at us. I hope Marshal's right about the cameras here. We entered. The interiors looked like every other Starbucks in the city. The number of coffee lovers was lower than in any other café, just like he had told me.

Marshal went to the counter and I followed him. Another camera behind the barista aimed at people who could place orders. I saw the barista mumbling to Marshal. It was inaudible to me. A minute later, he led him to the kitchen. Marshal turned, 'Follow me!' Going through the kitchen where a couple of workers stood workless, he took us to a door that had a security system installed. The barista stood at it and looked at Marshal and me. It was an obvious gesture, telling us to look away. The clang of a door unlocking sounded. It was now open. The barista told us, 'I'll bring you and Mr. Morgan something to drink. You may go downstairs!' Marshal went ahead and began climbing down. I went up to the barista.

'Black coffee for me, please!' He offered me no expression at all, as if he didn't care to listen. It was discomforting to meet his eyes. I turned and descended the stairs. Hospitality was very poor here. I made a note to put it in my feedback. Right after my thought, I heard the clang again. I looked up.

'Jim. It's okay,' Marshal said from the end of the stairs. I think I needed reassurance. Getting down, I looked to my left and saw a corridor that was an exact replica of the police station.

'What is this?'

'It's a replica of the lower cell of the LAPD. Castiel is more than an informer.'

What do these people do in here?

At the end of the space was a room with a door that looked like a slab of metal. There was no handle and no key hole. I thought it was a dead, end but on reaching it I realized that it led into a vault of some kind. At the wall beside it, right above my chest height, a high-tech biometric device was situated. Marshal lifted his hand and placed it on the black rectangular box. A green line of light appeared, scanning his prints from the top of his fingertips to the heel of the palm and vanished. The slab immediately shifted inside the wall. Marshal walked in, and so did I. The room he took me into was vast with white floor tiles, whitewashed walls, two white fans, one white table and a white chair and no provision for ventilation.

'Don't mistake this room for an ordinary one,' he said confidently. 'The floor tiles and paint are just a façade. The walls are originally made of hard steel and are held tight by unbreakable rivets.'

'I wonder what he does in this room!' I thought, looking around.

'Under the floor he keeps his armory of guns and explosives.'

'Wha… What?' I had absolutely no idea that an ordinary looking barista would be an informer. And now he said he had a hidden chamber of arms and explosives!

'Oh! I shouldn't have told you that.' Indeed, that wasn't appropriate when I was expected to be in a calm frame of mind to read a novel. The place wasn't like my comfortable study with towering bookcases on all sides with hundreds of books in them. The aura of the study enhanced my concentration levels. But this vacant room had to do for now.

The silence was going to support my next work as it would be a reminder of the seclusion that my study offered. Suddenly, the slab shut. We looked at it and exchanged glances.

'I think you should start reading!' he came to the point. My mind wasn't going to work till I got coffee into my system. He saw the tense look on my face and realized the state of my mind.

'You can relax. I asked Castiel for black coffee and some refreshments!' As he finished, the slab opened again. An arm carried in a tray with two coffee mugs and cookies. Marshal took it. As he turned, the slab closed again.

'That was quick,' I murmured. It was coffee time. I brought the coffee to my nostrils and smelled it. 'Ah! It's strong, just the way I like. So Marshal, what're you thinking of doing next?'

'Just watch you disappear again.' I figured there was both sarcasm and plain honesty in his answer.

'I'm not a magician, my friend.'

'But you do know how to pull that magic trick. I've a feeling that we can proceed only after that.'

'What makes you so sure?'

'First, I am clueless as to what to do next. Second, the madman got to you after you vanished. I am assuming once you come back from,' he paused, as if choosing the correct words, 'wherever you go, he'll come for you.'

'Do you mean to say that I am bait?' 'No. You are the bait.'

'Don't count on the plan, Marshal. I've fought that guy earlier. I've seen him kill trained cops back at the hospital. You've seen what he's done with people at the shelter. He's a professional killer. Even three cops would find it difficult to take him down!' My words got to him. He thought for a moment. The images of the dead bodies were probably flashing in his mind. Something made him look away in terror. Then, he looked back at me and nodded.

'You may be right. Things can't be this easy. What do you propose?'

'Let me just go through this,' I put the book on the table. 'We'll decide what to do once I show you the magic trick.'

# Chapter 13

I had trouble concentrating. My mind was gathering and projecting events after God's visit like a motion picture. Marshal sat in a corner of the room, his eyes riveted on me. I turned my gaze back to the first page and took a deep breath. I had to try.

Mitch was a regular guy with a regular MBA degree from an unknown college in Minnesota. The desperation to work under anyone and do anything was a guise under which he had learnt many trade secrets. His genuine goal was to understand how to make big bucks overnight. He had successfully discovered the science of conning people and after six months of practicing the art, he had mastered it. Though he conned people into investing their hard earned money in his venture, his wit ensured them high returns. The means he adopted were legitimate, so his supernatural growth couldn't be questioned.

Mitch had worked for three years at Marks & Anthony, a leading private insurance firm. Being the gatherer of all secret information critical for the functioning of the company, his value was solid. He was aware of dark secrets that could bring the company down. But he didn't speak against the company. Nobody was sure if his silence was bought by the Board of Directors or if he blackmailed them, but the result was that he made ten million dollars in ten days, got thirty percent stake in the organization for free and was now leading the firm. His name grew within the company at a considerable rate and outside of it. His presence was even more staggering. He became far more influential and wealthy beyond anyone's imagination. The Forbes magazine attempted to obtain a good hour with him for an exclusive. As anyone in the real world would have enough of his success, a few members of the board had enough of his growth.

They hired a supermodel, another professional con artist to con the man who had conned them. She laid an ingenious plan to capture his heart and then take control of the secrets of the company. Once she obtained those secrets, Mitch would no longer be a threat to the firm. So, he could be easily erased. Initially, the blonde gave Mitch trouble with her seduction but Mitch wasn't just witty, he was also exceptionally good at making women fall for him. As fate would have it, the two fell madly in love with each other and started taking the board for a ride, together. Despite the board's best attempts to get Mitch out of their way, their own game turned against them.

By the time I finished half the story, I had laughed many times. Every time Marshal looked at me, his expressions were serious, perhaps wondering what was making me laugh. The book had become a huge hit given my name on the cover and the cunningness of the central character. Only a few comic themed books had caused as much interest among readers as this one.

Like any other avid Morgan reader, Marshal seemed tempted to read it, as he had mentioned earlier that he had read it once and had burst out laughing at Mitch's wit. Later, he went on to read my other novels and seldom got a chance to go back to Witty Mitch, given his stressful work hours. Right now, his focus was more on the magic trick than the content of the book.

'Did you find any irregularity?' he asked.

'Yeah, lots of irregularities in the company's funds!' I laughed. The amazement of the fiction had captured my thoughts as I was completely into the story, forgetting the purpose.

'Jim, I am serious here!' That cut my amusement short instantly.

'No, not yet!' I went back to work. His eyes became sharper. He leaned forward with both hands on his knees. He saw my eyes slowly frowning. The expressions on my face eventually evolved to bafflement. The plain surface on my forehead changed by the marked lines communicated I had found something disturbing.

He got up 'Is that…' I quickly motioned to him to stay patient while I evaluated an odd page.

I didn't remember writing anything except satire, sarcasm and amusement. How had a serious page cropped up?

'You wanted to see a magic trick, come fast and grab my hand!' Marshal almost immediately held my hand. I knew that time travel was forbidden for anyone except me and that it would create irregularities in the timelines. My gut told me that Marshal had a role to play in my life and I was willing to take the risk.

# Chapter 14

It was just after dawn. The setting seemed bizarre. Railway tracks merged in the road, which appeared to be made of red clay. Abandoned train coaches over the tracks seemed to have been left without a care in the world. A railway station needing maintenance loomed ahead of us. It all seemed like a failed project. But the railways in the United States never had the word 'failed' plaguing it. A gust of wind blew my hair, its cold kiss sending a chill as we stepped ahead. It was my fourth time returning to the past. I still hadn't arrived at an answer to the question that had been giving me a headache. Yet, my gut instincts told me that the place where I stood with my newly-formed friend Marshal was going to reveal many secrets.

'We are,' Marshall swallowed, apparently flabbergasted by the magic trick. Unable to speak, he looked at the place, trying to figure out where we were.

'Somewhere in the past,' I said. He got the feeling that it wasn't merely a magic trick.

'I can't believe it!'

'Marshal, what we'll see and do here will have enormous consequences. There's a high possibility of finding our freedom back in time if we understand things carefully. We can set things right and avert a disaster.'

'Okay. So what do we do?'

'We don't do anything,' I said, watching him. The contradiction in my statement puzzled him. It had deep relevance, though. 'We only have to witness things here. If anybody sees us, it might alter history. If we so much as touch or move something, it will change things forever.' Marshal's bewilderment faded as I cleared our purpose. A troubling thought entered my mind. I don't know what I'm going to see now. I just hope I don't see nameless again!

'Are you okay?' he asked.

'Not really. Let's hope we don't meet my nemesis now!' I started walking with optimism, which I wasn't sure would help me. He followed, just a step away from my right side.

'He should pray that he doesn't bump into me or I'll snap his neck.'

'Don't you understand?' I yelled. I immediately muffled my voice as a precaution to avoid attracting attention. 'We'll stay away from him till we have no choice! We're no match for him!' He seemed annoyed at being spoken to that way - a fact that he wasn't prepared to accept. My mind began talking to me but my voice was akin to God's. 'Jim Morgan, you stand nowhere near finding your sins. There are secrets that have remained hidden from you because so far, you've only seen things with a plain view. It is time you let yourself see things from an author's eyes.'

Marshal was anxious. 'There's no one here! What do we do now?'

'Keep moving. Have faith, my friend. Someone will come for sure!' The hope in my voice wasn't forced. It was genuine and believable. I had the image of God stamped on my mind when he said, 'Everything has a purpose. Everyone has a purpose. Have faith!' His words followed me as I spoke to Marshal. Logically, Marshal could not accept my words or the feeling of time travel, and yet, intuitively, he had agreed to what I told him. 'Let's keep going then!' he said.

'This way!' a young voice resembling a school kid said.

'Take cover quickly!' I said in a hushed tone. We ran to the other end of the rusted coach and hid behind it. He hid behind me and I meticulously angled myself to stay hidden from sight. We tried to see who had spoken. My eyes traveled to the far end of the coach. A boy appeared from the other end. Another boy came behind him.

'That's just two school kids!' Marshal whispered in my ear. The uniforms they wore cleared the idea. We secretly listened to them and followed the boys.

'I don't see how this is going to be fun. We are supposed to go to school today. Dad will be really angry with us,' one of the boys said to the other. This one was taller than the second one. They both appeared to be of the same age, but I got the feeling that the taller one was a year or two older than the short one.

'Don't worry about dad. He never scolds me!' replied the other.

'But he scolds me and you know that.'

'I said don't worry, okay? I'll take care of dad.'

'You've always said that. Each time it turns out to be an empty promise!'

'This time, I swear dad won't say anything to you. Now you should trust me!' The taller boy didn't say anything and turned around. In that position he said, 'I will trust you if you swear one more thing! If we find the treasure, we split it in half.'

The shorter boy seemed reluctant. 'Well okay. What's yours is mine and…'

'And what's yours is mine!' the tall boy finished. 'Where did you learn the secret of this treasure?'

'I overheard dad talking to one of his bodyguards. He said, 'I hope that my items are well hidden underneath the signal at eighth track. Nobody must come to know about it." The boy had spoken as though he were his father.

'Dad will kill us if he finds out that we went near his treasure.'

'Don't chicken out now, brother. Come on, I'm going there. Treasure hunting will be fun!'

'I don't like the idea!' said the taller one. The shorter one grabbed his hand and pulled him to a signal that was not far from the track they stood at. The boy snatched his arm back away from his brother's clutch. 'I'm not going there and neither should you. There's a limit to curiosity!' he said, with his arms crossed at his chest. I watched the shorter one close in on him. He placed both his hands on his shoulders. At that time, something popped inside my head- Curiosity is persuasive! The shorter one's attempt to cajole him into unearthing the treasure was obvious. He said, 'Let us just see what it is. I'll put it back in its place myself!' The taller boy wasn't convinced. The shorter one released his brother. 'No more empty promises. Just do this once for your brother!' His persuasion brought a little frustration in his brother, who didn't want to participate in this. But it is a universal fact that a brother finds it difficult to say no to his younger brother.

'Fine. Let's go!' At this, the shorter one jumped up in ecstasy. 'But we'll put it back to its place once we see what it is!' They moved toward the eighth track from the platform and stopped on the sixth.

'There it is!' the boy exclaimed, pointing at ground that seemed to have been dug up recently. It seemed like he had located the place where something important to their father was buried. His brother's eyes followed the Earth ahead. It had a different texture compared to the Earth around them. The first one ran after it. His brother followed, but was not as excited.

'I think this is it. Come, help me out here!' Using both hands as a shovel, he started digging the earth. He turned around, 'What're you waiting for big brother? Come, let's find out what it is.'

The other boy was hesitant, yet his brother's excitement made him come. From two hands to four, they dug, grabbed and threw the Earth around them. It didn't take them much time to find what they were imagining to be a treasure. It wasn't too deep in the ground. 'I think we found it,' said the younger brother.

'It looks like a chest to me.'

'Quickly, remove the sand around it and then we can pull it out!' Their speed doubled. In some time, they unearthed to what looked like a wooden chest that had a lock in place.

'Give me a hand with this!' The shorter boy put his hands underneath one end of the chest. The other put his at the other end. 'It is too heavy,' said the younger. 'We can't lift it!'

'Ah forget it. I'm leaving.' 'Where're you going?'

'Don't know.' The boy said passively, turned and headed to the direction he came from.

'Hey, don't leave me here,' the elder boy called out but he didn't listen. He quickly spread Earth over the chest, although not covering it as it was earlier and stepped back on the track. He felt his foot twisting and then looked down.

'I'm stuck.'

His brother paused and turned on hearing this. 'Oh come on, stop fooling around! You can come out of it easily. I'm going.' Out of nowhere, in the deserted station, the loud horn of an oncoming train howled. Marshal and I had sneaked past their eyes and hid behind an old coach on track five. We heard the noise and realized that the train was headed toward the boy trapped on the eighth track. Fear settled over the boy stuck there.

'We've got to help him!' Marshal said. He stepped out and got pulled back. I pressed him against the train.

'We cannot help him. It is not our timeline!'

'How can you say that? He'll die if we don't!' His jaw dropped.

'It is hard as it is. Please don't make this harder for me!' The loud horn howled for a long time. The train took the horn away in seconds. Later, there was a long silence. We didn't hear the voice of either boy. Marshal ducked, continuing to feel helpless and sad for the boy. I glanced at the younger boy who was still alive. He was riveted to the spot, shocked as he looked at where he last saw his brother in one piece. His brother wasn't there anymore. Parts of his body were crushed and spread on the track. My eyes shot back at Marshal. I couldn't look at it. After a brief, intense moment, I dared to look at the younger one.

He wasn't the same boy who stood at the same place twenty seconds earlier. I knew that the accident would change him and his life but I wasn't sure how it would turn his life around. My thoughts lingered over the loss he was probably feeling. A strong wave blew past me. As Marshal dared to look, the boy fell.

Marshal wanted to help the collapsed kid. He barely managed to obey my instructions and stay focused on witnessing the scene. 'What do we do now?' he asked.

'Stop being human!' I never thought I would say something like that in my life. It was the coldest answer I had ever given someone. In just two days I had witnessed so many deaths. I didn't know how much more I would have to see. I didn't know what my sins in my previous life were. Standing there, watching the kid die and not doing a thing, I believed I was the sinner now.

'Come Marshal, we have to retrieve that chest!'

'But you said we can't touch anything. Won't that be wrong?'

'I can't explain it to you Marshal. You must follow me. I need answers and I think they lie hidden in that chest!' We trudged along our way to the fallen boy. Marshal didn't know what to say or do. But I had decided to take the chest with me. We stood just before the kid. I looked at him. His innocent face was spattered with dust. I looked at the footsteps that could lead us to where the chest was buried in a hurry. I started walking. Marshal followed. He didn't look at the boy, fearing it would soften his heart and change his mind. We didn't need to communicate our shared thought to know we shared it: Poor boy. Life can be so uncertain.

We got to the place and figured that it wouldn't take long to dig up and take the chest out. We started digging with our hands. Marshal kept digging along with me. As he did, he saw two drops of water become one with the sand. He looked at me and saw my face wet. The weight of the guilt and sadness overwhelmed me and took the form of tears. I kept digging deeper, and a couple more tears parted with my eyes. He looked at me for a moment as if there was something he wanted to say. 'There was nothing we could do, man,' he said.

In my heart, I knew he was both right and wrong. We could have done something. But it wasn't our time and I had to choose not to do anything. In no time, my fingertips scratched the chest as we had reached it finally. The place began to fade away. The red sand devoured the tracks. The sky turned white along with the Earth. Marshal became afraid. 'What's happening?' he asked.

I turned to him with the answer. 'We're going back to our time!' Above his shoulder, at a distance, the fallen boy disappeared. I began to feel something: I was the younger boy in my previous birth! This boy hadn't saved his brother out of negligence! He should have pushed himself while he could. That's unforgivable – if anyone had done something wrong in the past, it was this kid. I think I was him.

# Chapter 15

The chest was on the table. Marshal was examining it. I murmured, 'I was told that I had done a lot of wrong in the past.

Maybe the kid who saw his brother getting killed was me!'

He didn't hear me properly. 'Did you say something?' he asked. I didn't respond and remained in my speculation. Marshal looked at me and thought it best to leave me. 'Castiel's coming in just a bit. We'll be able to find out what's inside, in no time.'

Castiel entered the room with the all business and no sense of humor written on his face. He went straight to the table and began work. We gazed at the make of the chest as he began describing it. 'This is a very old, handcrafted piece made of walnut-colored wood and metal. It is a large pirate treasure chest.'

We already knew this.

'As you can see the corner guards, hinges, feet, heavy-duty handles and lid support are all made of the finest alloy!' I didn't know that it was made of the finest alloy. It looked plain, but was a strong metal. Judging by the way he described the object, I sensed that whatever he would say won't go in our favor. 'This is maraging steel.'

'What's that?' Marshal asked.

These steels are known for possessing superior strength, toughness and they don't lose malleability. These have high contents of nickel, titanium, cobalt and molybdenum. I think it is eighteen inches long, ten inches deep and twelve inches high in dimensions. It looks like it's an all pine with a strong dovetail construction. The quality of the wood and steel makes the weight be somewhere around forty pounds.

Marshal immediately shot a question at him, 'Can you open it?'

'If I try to hurt the body, the wood will send tremors inside. That will possibly damage the secret contents. Similarly, I can't melt the metal or try to break it without harming the stuff inside of it.'

'Can you make a duplicate key?'

'That sounds like an easy job but the problem is the steel again. This steel is notorious for not holding a good- cutting edge. The make of the key hole has many small irregularities. Nowhere in the 21st Century do you find such a keyhole. Modern machines that create replicas cannot create duplicates for such an intricate system. The make of the chest clearly reflects that it is crafted not long ago. It looks recently made but it feels like it is a chest that was made sometime in the 1960s and 1970s.'

I looked at Marshal, awestruck by Castiel's scrutinizing eye and knowledge. 'This chest is over forty years old. We brought it forty years ahead of time, so it hasn't aged,' I said this through telepathy. He seemed to receive it.

'We can't tell him about time travel,' Marshal reciprocated and I understood.

I looked back at Castiel. 'That's amazing. I mean, you are amazing but your information tells me that it can't be opened,' I said.

'Twenty-four hours,' he prompted. 'You mean you can open it?'

'He can do things,' Marshal pressed.

'You guys should get some fresh city air now,' Castiel said. He clearly wanted privacy.

Marshal said, 'I think he's right. I need fresh air. Come let's go outside.' I didn't question him, and followed him. As we walked outside Starbucks, I asked, 'You have something in mind don't you?'

Marshal raised a hand and stopped a passing taxi. The driver pulled the car in front of us. 'I like your magic. Let's get the tools for the next one.' He then turned to the cab driver who had the windows down. 'Take us to The Last Bookstore.'

The name of the store was ironic. It was California's largest used and new book store. Over 20,000 square feet space of the store was a haven for book lovers. It was situation in the Spring Arts Tower at 5th & Spring.

I remember promoting my initial novels there and after that I didn't need them. My name was enough on the cover of a book to sell it. Sadly, physical bookstores were being wiped out like dinosaurs from the planet from the meteoric impact of Amazon and other online platforms.

Before the driver accelerated, I rolled down the window for some city air. The basement at Castiel's was suffocating. The air of the city wasn't as fresh as that of my home located in the outskirt of New York City but it was definitely better than a basement with explosives and guns under the floor. I was relaxed now. Watching buildings pass as the car advanced slowly took away my inclination toward the dead boy and his brother. I began picturing my days as a writer in the city and time moved. In fifteen minutes, we reached the road to the store. Marshal told the driver, 'Stop the car at least fifty feet away from the store.' The driver did as instructed. He stopped at a parking spot and killed the engine. Marshal looked at me and said, 'Stay in the car Jim! I will be back in no time.' I agreed. I would draw too much attention.

'We need The Thrill of Lying,' I told him. He nodded and got out. I saw him walking up the sidewalk toward the entrance. In a few seconds, he cleared the distance and went inside.

Things were adding up but vaguely. The factory was burnt by an unknown person. Jason was definitely murdered by nameless. He hadn't committed suicide. Victoria's drunkenness was what his father and nameless wanted to show. They must have put her on drugs. But why? There's Holmes, his daughter, four partners and nameless.

They add up to seven then there's that underground chamber with seven planets and God said I had committed seven sins. The radio distracted me. 'Could you turn that off?' I asked the driver.

He looked back with an unpleasant expression. Then went back to his position and turned it off, grumbling. I had never seen a cab driver become uncharacteristically hostile to his passenger. Before I returned to my thoughts to understand what I did in my last birth, I rolled down the window completely. A pleasant breeze swirled inside.

'Whenever I went to past, I have only witnessed things connected with these seven people. That means, those kids at the tracks must be related with them. That place, the station didn't look like it was there like that in 1970s. It must have been ten or perhaps fifteen years prior to that time. God told me that I did all those bad things. Holmes, the partners and even Victoria have committed sins, but seven? No, it can't be them. The only person who has killed, spread sorrow and can be ruled out to make those seven mistakes is nameless.' I was rubbing my hands tightly as I thought I was about to know how I was connected with these people. 'That kid let his brother die because he didn't make an effort to save him. That's definitely the Sin of Sloth. If I am assuming myself to be that kid in my past life, then that kid grows up to be….' The picture of the reporter I saw at the university started taking shape in my mind. 'That guy who fell with me in my timeline, the one responsible for so many murders. After that train incident, the kid would surely become…'

It became clear to me as I spoke. 'It can't be…' I fumbled. 'He was me!' Words were stuck at my throat. 'I was nameless in my last birth.' Sweat formed on my forehead. 'He is me, I was him. Why God? Why?'

I wondered in anxiety what to do at the moment. I had to tell Marshal. I told the driver to wait and promised to be back right away. The driver didn't bother. He regretted taking me as a passenger. But with me gone, he could turn the radio back on. I stepped out of the cab, closed the door and headed to the bookstore. Before I reached the store, I heard the sirens of multiple cars. Many cars drifted into the lane and stopped twenty feet before me. I saw more entering from my left, stopping at the side. They blocked the street.

'Freeze!' a cop covered himself behind the car with a gun in hand, pointed at me. 'Put your hands in the air where I can see them!' His purpose was evident now. The look in his eyes was expected. I watched the man with an indifferent expression, since I had experienced plenty of guns and cops lately. Just when I thought I had all the answers in hand, I was cornered. I was about to be sent to jail for a long time for things I hadn't done in this lifetime, but in my last. Ten more cars entered the street from other corners and it appeared that over thirty armed policemen came to bring me in.

From one of the cars, I saw Captain Nash get down. I was about to raise my hands when he looked at me, but my gaze turned to the cop who was pointing the gun at me.

He got distracted. His head went above my shoulder. For a moment he looked like he'd seen a ghost. Whatever he saw sent him staggering backwards. Just when I thought that things couldn't get any worse, I looked back.

There was a gigantic truck heading straight toward me at high speed. The driver turned the wheel completely and the truck fell on the cab I was in a minute ago, crushing both the vehicle and the driver. Someone got out, someone deadly familiar. With a large machine gun in hand, this guy planted a crazy look and a cheeky smile on his face. Now it was I who became numb with shock. I had enough confrontations with nameless and each time, he upgraded.

I heard gun shots at high decibels. He started shooting everywhere. I couldn't move. I felt my breath. Those bullets weren't aimed at me. They were shot to kill everyone else. The bullets created devastation everywhere. Headlights of police cars were gone, bumpers were torn off. A running cop car clipped another stationary one. The hood opened with the impact of the crash and the car bent. A heroic yet foolish act from a cop who was gunning his car at nameless, was met with hell. Bullets flattened a tire and the car toppled, its body dragged along the ground, generating a shower of sparks. It sped to hit three cars that surrounded me from behind. The impact threw them off. Finally, the dragging car stopped. Multiple bullets grated against many cars. I covered my ears. The sound of several shots was ear- splitting. Behind me, nameless gave a hard kick to an open door of a car and broke it entirely. He made it a shield.

Impeccably trained to eradicate an entire army of cops when having guns, he advanced one step at a time, eliminating one cop after the other. The cops reciprocated after taking cover. Their shots added to the noise in the surroundings. Unlike the cops, his shots were deadly accurate.

What have I got myself into, I cursed myself. I need to get inside the building before he sets his eye on me again.

There was something ironical. If they killed him, they'll wipe out my existence. What tragic moment had life gotten me into? I couldn't even wish for someone who was hell bent on killing me to die because that would indirectly kill me. I collected my senses. If I moved quickly, my death could be delayed at least for a while.

I forced a little hope inside myself which was apparently needed for me to gather enough courage to get inside a shelter. Here goes nothing! I said to myself and ran the fastest sprint of my life toward the door of the shelter. No shots were fired at me during the sprint. Just when I took the first step at the stairs of the store, shots reached an inch just before my foot. I jumped and forced the door open. Many bullets pierced the windows. I covered the back of my head with my hands to save it from falling glass.

Marshal was lying low ahead of me. He shouted, 'Damn it! How the heck did the Captain find us?'

'I don't know. He isn't doing a good job keeping nameless busy.'

He thought about something and then shouted, 'Of course.' He reached for his collar and pulled out a tracker. The device felt like a pawn in the hands of the Captain. 'That cunning fox had this tracker planted on me all this time!' Recollecting his time at the LAPD station, he remembered that the Captain had given him a pat under the neck. He thought that the Captain would have intended to pat him on his back but missed it by a palm's length. That's when he had the tracker in place. Later, when the news of a massacre at the shelter broke, he was directly ordered by the Captain to reach the place as soon as possible. He had assumed that the sole purpose of sending him there was to rescue the survivors, but now it became clear. He was sent because the Captain had suspected Jim to show up there for Kathryn. It was obvious that Jim would only let him get close to himself for his affability.

'Darn it!' he crushed the device like a nut under his thumb. 'I got played.'

'You have a gun with you?' I asked.

'Yeah, but I shot all the bullets around that madman!'

Marshal was furious. He got up quickly and rushed to the help desk at the entrance where the manager was hiding. He laid his gun on the table. 'I need a clip!' The manager looked up and then slumped. Marshal grabbed him by his collar and pulled him over the table. 'I know you keep a Beretta and additional clips for security sake. If you want to live, I need you to give me your gun and all the clips you have.' The manager plunged his hand into his right pocket. He took out a set of keys and opened a drawer under the desk. His promptness conveyed how badly he wanted to live. He took out a loaded Beretta and an additional clip. Within seconds, Marshal had his gun reloaded. 'Stay down,' he told the manager, who had already sunk under the desk. He turned and tossed the secondary gun at me. I caught it reluctantly. 'I hope you know how to pull the trigger.' My knowledge on guns after intense research for a novel was fresh in my mind. I didn't need him to tutor me. I looked at him with a grim face.

'Now he's going to die!' He had decided to empty the clip into nameless' body. As he took two strong steps toward the window, I called out. 'Marshal don't!' My tone was firm. 'You can't kill him!' He wasn't going to stop, but the sudden intensity made him stop. He turned to me, with absolutely no idea of what was running in my head. 'Are you out of your mind?'

'If you kill him, you kill me!' I was too direct. My words seemed illogical, even to me.

'What the hell are you saying?' His brows were furrowed with tension.

'I was nameless in my last life!' That was perhaps the last thing Marshal had imagined. He stood there, shocked. The sound of gunfire didn't reach him, but an ugly truth pierced his mind.

'You what?'

'I am sorry. We truly can't do anything. If he dies, I won't even come into existence and the world will change.

We can't let that happen!' The direct answers were too painful. 'We can't do much but we must try to escape and stay alive.' He did not react. I was nervous as I said this and after having said it, I was unsure. Another window broke. The loud sound made him wake out of his frozen state. He shrugged instinctively. He looked at me with a look of regret on his face. He was aware of a fact that bit him from within. He couldn't have his vengeance. He stood, thought and turned to the manager who hid under the desk. 'Hey, is there a back door?'

The manager opened his eyes. His expression was one of surprise. The sounds of bullets being shot had taken his mind away. He stood up and began running. We assumed he was leading us to the back door. Marshal and Iexchanged glances and ran after him. The man ran through an aisle of books and clearing the section dashed to his left, there was a long aisle of vinyl records and graphic novels. He made past it and dived to his right. The two of us were equally fast in catching up with him.

'Did you find the copy?' I asked.

'No, I didn't get enough time, the bestseller section was on the top floor!' The store owner had deliberately put the bestseller section at the top floor so that all the visitors don't walk away just by grabbing a book and without seeing the magnificence of the entire store.

'Damn it!'

'We'll get it from another store. Right now we must find a safe spot! The Captain knows our hideout at Castiel's café.

We need to…' After another aisle, the manager reached the back door at the corner of the long hall. We both stopped. He wasted no time inserting the key into the hole. Since he was in shock, his hand shook and wasn't letting him twist the key properly.

'Here, let me do it,' the manager sidestepped and Marshal opened the door to another street. The manager ran outside without saying so much as a thank you. Marshal stepped out first and exactly when I was about to do the same, the neighborhood became silent again. A strange feeling crept inside me and I pulled myself away from the door, into the room. Marshal turned and seeing me stop he yelled, 'Jim, come on, we got to get on wheels and get the hell out of here.'

I wanted to walk out and run to a safer place, but I didn't. 'What the hell is the matter with you? He might be here any second!'

'Get us wheels, I'll be there in a minute,' I said and went inside.

'We don't have a minute!' he yelled, but I had already created some distance. 'I have to get my book and find the rest of the sins. He must be stopped before he kills more innocent people!' Marshal turned and with his gun, pointed at the first oncoming car. He stopped it mid-way.

'LAPD! It is an emergency, I need the car.' The guy inside the SUV wasn't going to object to a cop with a gun. Marshal got to the gate and opened it. 'Move it, I'll take the wheel!' The driver shifted to the other seat and Marshal sat down. He brought the car to the door. 'Come on Jim, make it fast.'

I reached the entrance and began climbing the spiral ladder at full speed. Inside, it was awfully quiet. I heard the thump I made on the stairs as I climbed up. With no book enthusiast inside, it appeared as if the store had just opened. It now needed revamping. Nameless had given the store free bullets on the outside and inside. I made it to the top floor and knew exactly where they kept the bestsellers. A large display board with glittering bulbs spelled the words 'International Bestsellers' adorned a section. My six novels were near the center, by the Harry Potter's entire series. I lifted The Thrill of Lying which was on the third row from the bottom. I ran down the stairs. It didn't take me long to reach the ground floor. Knowing the way to the backdoor, I hurried. I was optimistic as I ran. 'I can get out of here!' I thought. Next second, a bullet fired from behind me. I stopped after two long strides and became still.

'Turn around!' a voice sounded from the aisle where I stood. A cold sweat broke on my forehead. I turned around very slowly. Fear escalated in my senses. I saw a man with a gun in one hand pointed at the floor. He had the Captain by the collar, unconscious. I was expecting nameless. But the man I saw shocked me. 'Who are you?' I asked, without hesitation. It wasn't him. It was someone else. The man began to laugh. I stood riveted at the same spot. Blood covered the Captain's collar. His team of thirty men couldn't save him or me from this strange man. His laughter gradually ended.

'You forgot me in just a day!' I frowned after his answer. 'I forgot you… What?'

'I am the same man you threw from your window.' Sweat reached the tip of my jaw. 'How can it be?'

'The doctors in your time can do miracles. You crushed my face, remember?' He had plastic surgery. It usually took a patient months to undergo and recover from such a surgery. But he had the power of time with him.

I was scared more than ever. 'What are you going to do? Kill me?'

A sly smile formed on his lips. 'Oh no! I am not going to kill my future self!' His smile widened. 'I am going to take you with me.'

It had been over two minutes. Outside, Marshal grew extremely worried. 'Jim, what's taking you so long man?' he wondered. He looked at the frightened owner of the car with the gun in hand. He said, 'I'll be back in under a minute. Don't you dare go anywhere!' The man nodded. Marshal jumped out of the car and began moving toward the back door. The gun was ready in his arms. He positioned it exactly as he had done during his training. His duty required him to face such kinds of delicate situations. He pressed himself to the door. With his arm extended to fire at any threat, he entered the place. There was no one inside.

The Thrill of Lying lay face up on the floor with blood stains on it.

# Chapter 16

Sponge the blood off the body. Don't forget the floor. He will cry and scream. He will shout. If you so much as open your mouth to him, you will be risking your life. You will face horrifying consequences!'

I could never bear the sight of blood. I was in pain. More pain was inflicted on the Captain, who was tied to a chair. He was badly beaten up. The fear of losing my life in the hands of this murderer had me in its grip. I didn't open my mouth. I wasn't able to look at the Captain. His face was washed in his own blood. I was on the floor, hardly able to get up. His one punch to my stomach was enough to put me on the floor. I was infuriated at my helplessness. I let my lips finally talk. 'How can you do this to so many people? Why do you make him to suffer like this?'

'You can and you will! Just like you did in your previous birth!' he was right. I was the one doing all this. I was nameless then. I was Jim, now, a sinner. Fear and pain had paralyzed Captain Nash. He groaned loudly.

I looked at the bloody sponge in my hand. I looked at nameless, who watched me for a second and retreated. The sound of his steps ceased, leaving me alone with the nearly dead Captain in a dark room. An appalling silence prevailed around the two of us. A few candles were lit. The eerie coldness of the room was frightening. I looked at the Captain. My shadow loomed over his body. I watched it disappear the second the waning flames of the candles extinguished. The remaining flames of two candles were enough to keep my vision up for a hopeful ten more minutes. Minutes later, I scrubbed his face. His eyes opened. His hand grabbed my wrist, trembling. A shudder of horror threw me back like a thunderbolt had struck me. The poor man had lost a lot of blood. His suffering made me fearful of his approaching death. He gathered the remaining energy in his body. He managed to make a request before he lost consciousness, 'Help me! Please, I beg you to help me!'

I was strictly told not to even think about offering help. I dipped the sponge in the bucket of water and squeezed it. The sound of drops falling into the container was an exception to silence in the room. I saw the formation of red circular waves in the bucket; that electrified me. I couldn't attempt to look again so I turned to him. His eyes wandered quickly throughout the room and now they were fixed on me. His eyes shut then opened then shut again and then opened again. I had to bear the sight of a man I knew not much about. Hearing his agony as well without saying a comforting word was excruciating.

In the unending torture of remaining in the room, I heard two sounds: one, his intense groans; the other, water falling in the bucket. Working my bloody chore, I thought about the damage that one man's rage could do to another. The situation I was in and the thoughts that it brought to my mind kept worrying me. His bleeding worsened, neither God nor aid arrive leaving me to stay a spectator of the horrible event.

Why can't I take this poor person to help? What mystery lies behind this sin that I committed in my previous birth? It is pure rage, an act of wrath. How had he developed it? How did he get involved in the horror I gave birth to? Why was he lying tied up like this? What wrong did he do to me? What must have gone on in nameless' life that he decided to subject people to this gruesome torture? I had no answers. His agony made him groan. It was now unbearable for me. 'I cannot take this anymore, I will not quietly submit to the inhumane instruction that this monster has enforced on me!' I said to myself. 'Captain, are you with me? Captain?' Before he could answer, the door burst open. In came nameless, with a tool box and a steel rod in hand. The dim light that made its way into the room through the open door wasn't enough for me to see his face. He approached the unconscious body and stood there for a while. He took medicines out of the box and started dressing the wounds.

'What the hell? Did this guy have a split personality?' I wondered. I knew I wasn't going to get a reply. I didn't dare ask him anything. He bandaged several body parts.

He stood before the Captain for some time. He turned to me. 'Do you know what pain is, Jim?'

I didn't know what to say. He took the bucket and splashed all its contents on the Captain. The sadist raised the rod he held, and delivered a strong blow to his head and he went on hitting him. 'Stop it, you monster!' I was afraid I couldn't speak. He kept beating the Captain till the last dregs of his life were left in him. The moment he gave the last blow to his head, the Captain stopped sensing anything. That didn't stop nameless. After several blows, he was done. He threw the blood bathed stick on the ground. It made a terrible noise before it settled. He came to me and held my face tight like it was a sponge meant to be squeezed. He forced my eyes on the Captain. There were cuts on his face, flesh peeled off his shoulders. His torn shirt was covered in sweat and blood. There were wounds on his arm and both his legs. The aura of the room was frightful enough. Witnessing the nasty sight was a torment.

'I want you remember this pain forever!' he said loudly in my ear.

I understood now, why he had kept me alive. He wanted to give me painful memories that would kill me. My mind had saved the picture that I would see forever in my mind's eye. I would never be able to forget that look on his face: the unbearable agony and paleness. I would remember his screams. They would not leave my ears. 'Help me! Please, I beg you to help me!' I would never forget how his hand trembled when it reached and grabbed my hand. His helplessness bent him over. He released me from his clutch.

I used my palms to cover my face – and I noticed his blood on my palms. That sight wasn't going to leave my mind for a very long time. God knows how much he bled. I heard a voice in my heart. 'You suffered for not taking my advice. You cannot turn events that happened in the past. Try to make amends to the victim for the wrath that is showered on him!' I was surprised. It was possibly God's voice.

As nameless raised the bloodied rod to make me his next target, everything froze.

'If you want answers, you must go in the next room. Take out a key from your left pocket. Go down into the room after the stairs, open the wardrobe. You will see three drawers. The bottom one has answers for you. Bring it with you!'

The bottom one has answers? How was God so direct with me this time?

'Why are you doing this to me, to him? You are God, how can you watch all this?' I screamed. The walls of the room didn't respond. I could hear my heart beating, not giving me more words. I struggled to get up. My gaze went to nameless. Wrath had taken over him. He was frozen. Maybe time was frozen. I walked out of the room into the limited light and found myself on the first floor. I began ascending the dilapidated staircase. I rubbed my shoulders to warm them up. Why was it so damn cold? An old clock hung tall on the wall to my left. It was half past six. The area was silent but less darker than it was in the room. I crossed a window from where the last rays of the falling Sun caught my gaze. I had to hurry.

I reached the door of the room facing the stairs and took out the key that God had put in my pocket. I opened the lock. The knob made a noise when it turned. I went in and then heard a sharp, unpleasant noise. The rusty hinges grated as the door swung back and the door closed on its own. The creepy sensation of the evening made me uneasy. I looked around and turned to the only wardrobe and reached the handle. It wasn't locked. I opened it and carefully looked for an article that would be relevant. After rummaging through several unimportant contents I found some papers and took them out.

The title on the front page got my attention. It was a will left by someone. As I brought the papers closer I decided I would read them later. I had to go back upstairs. I pushed the door open and ascended the staircase. This time, I didn't care to look back when the hinges grated loudly. I hastened to the room thinking that God would be there. When I opened it, I said, 'God here are the papers…' I stopped short. There was nobody inside. The chair on which the man was held captive was vacant now. I saw a trail of blood extending from the chair to the door but not beyond. He must have dragged the body through the room and then lifted it to carry till it.

'God where are you? I have what you asked me to bring!' I held out the papers.

'What took you so long?' he asked, standing on top of the stairs. I turned immediately. Some anger and some frustration got hold of me.

'I suppose that you are done with me. Now put an end to this misery!'

'This place… What do you make of it?'

'I don't know, I just want to go back! This room is a torture cell and this house is a sad place. That poor fellow has left his last screams behind. This is where I committed my sins!'

'You look pale, Jim, are you afraid?' he asked. It felt like he was adding to my agony.

'Afraid? Are you asking a guy who has never seen blood before if he is afraid when he is left in a dark and dingy room with a tormented, brutally beaten man and a psychopath on a killing spree? Afraid? I am scared to death. You left me here unguarded, unsafe and without…'

'I warned you, didn't I?'

'I might have been a butcher in my previous birth but you know that I have humane instincts and I cannot stand idly and do nothing. I wanted to set the man free from his misery. I could not bear the pain!'

'Yes, I told you not to disobey me. You played with the timeline when you took Marshal along with you. You defied a direct instruction.'

'He has a part to play in this. I believe that he does. You can't punish me for having faith.'

'No, I won't. But that does not change the fact that you broke a rule!'

'Okay, I can handle that. It was my decision. What about the animal who was about to beat me?'

'Well, he isn't here now, is he?'

'So? He was there when I was his punching bag!' 'You don't trust me now, do you?'

'No! I trust you so much that I bathed my hands with blood with an indifferent face on because you are directing me to rectify my misdeeds! It is all Karma and you are witnessing it now!' I looked away.

'You look puzzled, Jim.'

'Why did you save me when he was about to break my skull?'

'Karma. It isn't your time to die.' 'Then what is this time for?'

'It is time you witness another sin.' My feet shifted from where I stood. Everything around us zoomed in. Three steps ahead of me there was a door. 'Where are we now? What is this?'

God was one step closer to me. 'You wanted me to help you. Beyond this door, is a sin. You can only watch it. No one inside can watch you.' I looked at him and then at the door knob. I put my hand on it and decided to go in. I sighed and opened the door. As soon as I opened the door, I saw Victoria lying on the floor, with her hands supporting her. She was facing someone. I opened it wide and saw nameless watching her very closely. She was his next target. Nameless scared her with his words. 'Your father is safe now. I've sent him to a place where no one can touch him or hurt him.'

'What? What do you mean he's safe?' she said, trying to distance herself from him.

'Now, you need not fear me my love, you're safe with me.'

'What did you do to my father?' her pitched reflected that she was crying. Her fear was evident.

'You will get your answers, but first…' he placed a hand on her leg and slid up to her thigh to execute his heinous motive. I couldn't remain like a spectator. I wanted to jump on him and impulsively shouted, 'No, you monster I won't let you!' In an instant, the place zoomed in again and my feet shifted back to the dark room I was in.

'God, please stop! I know what is going to happen. I must go back to my time now. I can't bear to stay here even a minute longer.'

'Yes, it is time. And you must take him too, with you!' I turned around. The Captain was dead and nameless was frozen. 'His body must go back to your time. His death was written here. But the body must be buried in his time.'

It was painful to have watched him die before my eyes. It was even more painful to carry him back to my timeline. God had a plan for me. I didn't know what it was, but I was sure that the worst punishment for me at this time was experiencing lifelessness and the development of the desire to die.

# Chapter 17

Marshal was searching the floors, I wasn't there. He ran to the top and was disappointed at not having found me. When he returned to the ground floor, he saw me sitting next to the body of the Captain. He realized that I went to the past again but he wanted to know how, without using the portal inside the book. He took his last steps from the steps and came rushing to me. Fear was evident on my face and he wanted to know what happened. His eyes were probing, trying to read what was in my mind.

'Marshal!' I whispered and looked at him. 'He's no more.' In the next few minutes, I painfully described what had happened.

Hanging his head in sorrow, he said, 'Let's go Jim.

There's nothing left for us here.'

'We must take him with us and give him a proper burial.'

He shook his head. 'Getting him out will be impossible. He's dead weight. He'll only slow us down!' He moved for the rear door. I stood to have a last look at the man who was just doing his job and got involved in the mess that I had created.

I left him, alone and peaceful. As I closed the door behind me, I realized that this was the last time we would see the Captain.

'This way! Hurry up!' Marshal called out. He sat in the rear seat with the owner behind the wheels. He figured that it would be safer for an ordinary man to drive the vehicle and not a man in a police uniform. When I reached the car, I heard the sirens of multiple police cars echoing through the street behind us. The man started sweating. I took the rear seat with Marshal and as I got in, a fleet of cars blocked the road behind us. A few other cars stopped other cars at the end of the road. They were coming closer. We ducked inside and I told the man, 'Step on it. Just don't stop the car.' A few cops got out of their cars. With guns, they motioned at our car.

'Go, go, go!' the cop shouted, trying to evacuate the area. The man drove us away. We didn't breathe easy till we traversed a good thirty meters. At a safe distance, we got up and sat on the seats. Riding in an anonymous car was good for us, but we had a problem.

'Where do you want me to take you?' the man asked us.

We were wondering the same thing.

'Does he have ears and eyes everywhere? He can come and go to and from our time and place, whenever he pleases?' Marshal seemed disbelieving of the extent of power nameless had. 'Man, how did he take you away?'

'The first time we fought, I threw him down the window from my second floor. He has my novel. Whenever I found a portal and traveled back in time, the page turned black.

Nameless used the same page of that novel to travel across time. But the worst part is that when I do it, I don't know when and where I will go. He has full control over his destination and time. His power has grown beyond our imagination!'

'How did he get that power?'

'I was told not to mess with time. I did exactly that and brought him here with me. Consider it a side-effect.'

'Can I use a page as a portal to go back in time?'

After a lot of thinking and arguing with myself, I finally told him. 'No, you can't. Only he and I can. God told me that time travel is not allowed. I shouldn't have taken you with me. It is not safe. God has given only me this ability. Nameless can travel in time because I was him in my last birth. You saw what happened to the Captain?' He looked away. 'You can't do it. Even if you try, I guarantee that nothing good will happen to you.'

'Don't lose hope quickly, Jim.' 'Why not?'

'You're still here, in one piece. You have God with you!' He had a point. I was a fugitive, I had come face to face with a killer. I had escaped the most ruthless and intelligent officer. But I was still alive. He had instilled hope in me. 'I think he has a purpose for you, my friend.'

I was frustrated at the turn of events. I responded in frustration, 'People around me are dying. Innocent people are getting brutally murdered. I don't understand what purpose I am here to serve!'

'Just have faith. We don't understand his will.' I looked at him. His eyes had a strange glint as he said this. The gun was no longer in his hands. He had put it in his holster. 'What's God like?'

'He takes a human form so I feel comfortable.' 'So he comes to you like a normal human being?'

'Yes and he has this childlike look on his face. He makes me feel like he's carefree. Sometimes, he is angry but he looks like he's in control!'

'He's God, he is in control.'

I described God. Marshal was fascinated. Judging by his listening skills, I deduced that he was a firm believer in God. After a while, the driver said, 'Um, excuse me sir, we're on the highway now.'

'Excellent!' Marshal responded. 'I sensed he had a plan, I told you, right?'

'Yes you did. I should believe in him.'

'You bet you should. I know someone in the department who might help us. He owes me big time!' Marshal looked at the driver. 'I would like to borrow your phone.' The man dug a phone from his pocket and gave it to Marshal. It was a smartphone with a screen lock.

'5537!' the man said. Marshal touched the numbers and went directly to the call option and started dialing a number. 'With the Captain out of the scene, we can breathe with relief!' I had not imagined that somebody's death would give me relief. Nobody answered the call. It seemed that the entire department was on the streets.

'Excuse me sir, are you the bad guys?' asked the innocent man.

'No, we're the good ones,' I said promptly.

'If we were the bad guys you'd be dead by now,' Marshal added. The man was nervous all this while. After the assurance, he seemed to feel better. The car accelerated at good speed. Someone finally answered.

"LAPD, how may I help you?" They offered to help, but ironically, they were hell bent on hunting us down. It was ironic. Marshal took a deep breath. 'I would like to speak to Mr. James Walker. I have information that I must share with him.' Marshal changed his voice to avoid being recognized.

'Who is calling?'

'Please tell Mr. Walker that it is his informer. Code 009!' There was no reply. Marshal spoke facing me. He had his hand on the phone keeping in mind that no whisper with me traveled through the line.

'No informer calls on the phone. But the code I have given will let Walker know that it is me.'

'Hello? What the hell have you been doing, Marshal?' somebody asked, quietly.

'Who Marshal?' Marshal replied.

'The line's not tapped, you can speak!' Marshal sighed. 'James I need your help.'

'Man, the whole department is after you. I hope you're not involved in all that's been happening in the city.'

'I'll tell you everything. First tell me, did the Captain bring a lady called Kathryn Morgan to office?'

'He did. She's still in his cabin. She's been ordered not to move till the Captain comes back!'

'The Cap's not coming back, man!'

'Why is that? He never leaves a case unclosed!'

'James, don't tell anyone now about this. Captain's dead!'

'What the-'

'Look man, I will tell you everything. But you have to get her to the Deltoro Stop after the highway. I hope you remember the exact place where the train stops for the crossing. Can you do that for me?'

After a short pause he replied, 'It won't be much trouble. No one's here, now, just the janitor who took your call. Half the department is at the shelter home and the other half was with the Captain.'

'Nameless did shake the entire department after all!' 'What did you say?'

'Nothing. I will wait for you at the spot. How long will it take you?'

'You forgot to ask how much you owe me.'

'Hey, don't act smart. You owe me a favor!'

'I want three grand for this!' Marshal exhaled sharply when he heard this.

'What's the problem?' I asked. Marshal pressed his hand on the phone's speaker and looked at me, agitated. 'He's asking for three grand.'

'Tell him if he gets the job done, he'll get five!'

'Are you sure?' I took out my wallet and showed him a number of credit cards. 'Right then!' he released his hand from the phone and continued, 'I'll give you five if you can make it there with the lady in an hour.'

'Consider it done then!' the man hung up. 'What did he say?' I asked him.

Marshal was about to give the phone to the man driving but he stopped and put his hand on my shoulder. 'You will meet Kathryn in less than an hour.'

After such a long time, I felt a tinge of happiness in his words. They relieved me of the danger I had imagined for Kathryn. 'Thank you so much, man!' I clasped his hand.

He smiled a little. It was the second time I had seen him smile. 'I told you, have faith!' I finally smiled earnestly.

'Yeah, you did!'

Marshal turned to the man, 'Please take us to-'

'I know the place sir, I heard you on the phone. It should not take us more than fifteen minutes to get there.'

Marshal's words were still on my mind. This man tempted it further. 'Faith!' I started to taste a layer of happiness that it gave me. For the next twelve minutes, we didn't discuss anything. My mind had twisted storms and it was begging for tranquility. We looked out of our windows and watched the landscape outside. At the end of the stretch, the man saw railway lines meant for normal speed cargo transportation.

'We're almost there!' he made an announcement. At this point, he felt relieved. In just a few minutes, he would part ways with us for good. Any busy corporate from Los Angeles wouldn't want to give a cop a lift, if he had pointed a gun at him, and a likely criminal covered in blood stains.

As the car roared down the swift highway, I whispered to him, 'I have to give you credit, Marshal.'

'Huh?' He was surprised as he looked at me.

'You have all these connections, a good hand on the gun and integrity. Surely you must have solved many cases. They should have made you a senior at the department.'

My complement piqued his interest. He laughed a little. 'To be honest, Jim, I'm not doing this for you. Back at the office, I solved cases. Sometimes, I was corrupt but I still tried to do the right thing. In many cases, I let the criminal go from right under my nose because I had to catch bigger fish. I tested my character and failed many times. Earlier, I used to ask myself if I had a calling or purpose in life and every time I used to tell myself that I did. But when you become a part of a system that sometimes does wrong things for convenience, life becomes faithless. The thing is, no matter what I did for my city, nobody appreciated me.

When I did something less dignified, I was rewarded. I sort of lost faith on the way!' He paused for a while. 'You never judged me like the others. Jim, you make me believe that I have a purpose in life.'

'What's your purpose Marshal?' I was curious.

'I think I am here to help a friend. I will be with you till the end of the line!' In all these years, I had forgotten what it meant. All those who came into my life came for transactional purposes. But this man was special. So far, he had only given, and received nothing. Maybe I was destined to come across this man who I would want to call my friend.

I extended my hand. 'Friends?'

He smiled and shared a firm handshake. 'Till the end of the line.'

'Even beyond,' I said. He laughed. It was the first time in many days that I had laughed so heartily. We were in our moment. We didn't realize that we had taken the road leading to a crossing.

'We are here!' he said.

'Can I have my cellphone back please?' Marshal tossed the phone at him. We got off and looked at the man. 'Well, good luck to you fellas!' he said. I waved, but he didn't care to look. He wanted to get away from us, alive.

'I hope he doesn't tell the cops about us!' Marshal raised his hand. I eyed the compact SIM he held with two fingers. He took it out before giving him the phone. 'I wish I were that intelligent.'

'You should join the department.'

'No, I will pass this opportunity. What do we do now?

Just stand here and wait for them?' 'We don't have any other option!' 'If you say so…'

We sat by the railway lines, on the warm grass that spread throughout the land. In about twenty minutes, we saw the first police car approach. We got up. Marshal took out his gun in an instant, just in case.

'Is it her!' I said, looking like I had doubt and certainty on my mind. The car slowed down. The man behind the wheel took it off the road.

'It's them!' confirmed Marshal.

Kathryn got out first. She was surprised to see me. I felt bliss. 'Jim?' she said.

'Kathryn!' We exchanged glances. I stood in my place, not knowing how to greet her. But that wasn't the sole reason. Seeing me covered in blood would scare her. Watching me as I was, her expressions turned to those of worry when we were together. I remembered the look on her face. She showed her love and care for me.

'Jim? Are you okay?' her eyes looked up as she came to me. 'What happened to you?' she turned to James who got out of the car. 'Please, the mineral water in your car.'

I grabbed her hand. She turned to me. I took her in my arms. 'I am okay Kathryn, and I am so glad that you're okay.'

James took a crate out of the car's boot. 'Hey, Marshal, I guessed you were going on a long trip. You will need this!' he handed the crate to him.

'What's this?' Marshal asked. 'It is a crate, can't you see?'

'I mean to ask what's inside it.'

'It has food and water for your journey, and bills for six thousand dollars.'

'Six thousand! What the hell?'

'It has bullets and two clips. I thought you would need it to assist the most wanted criminal there.'

Marshal looked at me, I was talking to Kathryn. 'Yeah, it's a long story, Walker.'

'They found Cap's body at The Last Bookstore. What a mess lies there!'

'You want me to tell you?' he cut in between.

'No, no. I better not know. Stay low for a month if you can. I can't promise anything for your friend here. But you'll be okay.'

'Thanks, man! I appreciate it!' James pulled his hand out in front of Marshal. 'Oh yes, wait!' He turned again to look at me, 'Jim, can I have a second, here?'

'Yeah sure!' I told Kathryn to wait. I went to him. He motioned toward James. I had my wallet in hand. I pulled out a gold card. '5535, the card has a credit limit of $20,000. They're all yours.' James' jaw dropped. He hadn't expected generosity from a fugitive. He tried gaining control over his expressions. 'Thanks! It was nice doing business with you!' he said. 'Marshal, if you ever need me, call me. The train will be here any minute!'

'Yeah, I am anticipating it. I hope we're not being tracked.'

'No, no. The department is busy with the mess you created. I had the lady checked at the office to see if a tracker was planted on her. She's clean. That car there is old. No camera, no tracker. No one has eyes on you now.'

'Okay, good!'

'See you around. I better leave.' In a minute, his car was gone. He seemed the rash driver that the LAPD was partially known to be. A train approached. Its speed gradually slowed down.

'Why's it slowing down?' I asked Marshal.

'I told you about the criminals that we let go from under our nose, right?'

'You did, yes.'

'Well, that's the train through which I let them escape. And now that we're criminals, we'll take the same transport.'

'You're criminals?' Kathryn shouted.

'We're not. You know I can't be one. Come, I will explain all this to you!' The train stopped a little further ahead of us. I heaved open the massive door and helped her up. I got in after her. Marshal lifted the crate and I took it from him and pulled him in. Marshal extended his hand outside and waved four times. It was a signal for the train to proceed. Almost immediately, we felt a jerk as the train began moving. Marshal and I closed the gigantic door. The compartment was pleasantly posh. It looked like it wasn't a compartment at a cargo train but an empty compartment with three bulbs illuminating the space, a room with two beds and a toilet, which was hopefully functional.

'You're doing a great job, Marshal,' I complemented him.

'Yeah, the criminals are luckier than we are!'

We got a good look around the coach. Kathryn watched me and finally asked, 'Jim, what's going on?'

It was time I told her everything. We sat on the floor. I was about to begin my story when it occurred to me to ask Marshal something. 'Where are we going anyway?'

'We're going to where it all began. New York.'

# Chapter 18

So things you see of your past life are a string of clues that will eventually lead you to know what you did to someone?' Kathryn asked, half-understanding my narration. Her eyes didn't move an inch from me throughout the time that I explained.

'They are not quite a string of events. I think my visits have something to do with me being an author. I imagine and then write. I think I have to use these visits as points to make me imagine and construct a story. If I am imaginative enough, I will find out what I did against whom.'

'And these lockets, these keys that you talk about, what do they do?'

'At first, I wasn't sure. I thought they opened huge planet-like balls that might contain drugs or illegal stuff. Why else would a mafia kingpin protect them? Whatever's inside them, Holmes badly wanted to keep them a secret. It seemed to be very precious to him.'

'Right. So what do you think about them now?'

'First, according to what I have seen and heard, Holmes is dead. Next, if that's the case, I won't be able to find the other lockets to open the planets. I hope he has changed his appearance and is alive. Second, I think these planets have something to do with my sins.'

'How can you be so sure?'

'That has to be the case. I don't see any other possibility!' 'So you mean to say that if you open these balls, your sins will be forgiven?'

I needed a moment to gather my thoughts and answer. I shrugged as I said, 'I'm not sure about this too,' looking down at the moving floor with a blank face.

'Don't mind me, Jim, but this seems illogical. Noah used to tell me that a man has to go through severe ordeals to atone for his sins. This sounds too easy!' I watched her eyes for a spark of hope. I didn't get any. She seemed right.

'You are right,' I admitted. 'There has to be something else.' I looked at her, disappointed. I wish God were here to answer.

'Can I have a look at the keys?' I opened the top two buttons of my shirt and pulled out the one Mark had given me. 'Here you go.'

She held it in her hand and looked closely. 'Magnificent!' Marshal was equally amazed. 'So this is it!'

'Yes, it's supposed to open up the planet.' 'Which one?' asked Marshal.

'This green stone is emerald. It is the stone of planet Mercury. I guess it should connect with Mercury.'

'What do you do with them? Place them on a slot in a sequence and wait for the planet to open up?'

'I don't know yet. Mark told me that all the keys may have to be at that chamber, at the same time.'

'I'm not sure if you should wear them,' said Kathryn. 'Why's that?'

'If they are made of the gemstones of the planets, they have an impact on the bearer! Noah told me that every person is governed by a ruling planet. The person can only wear gemstones related to that planet or planets that are friendly to the one that rules the native. Any gemstone that belongs to an inimical planet will bring nothing but harm.'

'Care to elaborate please?' I asked.

'I don't remember precisely. I had little interest in this science. Noah said that Saturn and Sun were enemy planets. If your horoscope's ruler is the Sun, you shouldn't wear Saturn's gemstone as it will only cause you harm. Noah had a gemstone for me to save us from falling apart. I refused to wear it in my ring finger. I guess I should have taken a chance.' I didn't know how to react. We were all silent. The journey was long and we needed rest.

'I thought that if I was able to open the planets and blow open Holmes' hidden businesses, I will have paid for my sins!' I realized that there was more to it than met the eye. I looked at Marshal and Kathryn. Kathryn got up. It looked like she was planning to sleep. As soon as she got up, a thought hit my head. Where was God when I needed him?

'God's always with you!' a voice reached my ears but I didn't know from which direction. I looked around. No one was there. 'Did you hear that guys?' I asked the two. The two didn't respond.

'Kathryn!' She was motionless and didn't respond. 'Marshal?' He was also frozen in time. But the sound and movement of the compartment told me that the train was on its way.

'You seek answers but you never look within,' the same voice hit my ears again.

'Is that…?' I felt a hand on my shoulder.

'What's gotten into your imagination, Jim? I expected you to solve half the mystery but you look like you're going in the wrong direction!' There he was, standing behind me. The same jolly face, only this time his eyebrows frowned. There was care in his eyes. I turned to ask him something but he had the answer prepared. 'Don't worry. I froze them for some time.'

'You went missing for such a long time. Where were you?'

'You know all this keeps me busy. I take out time from my busy schedule for people who call me!' he said. 'You called, so I'm here!' he took his quirkiness to a higher notch.

'That's very thoughtful of you! I'm sorry, I don't have a seat to offer today and make you comfortable!'

'Oh, so what's that I see over there?' I looked in the direction in which he pointed. A wooden rocking chair and a purple bean bag were placed at the center of the compartment. I looked back at him with an 'I saw that coming' look on my face. 'That's very thoughtful of you, Jim!' The joke was on me now. 'Come, I love the rocking chair. We have to make you work your mind now!'

'Okay,' I said, puzzled. The feeling contradicted my response. 'How're we going to do that?'

'Remember this purple bean bag?'

I looked at it. It was vaguely familiar. 'I don't recall it completely. I remember sitting on a purple bean bag in my school days.'

'What did you do when you sat on it?'

'What do you mean? Anybody who sits on a bean bag rests or relaxes.'

'See, that's why I said, that we have to make you work your mind now. You have to make your mind work or you won't make it past the first question.' He made me a part of a quiz competition I didn't sign up for. He, as his nature would have him do, had ways that were beyond my power of imagination.

'Why do I have to go through crooked questions and even more crooked answers? Why can't I get straight answers?'

'Because, Jim,' he began rocking the chair, 'life is not a straight line. It has lots of curves in it. Besides, where's the fun when you don't break rules and snake your way through the curved path.' The point about breaking rules didn't go down well with me. God telling me to break rules was beyond belief. 'Now Jim, what did you do when you sat on it?' I must admit that at the time, his presence strangely made me feel like a kid. I had no option but to participate in the question-answer game. I lay back on the bag and started thinking. I let out a sigh before I looked at him and answered. 'I would think?'

'Not bad, that's a good start. Now try a little harder.' I looked at my legs trying to figure out an answer. What had I done back when I was a kid? I started to construct thoughts. A dreamy seven-year-old Jim played with two action figures in his room. He seemed immersed in the game just like any kid his age. After a friendly fight with Batman and Superman, little Jim took the purple bean bag... With both action figures in hand, little Jim imagined himself as Batman and how he would save the day using his wits before Superman.

'I got it!' I turned to God. 'I used to dream of becoming a savior of a city one day. Just like Batman.'

'Nice. Can you put this in a way that resembles how a teacher instructs you to do what you love to do?' God gave me the hint I was looking for and so I spoke before he gave the entire clue.

'I used to imagine.'

'That's brilliant, Jim. You found the answer!' I wasn't impressed with myself, knowing that it was an easy question. 'So Jim, I have one more for you!'

'I'm ready,' I replied like a confident student who had studied well.

'What have you been doing lately?'

'What kind of question is that?' I argued. I didn't understand his intent.

'The answer to this question lies in your answer to the previous one.' I began to recollect all that had happened in the last two days. None of it seemed to match the previous answer. 'Can I get a hint?'

'Why do you want a hint, Jim?'

'Because I read that God helps those who help themselves and I am trying to help myself here and I need you to help me.'

'When did you start offering such amusing responses?'

'Just lately!' I felt a ripple of excitement spread in me. Imagining lately. But his question was what I hadn't been doing lately. It didn't take me long to answer this one as well. 'I haven't been imagining like I should.'

'Ah! You're getting good at this. That's absolutely correct!' Sadly, the answer didn't make me happy.

'I think now you know what you must do more than travel in time.' I got up. Imagining on the bean bag had done its work for me. 'I have to connect the dots in my writing style, right?'

'You should. Then you can go travel in the past.'

'But how do I do that? I don't have my book with me!' 'Who're you talking to, Jim?' Kathryn's voice sounded from behind me. I turned and saw her standing and Marshal getting up.

'How'd you get over there in a flash?' Marshal got up and asked.

'Hey fellas, meet…' I turned to see that God, the rocking chair and the bean bag had disappeared. 'God!'

'Are you talking about this book?' Marshal pulled out the novel I had with me at The Last Bookstore. I figured that he had taken it along in case I would need it.

'Marshal you're the greatest.' I went up close to both of them. I took the book from him. 'I wanted you to meet the creator but I guess he only likes me here!'

'Do you mean…?' asked Marshal.

'Yes, my friend, and he has instructed me to imagine!' 'Imagine what?' Kathryn asked this time.

'Actually, that's what the writer in me will answer in a while. I wish you had a coffee machine installed in here but I guess I will have to work without it!'

'What do we do?' Kathryn asked.

'I think you should get some sleep, both of you, while I solve the mystery.'

# Chapter 19

The sound of the slowing engine made me wonder. We were nearing New York. The train decelerated and came to a halt. I turned the lock and slid the door open.

We stepped out of the compartment into the vast grassland that brought in the badly needed fresh air. Three days inside a train was terrible. Luckily, I found a blank diary where I wrote the entire events in the pattern of a story. Till now, it had shaped into a novel and I was even planning to make it my seventh if I come out of the mess, completely clean.

Marshal began to lock the door behind us. The engine was still idling and the sound escalated in less than ten seconds, taking the train away, to its destination. The terrain was grassy, unlike the concrete outskirts of Manhattan city. We were well away from the city and that was safe for a convict like me. A direction board that stood a couple of yards north of us on a road leading to the city made us aware of our current location. New York was about 50 miles away from the place we stood and I was about twenty away from my place and a hot brewing black coffee.

Kathryn and Marshal looked unsettled. The journey was less than comfortable. The story that I narrated of the events and how I was responsible as nameless, surprisingly believable. They admitted before getting down that the way I had imagined things and connected the dots, was mind blowing. Whatever Itold them, made perfectsense. Marshal recalled how I narrated it. Through my imagination, I was able to conjure conceivable events and circumstances that explained everything about my previous birth and how it led me in this life. But I still was far from unraveling the mystery of the seven planets and how I was going to get myself rid of my last birth sins.

'So we find Holmes now?' asked Marshal. I nodded. 'But we can't be sure of his existence. You think he's here? What you told us is still a story!' Kathryn said, seeming skeptical.

'I have a purpose here. God doesn't come and meet everybody in person. We'll find him here and like I told you, I've a pretty good clue about his existence and changed identity.'

'Then we should go and get that...' she stopped before saying a curse word. Kathryn liked to be part of a civilized world just like I did.

'We can't just go there with guns and expect him to cooperate with us. He's exceptionally powerful within his territory!' said Marshal.

'Oh, he will cooperate, but not with us,' I said. 'Then with whom?' Kathryn asked.

'Nameless has a score to settle with him. Let him have his game of destruction inside Holmes' world. He'll wreak havoc there. Afterwards, I expect to collect clues that will take us closer to solving the mystery of the planets.'

'What do we do now?'

'We change first, and then relax.' Marshal seemed to hesitate. Seeing the confidence I had in my story and feeling the determination in my words, he deemed it in our best interest to do as I said. His trust intensified under the realization that I had a plan in my mind which would solve things once and for all.

I had a plan. I didn't want to share it with them since I knew it would ultimately lead us to a confrontation with nameless. My instincts made me dead certain about it. The plan was going to have to wait to be shared.

'There's a mini truck coming from that direction,' Marshal pointed and ran to the road. His uniform made the driver stop. 'This should take us to your place Jim. I hope you don't mind getting in!' he said.

'No, not at all. I can't wait to take a bath and change!' The loader was a two-seater. We jumped into the back and let the driver drive without being bothered. The carrier coursed down the grasslands. At the back, I sighed. Breathing the countryside fresh air and knowing that after the longest and most turbulent days of my life, I had a break. Marshal sat on his hips, hands on his lap, still not letting his senses relax. The police training had a stressful impact on the daily conduct of every cop. Kathryn sat next to me. The wind made her hair blow, reminding me of how I would run my hands through her beautiful curls.

Marshal looked at his watch probably wondering how long it would take us to get to my place. I read his thoughts. 'Another fifteen minutes tops,' I assured him. As the car speed toward the city, I found myself wondering how to talk to Kathryn about us.

'Excuse me, can I borrow your phone?' I asked the driver from the open window behind him. I wanted to call Sebastian and tell him that we're coming.

'Sure!' he pulled his phone out of his pocket. 'I'm afraid it won't be of much use.' I took it from him. Seeing the faint signal turn dead before my eyes, I grumbled. 'You're right man!' I returned it.

'Your friend told me you live near this area. You should know that network service is poor here!' he said, glancing at me in the rear view mirror. 'The service will improve once we're in the vicinity of the city.'

'Slipped from my mind,' I mumbled.

'But you don't want to go there, right buddy?'

'Yeah,' I looked up to figure our current location. 'There's a road connecting with the one we're on. Can you take us two miles on that?'

'No mister, I will drop you at the junction. You can walk from there!' I felt a sudden surge of frustration. We were lucky to manage a lift from him.

'Please sir, we will really appreciate your kindness!' Kathryn said. I looked at her. 'You've been kind enough to get us this far. If you can just take us two miles further, we'll be indebted.' The man thought a while. Kathryn's mellifluous voice was too persuasive for any man. 'Yeah well, what the hell is another two miles. I'll take you there, lady!'

'Thank you, Sir, I wish people were as nice as you are!' 'It's okay, lady. No problem.' We sat back. She didn't say anything, but smiled. I responded with a nod. None of us spoke for the next couple of minutes. I had been writing continuously for nights now. My eyes began to droop, but I didn't want them to close. I shook my head and turned to face the oncoming view. My eyes stretched through the length of the deserted road. It seemed to be an unending road, melting at the point where the Earth and sky met. It reminded me of the road to heaven that I had seen at Victoria's Garden. I looked at the road before I was about to get off. My vision went ahead, where there was an image of a man standing at the center of the road. I widened my eyes to get a clear view.

'Stop the car now!' I told the driver.

'What for?' the driver asked. Perhaps he couldn't see the man.

'There's a man straight ahead, do you want to run over him?' The driver didn't reduce the speed. I looked up again at the man. My eyebrows rose after seeing the man. Nameless stood with a gun in hand and a smirk on his face.

He didn't take a second and I heard loud gunshots from his end.

'Shit!' I cried loudly and ducked. My eyes opened. I had snapped out of a nightmare.

'Are you okay Jim?' Kathryn asked, perhaps seeing the horror on my face.

Marshal saw me shaken. 'You look like you saw a bad dream man.' I took ten seconds to relax. I kept blinking to check if it really was a dream. 'Don't ask about it. I saw nameless before us on the road with a machine gun in hand. He had the familiar intensity in his eyes when he started shooting at us.' Marshal looked at the road. 'Let's hope your nightmare doesn't come true!' he said.

'Ah, it won't!' I said. But we will see him tomorrow! I sat up and initiated a conversation to cool things down. 'Do you think Castiel has opened the chest?'

'Castiel takes enormous care with his work. He will take time if he must. The important thing is that the articles inside don't get damaged!'

'I hope he takes extra precautions because that chest is the only thing we have against Holmes.'

'He will, I can bet on it.'

'We'll confirm with him after we get home.'

'No,' Marshal's instant refusal came to Kathryn as disturbing news.

She asked in confusion, 'Can we not initiate contact with him?'

'The Captain found out our hideout. Castiel will give his life to keep his chamber away from the department's eyes. Since they don't have any evidence against Castiel, they can't take him in!' Kathryn's eyes were still curious to find out why we couldn't contact him. Marshal continued, 'There is a protocol of follow up action in the LAPD. The department will always eavesdrop on suspects' conversations. This is common. Since we're under their radar, we can't talk to him for three more days. That's how long the department keeps its ears on you.'

'If you'd read my thriller, dear, you would know this!' I said.

'Your books have done enough damage to us. I'm not going to even talk about them!' she said. After her comment, the silence between us accentuated the sound of the car. I broke into a light sweat. My madness for work was the only thing that took all the time I had for her. That separated us.

Seeing the two of us in an awkward situation, Marshal attempted to lighten the mood. 'From where I see it, you are together in a catastrophic circumstance. If you removed the ego, you can see that you care a lot about each other.'

We looked at each other slowly. Marshal's words were comforting. I looked down at her hand, which supported her on the floor of the car. Moving my hand up to hers and holding it, I said, 'I'm sorry, Kathryn.' She felt my hand and sensed the genuineness in my words. 'I was driven by the limelight. I overlooked what mattered most to me.'

Kathryn looked away. Her eyes were dewy. 'You're not the only one who made mistakes. I shouldn't have given up on you!' she said, in a tone that told me she was crying from within.

'You didn't,' I held her hand tighter. 'You still have my name with you.' She turned back at me. After many years, we hugged again. For a brief moment, I was lost in her arms and she, in mine. Watching us together again, Marshal seemed happy.

'Is this the road you guys have been talking about?' The driver brought his vehicle to a stop before a road that was connected to the one we were on. The three of us looked at it. It was the one.

'Yes, this is the one!' I said. He took the road and we cleared two miles in two minutes. He dropped us just before my large mansion. We thanked him, but he only paid attention to Kathryn and Marshal. I didn't mind. As we walked toward the front gate, I was surprisingly calm. The gravity of the situation struck me. I was being hunted by me from my last birth. I was a sinner, trying desperately to figure out how to solve an enduring mystery to atone for my sins. The fact of having Kathryn and Marshal with me lessened the burden I felt was only mine. I now had my wife back and a friend who would give his life for me. And having figured out most of the mystery gave rise to the prospect of performing God's given work! Kathryn's first step on the cobblestone laid pathway reminded me of my pleasant memories with her in our mansion. It curved to the entrance where we saw my butler, Sebastian come out. He was surprised to see Kathryn return.

# Chapter 20

I had slept for nearly eight hours. For me, the morning was the best time to sleep. After changing my clothes, I went down to the living room facing the veranda. My black coffee, Kathryn and Marshal were waiting for me at the table. I hadn't taken my first sip when Marshal fired a question. 'I still don't get it. Why would nameless want to harm him and not you?'

'I assure you he has intentions of harming me but at the moment, he is delivering vengeance!'

'I don't understand,' said Kathryn.

I took a sip and went onto explain. 'Nameless is Holmes' adopted son. Since he was an underworld don, he needed professional assassins. He made nameless one. He became exceptionally efficient as an assassin after the promise that Holmes would hand over his throne to him.'

'If he had him trained to take over, I don't understand why he wouldn't just retire and give his empire to his son!' Kathryn was puzzled. A news channel on television ran the news of the destruction that nameless had caused.

'Greed, Marshal! Greed for power had become an obsession, a habit he couldn't get rid of. They must have had a fight initially, but Holmes' men must have overpowered him. Holmes thought that nameless wouldn't be a threat, but nameless took away his daughter, Victoria. Assuming the extent of rage nameless had for his father, he changed his identity to that of the Chairman of a university. Who would think that a man running an empire in the education sector would be a kingpin of the underworld?'

My imaginative story seemed to explain why things we were watching happened as they were. I told them that according to me, Chairman Prescott was Holmes, the man I had met during the promo event for my novel that Noah had arranged. The words "Breaking News" began to flash on television. The anchor said that the adopted son had figured out his father's hidden identity and was taking his rage out on his father's new empire. The news made the university look worse than I had imagined.

'This guy's a total annihilator!' I murmured. Sebastian entered with coffee mugs placed on a silver plate. He arranged them on the center table. 'Ma'am, just as you preferred, light coffee in a small mug.'

'That is very sweet of you, Sebastian.'

'I am baking cookies for you, it shouldn't take long!' he said. I looked at him with a peculiar eye. It hadn't even been a day since she had entered our mansion and Sebastian had forgotten me altogether. Kathryn seemed to have read my mind, because she fixed me with a devilish smile.

Normally, I would have yelled at Sebastian for making my coffee light. But now, I didn't, because she always got to decide what I would eat or drink. Sebastian nodded as he smiled and disappeared into the kitchen. Marshal glanced at me, trying to empathize. 'Marriage is still a long way ahead for me!' he mentioned.

'You won't need to wait that long, I know someone you'd be interested in!' Kathryn said. Marshal was amused. The news channel appeared to irritate her a little. 'Americans!' she commented in a hoarse voice.

'You aren't American? Do you not like Americans?' 'Don't get me wrong, Marshal. My distaste for Americans extends to politics and war. I am not originally an American, my family shifted from the UK, when I was young. I love this country and the people.' Seated on the sofa beside me, Kathryn began drinking coffee and bit into a chocolate chip cookie that Sebastian had brought. Marshal joined. The effect of the late afternoon snack was welcoming after a long journey on the cargo train.

I got up. 'Marshal, it is time to go to the university. I have a feeling we must go there.'

'No way am I letting you go there!' Kathryn got up. 'It is dangerous there! Look at the news. I don't want anything to happen to you.'

'Nothing will happen to me, I promise.' She wasn't convinced. Marshal was ready to get into action. I took my car keys even as Kathryn protested. We left the room when she shouted, 'I don't want to lose you, Jim! Don't do this to me.' I turned around saw fear writ large on her face. I went to her and hugged her.

'I will be okay. I just realized that whatever's happening is becoming a part of my seventh book.' Kathryn was surprised. 'I am the author of this story and I am going to write the last page and come back to you!' She didn't understand what I meant. She released me from her hands. 'Kathryn, whatever happens next, is exactly what I want. God hasn't only given me the power to travel through time. He has also given me the power to make my last book become real!'

# Chapter 21

There were cops everywhere. They had sealed all the roads to the university. Unconvinced by my explanation that I was going to be okay, Kathryn had insisted on joining us. I parked near the sealed area. As we walked toward the road leading to the main gate, I felt as if we were being watched. Marshal said he could get in with his police ID. 'Wait here. Let me find a way in, I might know a few cops here who will definitely help.'

'Okay, but be careful!' I said. His expression assured that he would take the best steps. He crossed the restricted area and began sneaking past a few cars. The police stood a good distance from us. We lost sight of him as he entered a car crowded area. We stood facing the area, waiting for him. Suddenly, someone pressed a gun against my back.

'Turn around, Mr. Morgan.' I did as told. Having seen the person, I said, 'I never thought I'd see you with a gun!'

'I see you underestimate my capabilities!' It was Monica, the announcer of my event at the university.

'Oh no! I mean you hardly look the assassin type.'

'I am flattered!' she said with a casual look. 'I hope you know it is unwise to test my intentions. You see the black car around the corner?' I tried looking for one and caught a glimpse of the black Audi before I turned back at her. She sidestepped and motioned her gun to it, instructing us to get to it.

'I knew you were interested in me. But, I must say that I didn't imagine you taking me hostage!'

'Disillusioned, are we Mr. Morgan? A lady knows how to get a man to wag his tail for her. I hate to break it to you but I am here because I was asked to deliver you to my boss.' She swung her gun in Kathryn's direction and back to mine. 'Enough of the sweet talk. Get moving, you two!' her voice was stern, like the determined expression on her face. We walked to the car slowly.

'And here, I was a fool to think of you as just the master of ceremonies!'

'Again, I see you greatly underestimate the killer instinct of a woman Mr. Morgan!'

'I wonder why a gorgeous lady like you would work for Holmes.'

'What?' Monica was thunderstruck. She stopped. There was no way anyone could figure out the Chairman's true identity as Holmes, the underworld kingpin. It was beyond her wildest imagination that a harmless writer like me would be able to know this.

'Stop!' she said. Her hand lost its tight grip on the gun as she lowered her hand. We turned. 'How do you know that-?'

'So now you want the sweet talk!' Kathryn cut her short. Monica didn't pay attention to Kathryn. Her eyes were fixed on me.

'It doesn't matter. I am paid to do what I am doing. Knowing how you got the secret doesn't concern me. Turn around and keep moving.'

We didn't move. I figured that I had put a little pressure on her now. 'Monica, you don't need to do this,' I declared.

'Do as I say,' she commanded as she raised her gun. 'I will not hesitate to shoot ifyou don't follow my instructions.'

'If I know better, Holmes sent you here to collect the both of us… Alive!' I stressed on the last word. She broke into a sweat. My statement hit her harder than I intended for it. Her worrisome expressions took away the camouflage of her sharp words. Compared to the crude assassin that nameless was, Monica was a new recruit with a gun in hand. I had already predicted that I could make her uneasy.

She seemed to firm her resolve. 'The boss will sort that out when I turn you in!' she said. Her eyes were back on me, only this time, they weren't as determined. 'I let you speak enough.'

Kathryn saw the surge of apprehension on her face. It was time to keep the pressure building. She added, 'Everyone around that man dies, Monica. You may do your job with us but you can foresee death coming your way too.'

'Shut up!' she screamed. Her hand began to tremble. 'One more word and I will shoot you!' She swung her gun at Kathryn.

'Don't do it,' I raised a hand at her and the other at Kathryn. She pulled the trigger in anxiety. The gunshot made Kathryn duck reflexively to avoid being hit but the bullet had already gone over her head.

'We'll do as you say,' I quickly said and turned Kathryn around with me. 'One more minute, just do as she says,' I whispered. I felt the barrel of the gun press against my back.

'Now move,' her voice was more confident, 'and don't try to do anything silly!'

We moved across the road toward the car. Kathryn looked at me and I could read her eyes. We have to do something. I was counting seconds as we moved and somehow my eyes assured her that we were going to be fine. Monica was too close to me. Sensing that I could take a dynamic leap to snatch her gun from her, she repositioned herself by increasing the gap between us. Now well out of my reach, she became more confident. We reached the car. There wasn't a driver.

'You, takethewheel. She'llsitwithyou!' shecommanded. I was still counting seconds. I didn't disobey her. I moved to get behind the wheel. Kathryn stood at the navigator's door. Monica's car key unlocked it when she came near it. I stood at the door and paused a moment, seeing her point the gun at me. 'Get inside now,' she pressed. I opened the door and as she was expecting me to get in, I stepped backwards.

Monica froze when she saw me disobey a direct command. Kathryn didn't move. I turned and looked above her right shoulder. In a second, I made up my mind and decided to disobey her. I said, 'Sixty!'

She frowned. Sixty? Having no idea what was running in my mind, she recalled my last gesture. I saw something above her right shoulder that made me say the seemingly out-of-the-place word. Sensing danger, she felt a surge of panic. She immediately swung with the gun but before she could position herself, Marshal came swiftly and struck his big right fist on her face. The sudden explosion on her face sent her falling backwards onto the ground. Her nose shattered. She received a slight cut above her eyebrow and blood began to run from it as well as her nose. With blood blurring her vision, she wasn't able to process Marshal's exact position. Unfortunately, even with unclear vision, she had the gun in her hand outstretched at Marshal. That stopped him from making his next move.

Kathryn acted faster than the speed of light, assessing Monica's position to use it to her advantage. As she tried to get up, Kathryn clutched her hair and pulled her down hard. Monica shouted before she fell, head first. There was a loud thump that reverberated. The gun flew from her hand, and she lost consciousness. Kathryn sighed once she realized that Monica was unconscious.

I walked quickly to them. Marshal checked Monica for a pulse. I looked at Kathryn and said, 'I told you, one more minute.' She didn't seem pleased.

'She will live, but we must take her to a hospital!' I was afraid he would say that. He began to carry her. She was far too heavy. Turning to Marshal, I calculated the risk.

'It is better we leave her. Cops will be here any minute, they can handle her!' Marshal thought about my idea and felt best not to argue. He put her back on the ground.

Kathryn was going for the gun when I stopped her, 'No don't touch it.' She turned and realized I was right. The last thing I would want was for her was to get her fingerprints on the gun and make her join the convicted club.

'All that remains here for us is to let her and the gun stay as they are.' A moment later, leaving Monica unconscious on the ground, we took the car and headed for Victoria's Garden.

# Chapter 22

The sprawling 105-acre estate of Chairman Prescott was located on the outskirts of New York City, twenty minutes before Victoria's Garden. His estate was popular for having two man-made lakes and a man-made 100 feet high mountain. One could easily see the artificial waterfall from the freeway. It had become widely known as the Kingdom of Dreams. I brought the car to a shuddering stop at the face of an imposing gate. There were more security guards stationed than I had imagined. A sharp security officer with a rough expression on his face came to check me. He stopped right by my door. My eyes rolled as I sized him up and caught sight of a pistol in his utility belt. He frowned, finding only me in the car. The sternness on his face changed into apprehension. I could read his mind. He was expecting Monica and was puzzled after not having found her at the rear seat.

'I am here to meet the Chairman.'

Sweat accumulated underneath his cap. He adjusted it to get some air. 'Private vehicles must be left at the gate, sir, for security reasons. I request you to take one of our vehicles.' I stepped out of my car and saw him wave at a guard sitting inside a watch tower of sorts. I noticed three land rovers parked near it. 'You guys get great treatment!' I said to the officer. He didn't find my observation amusing. One of the guards inside the tower appeared to be writing something before coming out. I saw a key in his hand before he put it in his pocket and got inside one of the cars. He started the engine and brought it to me. The officer opened the door. 'Please sir,' that was my cue to get in. Once I sat inside, another guard at the gate swiped his card on a panel that triggered the gate's sensor system. The gate swung inwards. Sitting inside the car, I stared at the long path that led to the entrance of the gigantic estate. The mansion appeared like a speck, and was a good 500 meters ahead. The car moved in and as the gate closed behind me, I felt sweat collect around my neck. I was nervous about getting inside the lair of a kingpin.

'You don't talk?' I asked the man driving the car. There was a small pause.

'Sir, I am instructed not to engage in conversation with guests.'

'Do you want to make some money? You only need to answer a few questions!' He seemed curious. I held out a few hundred dollars. He looked them. People connected with Holmes had one thing in common: love for money. The scent of the fresh currency notes had him convinced yet he took precaution.

'I hope our conversation stays inside the car, sir.'

I smiled, 'You sure know how to make easy money, my friend!' I stretched to touch his shoulder and he immediately took the cash and put it in his pocket. 'You can do something for me.'

'Sir?'

'Deflate the tires of the car your boss uses to commute.

I hope it won't be much of a task.' 'No problem, sir. Anything else?'

'That's all. Thanks!' I didn't say anything more. We had reached by then.

The building rose like a gigantic castle amidst a sprawling golf course. A woman came forward and opened the door for me. As I got out, I thanked her with a sincere smile. She was too pretty to be a bodyguard in disguise. Two women clad in business suits stood at the door. Holmes preferred flamboyance throughout.

'Good evening Mr. Morgan, it is a pleasure to have you with us. This way, please!' Her pleasant tone and manners effectively communicated cordiality. She led me to the door. I was expecting her to open it for me but she didn't. When we stood right before a very expensive door carved of oak, it swung open from inside. Another woman greeted me with an alluring smile. 'Sophie will escort you sir. She will do her very best to make you feel comfortable,' the one standing with me said.

Who would not feel comfortable when ladies give a five star treatment? She left me with this lady named Sophie and I went inside.

'This way please,' Sophie began to take me to the meeting room. My eyes rolled to register the finest crafted paintings, hand-made decor and other interior embellishments. Holmes was filthy rich! She led me to an opulent living room. While entering, my nostrils received the pleasant aroma of lavender with traces of Cuban cigar smoke. He shouldn't have been smoking at this age if he wanted to live long.

'Please make yourself comfortable, Mr. Morgan. Mr. Prescott will join you in a few minutes. If you need anything, please don't hesitate to tell me. I will be grateful to be of amiable service.'

'Thank you Sophie, for your hospitality. I already feel at home!' She smiled. 'I would like to watch some news.' A gigantic LED television hung on the wall facing the most comfortable sofa. Sophie picked up the remote control lying on the table at the center and held it out for me.

'Anything else, Mr. Morgan?' 'Not for the moment. Thank you.'

'I am here in the room if you need anything.'

I preferred not to have an eye watching over me so I said, 'I am fine Sophie. There's no need for you to stay and trouble yourself.'

'I feel no trouble in taking care of our guests. I have instructions to be with you all the time!' That settled it. She would keep an eye on me even if I didn't want her to.

'Okay then, I will just sit down and watch some news.'

'Very well, sir. The news channels begin from channel number 100. I am here in the room with you in case you need anything!' She went back to the door and stood like a guard. I looked at her, and felt she would stay that way for a while. I turned my attention to the television and started watching. As I surfed channels, I found that all of them had the same news. Every news channel couldn't get enough of the day's catastrophe. Several journalists covered the news at the university. Watching the news for about four minutes, I heard some footsteps advancing.

'The insurance company will take care of this mess.' I turned and saw Chairman come to me with three armed female bodyguards. He had a way of making an entrance.

'I hope you don't mind late-night visitors Mr. Chairman!' 'No not at all. In fact I had sent Miss. Monica. But it seems she is an incompetent escort.'

'For the record, she did her job well. Take that as a positive appraisal. But you didn't anticipate your client to be more than a naïve author. So I would say the person who is incompetent, is you!'

The bodyguards raised their guns immediately after my remark. He looked at me and without changing his expression, said, 'Is that the way to treat your guest, girls? Lower your guns please.' They obeyed. 'What would you like to have, Mr. Morgan? I heard that you're quite a drinker!'

'People tend to make that mistake quite often, Mr. Chairman. They give you wrong information. On the contrary, I detest alcohol. I am only a…'

'A coffee connoisseur. I am aware. I learnt that the first time we met!'

'Then you may know another thing about me!' He wasn't anticipating this, clearly. 'I know who you truly are,' after a brief pause I said, 'Mr. Holmes.'

He didn't react. 'When I first heard that you were working on a thriller, I didn't expect to be made the villain. You pique my interest with your assumption.'

'I am honored.'

'Leave us now,' he instructed his bodyguards. They left immediately. 'What do you want?' He turned serious now.

'Let's sit and talk, I am a little tired!' I sat, but he didn't. 'Looks like you're not in a mood. To be honest, even I am not.' I got up and started walking around the room. 'When you disappointed your step-son, you had a firestorm of hostility coming from him. I happen to know that he despises you.' He eyed me. His look clearly reflected that he was ruminating over the possibility of my knowing everything.

'Then you had your identity changed so that nobody would even smell a rat.' He looked unconcerned till yet. 'Believe me, I know more about the seven lockets than you can ever imagine.' My discovery rubbed against his pride so hard that he lost composure. The instant turn of confident expressions into weary one made it evident to me. He would be thinking that the game was in his hand and now I had him in mine.

I continued, 'We both have committed seven sins and we know clearly that we're heading directly to hell. And we don't want that.' I let him show some fear through his eyes and went on, 'You spent a fortune to identify the key bearers. You wanted to have them so that you could atone for your sins. Changing identity didn't stop you from committing further crimes. Under the guise of the university, you continue your illegal businesses. But you don't have all the keys do you?'

I could sense apprehension brewing in him and I went on, 'I have a few with me. Here's one,' I took out the emerald locket with the initial M. His eyes widened at seeing it. 'All that's left with you is to convince your step-son to hand over the final key to you.' He didn't like hearing this one bit. 'I know that he possesses the final locket.'

There was silence in the room for some time and then I finished my monologue, 'We both have limited time.'

After a brief pause he went back to his calm state and said, 'Sounds to me like we have a common interest.'

'I will be waiting for you at Victoria's Garden. Be there before midnight.'

Although he understood my proposal, he was hesitant following my instruction. Considering that he had no choice, he said, 'You should know that I am old now. My protection team will not allow me to go anywhere alone.'

I was counting on this reply. I was aware that he had spent his life trying to keep his crimes hidden. Now, he was keeping himself hidden in his fortress. If he comes outside, he will have to face nameless.

'When did I say that you have to come alone?' He was a bit shocked at hearing this. 'You need time to think. But you should know that time is a luxury neither of us has. We just have one more day. If one of us can't have all the keys, then both of us will enjoy the same fate- the road straight to hell.' I turned and was exiting.

'Wait! I will be there by midnight.' That came faster than I had anticipated.

I stopped but didn't turn and then left the building. The same driver took me outside. Upon getting down, the driver whispered, 'The job's done sir.' I smiled, got into my car and drove away.

# Chapter 23

I reached Victoria's Garden at eleven thirty. It was dark as expected. Marshal and Kathryn were waiting for me at the gate.

Kathryn rushed to me, 'Are you okay?'

'Yeah, I amazed myself back there. He will fall right into our trap!'

'Where's the trap?' asked Marshal as he was puzzled. 'That's a wrong question. You should ask, 'Who's the trap?''

'Oh don't tell me that he's…' Marshal became a little anxious.

'He will come here to exact vengeance against his father.'

'What makes you so sure that Holmes will come here?' asked Kathryn.

'He will come for sure. He has no other option. He lost hope of survival and gave up on the lockets. I just gave him his last chance. He will come because he doesn't want hell!'

'I found this in Monica's car,' Marshal handed me a gun. I took it. 'I have mine. I think we'll need it with Holmes's men and our beloved assassin coming here any minute.'

'Holmes will take him. Kathryn, I want you to be safe. Go take the car and go back home. This is one fight I will have to fight on my own!' I placed the key in her hand.

'I am coming with you,' said Marshal.

'I need your help, Marshal. Without you I couldn't have made it this far. You had an important part to play. But now I need you to take care of her.'

'Why can't I come,' Marshal pitched.

'Because I must fight this battle alone. It is mine and mine alone. Now please go.'

Kathryn hugged me. 'Will I see you again?'

'Make sure the coffee's ready in the morning!' I kissed her. 'Go now!' I said and went inside to take my position.

Kathryn watched me walk and then Marshal called me. 'Hey!' I turned and he approached. 'Aren't you forgetting something?'

It dawned on me. 'Yeah, I almost forgot. Do you have Saturn's blue sapphire locket with you?'

'Yes I do. Here!' he took it out of his pocket. I wore it. He extended his hand. I shook it. 'I will wait for you, my friend.'

'Take care of her. I will meet you soon.' I turned and walked on. After many steps, I heard my car's engine start and the noise went away with the car. 'Take care Kathryn.

I hope everything happens like it should.' I stood at the building, watching it closely. 'So this is where it all ends.'

*****

The sound of a car entering the garden was heard. The gate burst open. I saw the old model BMW entering. The driver drove recklessly till it came to a halt near me. The door opened and Holmes emerged.

'You took some time coming here. It wasn't a long way from your place,' I said.

Holmes was furious. 'You! You did that to my tires!' 'How does it feel to not have time and to be late for your last chance?'

He contained his anger. 'Well I am here. Where are my lockets?'

'Your lockets?' I smirked. 'I think I locked them inside this building. Do you care to open it for me?'

He took a gun out of his coat and pointed it at me. I ducked as he began shooting. The lock at the huge entrance door to the building opened with the bullets. I looked back and then back at him. 'I am old but I still know how to shoot.'

'And you also know that the lockets have to be passed on willingly. You can't force me to give them to you!' My smile clearly irritated him. 'I am going inside. I hope you can walk.' I began walking and he followed. I entered the huge hall which was dark. Limited moonlight entered and illuminated the place enough for us to see where we were walking. I saw rows of chairs stretching from the entrance to the end of the hall. It looked like a church.

'Morgan, I am through with your games. Now tell me where my lockets are!' I turned around and let myself see the desperation on his face in the dim moonlight. 'Where are they?' he shouted, coughing.

'I am wearing two of them. I bet you have three. The ones you got from Jason, Victoria and your own piece.'

'Where is the red coral?' he asked after recovering from his coughing.

'You're asking the wrong guy!' His eyes went past me and grew wide with fear. Nameless emerged from the corner shadow of the hall.

'Are you looking for this father?' he said as he advanced and showed his locket from his neck.

'How are you here?' Holmes looked like he had a heart attack. He was thrown back at one of the seats. I sidestepped to let the man see his creation in flesh and blood. Nameless stopped at a distance from us. 'Wondering how I am young, alive and here? Keep wondering, father, because I am here to bring hell to you.' I took another step behind. Nameless said, 'You're coming after him!' His words were directed at me.

'Wait! Before you do something, I want to know where the locket of Michael Welsh is!' I turned to Holmes. 'I understand that Victoria must have given her diamond locket to you and you must have convinced Jason, too, to give yellow sapphire locket to you. But Michael was selfish. He would die before he would give anything to you.'

'Shut up!' shouted nameless. 'I don't care about your lockets. You both are going to die now!'

I didn't look at him. My focus was on Holmes whose focus was on his son. 'Tell me Holmes, where is it?'

His face was struck by the sight of step-son. His lips began to move. 'He hid it in a treasure chest. My men could not find it.'

It struck me like a lightning bolt. The treasure chest that I had found near the railway tracks was actually kept there by Michael Welsh. I had imagined it to contain secrets of Holmes' businesses. How had I not thought about that?

All of a sudden, Holmes started to laugh out loud. His laugh echoed inside the hall. Neither nameless nor I could understand his state of mind. Soon, he gave his laughter a rest and turned to me. 'I don't need Michael to give me his locket!' He put his hand into his shirt and took out a glittering chain. 'I am the kingpin and I take what I want.' I was shocked to see it in his possession. 'How did you…?' He had me locked in his hand with the pearl locket. 'You didn't think I would come here unprepared, did you?' He turned to nameless. 'You thought you would bring hell on me! You are forgetting something, Matt Holmes!' his step- son's forehead was filled with lines as he tensed up. 'I am your father. Let me show you what hell is.'

The sound of a car increased. Lights were turned on inside the hall. Things grew visible. Before I could prepare, an SUV crashed into the door and rammed it inwards. The door fell on the first few rows, throwing me to the side.

Holmes took cover behind the chairs. Nameless began shooting at the car. After a couple of shots, there were shots that came in nameless' direction from inside the car. He dived for cover. A man stepped out of the damaged SUV and began shooting at me and nameless. I covered myself.

'I want them alive, Castiel! I will skin them myself!' Holmes instructed his assassin.

'God, I can't believe it. That's how he got Michael's locket. Castiel sold himself for money!' I thought. The chips of the marble floor and shards of the wooden seats came off and fell around me. I started crawling to the end of the row, away from the firing. My hands and legs swiftly moved. I intended to go beyond the wall where the initials of the planets were glowing in the presence of all seven lockets. Holmes got up in position and then with Castiel, he started shooting recklessly at nameless. Nameless took cover behind a pillar with an evasive manoeuver. Noticing his clip-end empty, he threw the gun away. Castiel, after having seen the gun being thrown away advanced in caution. He stopped firing and loaded his Beretta.

'What are you doing, you fool? Don't give him time to…' Before Holmes could finish, nameless began firing a machine gun. Amidst the violence, I crawled past the hall. Realizing that I was near the symbols, I took out the emerald locket and placed it on symbol M, which was glowing green. It worked. I got inside the chamber of the planets. Inside the hall, nameless emptied his machine gun and reloaded it. Seeing the opportunity, Holmes got up and yelled, 'Give me cover fire and take care of this jerk!' Castiel didn't stop shooting at nameless' pillar till Holmes went past the wall. Nameless returned fire without looking at Castiel and managed to only hit the chairs and the floor.

Holmes used his pearl locket and placed it on letter M, which shone white. When he got inside the chamber, he didn't see me. I hid behind Saturn. He advanced quickly, thinking I didn't have a weapon with me. From my cover, I took out my gun and shot at Holmes. The gun didn't work. I realized that maybe this chamber was magical and violence was forbidden. I came out from under my cover. Holmes saw me and aimed at my leg. The gun didn't work. He took a quick look at it and cursed, 'Damn it!'

Back in the hall, after hundreds of misfires, the sound of mad laughter was heard. It came from nameless. Castiel took precautions and slowly tried to position himself to the left of the pillar. Just after the laughter stopped, nameless announced, 'You thought that you could match me, you insect!' Castiel fired two bullets at the pillar. It was thin, but strong enough to block shots.

Castiel replied, 'I will have the last laugh when you'll be under my feet.'

'You can match my bullets. I give you that. Try matching this!' Three pins fell on the floor. It echoed a little. Castiel looked up. Three grenades fell around him. He turned and attempted a quick dash but the blast took him in its grasp. Nameless ran behind the great wall. As fire was about to wrap him, he entered the chamber.

Seeing him enter, Holmes realized it was the end for him. Since he couldn't use guns inside, and couldn't fight, his game and life were over. Nameless advanced toward Holmes. The latter withdrew in fear. He saw me near Saturn and said, 'First, I will snap your neck, father. And then you're next!'

Holmes fell on the ground that looked like an endless space of the galaxy. He crawled toward the Sun when nameless almost got to him. 'Get up!' he said.

Holmes was scared and was slow to get up. 'Say your prayers!' Before he took a step ahead I shouted, 'Stop!' He smirked as his gaze reached me. 'Who's going to stop me? You?'

'No,' I replied. 'But this will!' I touched Saturn's rings and just like the last time, all the planets came into motion.

'Huh! What is this?' He looked around at the planets. His eyes fell on Saturn while I ducked. It was a slow moving planet. Others were relatively faster. I stayed in position till one rotation ended, when he said, 'That's going to stop me?' Holmes looked at the planets first and then his eyes went after nameless and widened.

I looked less than an inch above and whispered, 'No, but that will.'

Nameless saw Holmes' eyes. He half-turned, and the fastest moving one, Moon, hit him directly. The force was immense. It sent him flying away and he fell. The Moon took Holmes along, too. He was thrown hard and I knew that he wouldn't survive the fall. I rolled away from the rotation. When I got up, I saw nameless struggling to get up. His bones were probably broken, given the struggle he displayed. Just when he planted his feet, he got another hit by Mercury, another fast moving planet. Nameless was down for good. I didn't know when the rotation would stop so I kept away, at a safe distance. I looked at Holmes first. He was certainly dead. Nameless wasn't showing signs of movement either. Ihad lost my chance in our fight. Without their consent, I would not get the remaining lockets and so, I was not able to ask the planets to forgive me for my sins. Right when I had lost all hope, a voice reached my ears. 'Giving up already?'

My senses sharpened. I saw God come into the chamber. With every step he took, the rotation slowed. When he reached the middle of the planets, they all became still. 'I blew this. Without the lockets, I don't stand a chance for atonement!' I said.

'Why did you do it, Jim?' he asked politely. His voice didn't make him sound upset.

'I couldn't risk Kathryn's and Marshal's lives. If I let nameless get away, he would have certainly harmed them.'

'I knew you were special, only you didn't realize it.' 'Special? It is all over, God. If I were special, things wouldn't end like this.'

'Tell me, Jim. What makes you think it's over?'

'Look at the two. I needed the lockets with their approval! Holmes is dead, nameless or Matt or whatever his name is, looks as good as dead. Now these lockets are useless.'

'You know that these lockets have to be passed on. What you don't know is that this rule applies in your world. This chamber you are in is in a completely different dimension. Rules that apply in your world don't apply here.'

'So?'

'So, Jim, you still stand a chance.' I didn't believe him at that moment. But when I looked at the two lying on the ground, I felt that I really did have a chance here.

# Chapter 24

I held all the seven lockets in my hand. The following moment, all of them lit up. The blue sapphire key floated and became one with Saturn. The red coral went into Mars, pearl into Moon, yellow sapphire into Jupiter, diamond into Venus, emerald into Mercury and ruby merged with the Sun. The seven planets floated just inches above the ground started changing. They took the form of the people I had come across. I had foreseen this.

The Sun became Steve Holmes, Mercury became Mark Hawk, the Moon faded and Michael Welsh appeared, Mars vaporized and Matt emerged, Venus turned into Victoria, Jupiter became Jason Smith and Saturn became Stephen Malcolm.

A voice sounded around as these deities watched over me. 'Only the one with the seven keys can receive the blessing to see us. Only you, Jim Morgan, have emerged as the one with the seven keys and the one with a good heart. We have the power to free you from your punishments.

You are the one who bears all the keys. Before you speak to us, you must answer three questions. If you have a pure heart, you will pass the test. If not, you may live the limited time that is left with you. After that, the door to hell will open for you.'

That ruled out two of them. Even if nameless and Holmes had come this far, it would break their hearts and crush their minds to know that they weren't pure enough to pass this test.

'Your first question,' the voice said, its tone sharp. 'What is that one thing that you, Jim Morgan, regret?'

I recalled the bitter things that I had done in my life that gave birth to regrets. After a full minute of pondering, I realized that I had none. This had to be a trick question. I am here to rid myself of all sins. That meant that I had to make efforts to achieve a goal. A man's goal was to serve and protect his family. Now that I had Kathryn, there was no regret from the wife's end. I found a friend in Marshal, but our friendship had begun only recently. So far, I had fulfilled my duty as a friend. But as a son, did I take care of my parents? I looked up at all the deities and announced, 'My greatest regret is that I didn't serve my parents the way I should have.'

'Is that what you truly regret?'

My head was down. I gently nodded, 'Now I do.' 'Indeed!' the voice sounded unaffected. There was a momentary pause. 'What is that one thing that you, Jim Morgan, loath the most?'

Another trick question? I suspected that there was something strange about the simple question. Flashes of my writing days started coming to me. I stood among the top shots in the writing business with money and fame. I was successful but not happy. I didn't have Kathryn with me for so long. I immediately got my answer.

'My decision to leave what mattered most to me, my family, my wife. That is what I loathe the most.'

'And do you, Jim Morgan, believe that the one you think to be God, to be God, truly?'

I looked at God. He smiled at me. The way these deities were floating before me, not paying heed to God, made me suspect that he wasn't truly God. Anyone would expect God to be supreme and above all. Given this notion, the deities did have to show reverence to this figure that stood near me. His smile stayed the same. I recollected all the time he was with me, through my ordeal. His will was primary. His existence was second to none. Everything that happened had happened because he wanted it to, in the way it did. I raised my head and spoke. 'Yes, he is God. I do not need a reason to have faith in him. I believe in him because I choose to.'

'Your heart is pure and true. You may pass and receive the privilege of facing the deities that rule this solar system and the lives of all living beings in it.' With this, the voice resonated for the last time, leaving me prepare myself for what was about to come.

Stephen came to me, still floating in air. He appeared taller than he was, the last time I saw him. He smiled as he was directly ahead of me. As I stared at him, in bafflement, I had the sensation that I was expecting this to happen somehow. 'You'd be?'

'I am Saturn, the planet of hard work, discipline, old age and misery. I have been waiting for this moment Jim!' His voice sounded like a wise old man speaking with a lot of control: not fast, not slow, just perfect. I wondered why I saw Stephen. 'We have a form that you learnt about in astronomy. We are situated in the cosmic sky but in this chamber, you activated us through our keys. We have taken the form that you understand. I took this form because you relate Stephen with the qualities that I possess.' With his reply, the intelligence bulb inside my mind blinked to life. 'Now, it is time you answer my question and let me go back to my eternal duty.'

My eyes were fixed on Saturn. 'Jim Morgan, what sin, related to my work did you commit in your previous life?'

I was confident of my answer. 'That's easy. I was Matt in my previous birth. As a child, I didn't rescue my brother who had died in a train accident. I stopped myself from doing what I could have done. The sin I committed was the Sin of Sloth. Since you, Saturn represents laziness and restriction, I believe that is the sin related to you and that's how I committed it.'

Saturn watched me for some time and without saying a word, went back to his original form as the gigantic ball with beautiful rings. God was amused. My gaze went to him and I said to myself, 'Looks like that's one less sin to deal with. I wish Saturn had responded better.'

Mars came forward in a flash. I got a jolt from his energy. He was quick and straight to the point. 'Jim Morgan, what is the sin connected with me? How did you give it life?'

I didn't want to spend time with Mars as he appeared as Matt, the man who was hell bent on killing me. I responded with promptness, 'You represent energy and anger. When they go beyond a man's control, the Sin of Wrath is committed. I took many lives with my hands because I was a victim of rage. It consumed me and…' Before I could finish Mars vanished and the dormant ball appeared in its original position. I turned to God again. His smile was still the same. 'That was quick wasn't it?' I thought. I was pumped with the answers I was offering. I believed that I was getting rid of the sins that had latched onto me.

It was time for the Moon to come forward. It was in the form of Michael Welsh. It didn't come forward, but floated in place. I didn't understand what it wanted to convey. I realized that after the previous answer, its facial expressions saddened. I wondered why. As I contemplated my progress, it called out. 'You know the question. You may answer it straight away.'

I was eager to pay my debt. I didn't waste time answering, 'Greed! You represent emotions. The one sin that overwhelms every other emotion is greed. It makes man emotionless more than any other sin does. As nameless, I mean Matt Holmes, I was greedy. Those papers I saw at the place where I murdered Captain Nash and did that horrible thing with Victoria, were dedicated only to Victoria. Right from the beginning, I wanted Holmes's throne and entire property. That was my sin.'

Moon's brows furrowed. Its eyes misted over and it vanished with a cloud of vapor around it. 'Am I not right?' I asked and didn't receive any response. The Moon was back to its dormant form.

I expected the Sun to ask me next, but Mercury emerged. Mark Hawk, the human form of Mercury was the only planetary deity that stood next to me. 'So Jim, what do you think I signify?' It was friendly, unlike any of the other deities. 'Definitely intelligence and communication. You signify that.'

'I guess this answers my next question.'

'Yes it does. I was envious of my elder brother who was perfect when I was a kid. My father liked him more than he liked me. I was envious of my sister, Victoria, who got everything and I didn't. I even drugged her and made Holmes think she was a drunkard. Because of my envy, I crippled my intelligence and broke all communications with my family. That's my sin.' Mercury laughed. I guess it had some of humor. I joined with a fake laugh. 'Good Luck Jim Morgan, for other questions.' I looked to my right. Another deity took its natural form.

'Many have come and most have failed!' a sermonic voice came from another planet. Jason Smith appeared from Jupiter with an air of calmness. He looked directly at me as he descended. 'Most people are not able to sense what I am asking as they focus on the words while missing the depth of the question. Do you have the wisdom to answer my question correctly, Jim Morgan?'

'I will try.'

'In order to fully understand my question, you must become a student and let me become your teacher. When you become the student, you must give your all to me to advance from intelligence to wisdom.'

I shrugged and replied, 'I will try.' 'What is life?'

In my extensive research I had done for my novel, I had never touched a philosophical tangent. I had never received knowledge or learnt about life under a bona fide spiritual master. So, I didn't know the answer. Instead of playing with words and speculating, I gave a firm answer with a little disappointment. 'I do not know what life is.' His expressions remained unchanged, as if he was expecting me to speak further, in anticipation of the correct reply. I continued, 'I do not know what life is, I wish I had someone in my life who could tell me that. Will you teach me please?'

Jason, the planet Jupiter, smiled. 'You are an enlightened soul, Jim Morgan. Not every question is to be answered in speculation. May you enlighten people around you! I will share my wisdom with you after you have pleased all the planets and have cleansed yourself of your sins.' He gave me optimism with his presence and words of wisdom.

'Now is the time for me to ask you the question, answering which will rid you of one sin. What sin did you commit in your previous birth?'

Noah's explanation of Jupiter's expansive qualities had given me a hint that if Jupiter symbolized expansion, fat or gluttony was the sin related to him. Nameless never drank or smoked, as faras Iknew. Iwas thinkingofsomethingthat multiplied exponentially, something that I, as nameless, went on consuming. My mind drifted to something more meaningful than just body fat or consumption of alcohol.

'I believe that as nameless, I mean, Matt, I went on consuming revenge. I became vengeful. I hated my father who had abandoned me. As Matt, I hated Jim Morgan. I fed myself with revenge. That's what I committed! I drank myself with vengeance!'

'You are wise, but you are a fool. You are both correct and incorrect!' With the statement he immersed into the giant ball of Jupiter and became inactive.

'Wait! Have I answered it correctly?' he was gone in an instant as I tried to reason with him. Wise but a fool, both correct and incorrect! What did he mean by that? My head started spinning.

God spoke to me, his expressions normal. 'You answered the question correctly. But you still don't know what your sin is.'

'If I answered correctly, that would mean that I know what my sin is!'

He smiled and said, 'Someone has a question for you, Jim.'

I turned and saw Venus floating before me. I felt ashamed. Looking at her reminded me of Victoria and the horrible incident. Answering her was critical for me to rid myself of the sin of Lust. Even then, my feelings didn't diminish the majesty and unparalleled beauty of Venus, the Goddess of beauty, love, romance and relationships. She looked at me as I stood in grief and astonishment. I didn't want to face her for long, for it would kill me from within. I had to answer her and move onto the next planet quickly.

She spoke, 'It seems that my appearance bothers you a lot!' I didn't need to nod to affirm. 'You respect women. As a token of appreciation, I will reveal something to you before you answer my question!' I didn't expect her to say this. 'Kathryn, if ever she conceives, will give birth to a girl. This child will have the best qualities that I will offer to her as a gift.' I didn't know what to say. I was confused by Jupiter's response and God's answer. I was surprised at Venus' blessing to me. There were so many emotions running in me, that I felt an ache in my head.

'What sin did you commit, Jim Morgan, that is related to me?'

'The sin of Lust against Victoria Holmes!' I looked away and replied. I couldn't face her.

Venus was still looking at me. I struggled to meet her eyes. When I managed to, she said, 'Oh Jim! I wish you had found out the truth. I'm afraid what you said is true in the mentioned sense but not true to you.'

'Huh? I don't understand!' She closed her eyes and went back to her dormant state. I was clueless about what was happening.

Finally, the Sun, the ruler of all planets, emerged. There stood Steve Holmes, a person I disliked. 'Can you feel my warmth, child?'

I was still puzzled. I didn't know what to say. 'Was I answering correctly or not?' This question was continuously bothering me.

'Listen to my question and answer well. What is the sin that is connected to me?'

'I know the answer but will it be right? I don't know, I have to try!' I said to myself. I met his eyes and said, 'Pride. The

Sun is the king and the ruler. He should not lose himself to pride. I did that. As an assassin in my previous birth, I had great pride in my abilities: so much pride, that I became blind to reality. That was my sin and that led to my downfall!'

'You are a fool, Jim Morgan!' The Sun's tone was penetrating. 'You received an opportunity and you wasted it. I pity you.' His words pierced my heart.

'What? Please, I have answered all the questions correctly! What is it that I got wrong?'

'Fool! Your imagination has let you to think wrong, believe wrong. Before I go, I will tell you the greatest mistake you made here. You made a mistake of thinking yourself to be nameless.'

'What?' I fell on my knees. My eyes stayed with the Sun's eyes. 'It can't be!' My arms stretched forward and went numb. All the planets were dormant in front of me. They were gone and so were the keys. The revelation caused me a great deal of sadness. The harsh reality of not uncovering my true past life identity gripped me. I pictured all the facts I had gathered and connected them. Where had I gone wrong? I had to have been nameless in my previous birth. Only he had committed all the sins. The Sun's words had me in deep confusion. I saw no one else in my past except for nameless, who could have done horrible things.

'Murder is the outcome of a strong misdirected sentiment!' God's voice bellowed in my ears. 'Our decisions can lead someone in the wrong direction. It is not the victim who committed the sin, but you who made someone become a victim. And so, crimes committed by the victim are generated by a misdirected sentiment created by you. Therefore, you are the sinner, the originator of the sins.'

I quickly outlined what I had thought of previously. 'The murders, Victoria's molestation, the killing spree, all these things point out to him and him only!'

God placed his hand on my head. 'You still cannot look beyond it, can you? Let me show you.'

My eyes looked up at God. A voice from my past that was buried deep inside my subconscious mind had come to life. The childlike voice was vaguely familiar.

'Do you hear that?' My expressions confirmed that I did. The surroundings changed into another place. The view of the railway tracks I had seen earlier with Marshal appeared. Two shadows belonging to children moved ahead of me, across the tracks. Then, the view became clear. It was nameless and his older brother. They moved into the light when they were going to unearth the mystery box that belonged to Holmes, their father. I got the feeling that I now knew who I was in my previous birth, but my intelligence wasn't gathering facts to support my feelings. It couldn't be!

'As the older brother, you should have stopped him from crossing a line. Had you stopped him then, he wouldn't become nameless as you know him now!' I turned to nameless, who lay unconscious on the floor, his chest alive as he was breathing very lightly.

'You were not nameless. You were his older brother, whose ignorance created a killer within!'

# Chapter 25

I was in tears. I had it all wrong. My head was in my hands and I didn't know how to react. Should I be angry or frustrated or sad? 'It is all over now.' I wiped my tears and soaked the rest with my hand and shirt. 'It is all over now. I am sorry!' I said to God.

'If you think it is over, then you're right!' he replied, still standing by my side.

'How does it matter what I think?'

'It matters, son!' For the first time since he met me, he had called me son. I wanted to thank him for all that he had done for me. I wanted to tell him how grateful I was to him for giving me life, happiness and opportunities. I felt terrible at having disappointed him. 'You can release some of the weight from your chest.'

'This weight will stay here forever. It won't leave me.'

'I am not talking in an emotional sense, Jim. I mean it, literally.' I frowned. Release some weight? I put my hand over my shirt, under my jacket. I felt something plain and hard. It was the diary in which I had penned my seventh novel. I opened my shirt's buttons and brought it out. Turning the pages and seeing the ink on the paper I whispered, 'I thought you had given me the power to make everything I write here become a reality. I was such a fool!'

'You are a fool to think that I didn't give you that power!'
'You are just saying it to make me feel better, aren't you?'

'So far, everything you have written here has come true! You wrote about the Chairman being Holmes, about Matt being his discarded step-son. You also wrote about how you'll get inside his mansion and come out alive with him in your palm. Not to mention you wrote that Marshal will knock down Monica exactly after sixty seconds!' He was right. I did write all of this. 'Whatever you wrote there has come true, except…'

I looked at him and said, 'Castiel's entrance!' God didn't need to smile this time. I got the feeling that he was opening a closed door for me. 'Do you want to tell me something God? Can I still do something?'

'You have the answer in you palm.'

I looked at the copy. 'If I created my seventh book, that is where the seventh portal lies. The seventh portal is…' I flipped the pages and came to the one where Castiel made his killer entry.

The chamber turned white. I felt that I was going into the past again. 'Where am I going this time, God?'

'This time, you can decide.'

I can't change the past because it will change the future. My biggest mistake was not showing my younger brother Matt, humanity. I know what I must do.

I decided to come to the immediate past. I lay on the floor, the rotation of the planets was still happening. Holmes was dead and Matt was struggling to get up. I got up immediately and saw that he had almost planted his feet and Mercury was facing him from behind. I made a quick dash at him. In my three seconds of sprinting, I made up my mind to save him. In the third second, I pushed him away from the oncoming planet but made way to get into a direct collision with Mercury. I was ready for my end. Just an inch before I made contact with Mercury, God's voice resonated, 'Stop!'

Everything froze. I was in mid-air, just an inch away from Mercury. The rotation of the planets stopped. Every planet became still. Matt was almost flat on the ground but his eyes had captured the moment I threw myself at Mercury to save him. I guess I had shown him some humanity. I saw from the corner of the eye, God was coming toward me. He held my hand and brought me in motion. I was pulled away from Mercury. After a snap of God's fingers, everything came into motion. I walked away from the rotation and pulled Matt with me. He groaned in pain.

'Why? Why'd you do it?' he asked. I put him down and calmed my breath before I replied to him.

'I did it because I am your older brother. Matt, I did it because I am your older brother.' The look in his eyes changed.

Looking at him, I felt that he had been waiting for a long time for something like this to come from his brother. I felt that in that moment, I had brought emotions in him. A moment later, just as the color of his eyes changed, the color of the surroundings changed too. A sharp light forced me to close my eyes. I put my hands over my eyes and as the blinding light disappeared, I opened my eyes to find myself in my current time.

Nameless, my younger brother from my past life was alive. I had rescued my brother from the killer. Holmes was dead. I got up and went to Matt. I extended a hand to him. This was the first time in his life somebody lent him a hand. He didn't know how to react. So I tried to help him with words.

'It's okay. I'm here with you!'

He looked up at me and after a brief moment, he extended his hand. Shockingly, his hand went through mine. I looked at his hand. It was disappearing. Then, I looked at him. He was also disappearing. Before he faded completely, I heard, 'Thank you, elder brother!' He vanished right before my eyes. I stood in place, trying to understand what had just happened.

'He went back to his timeline!' God said from behind. That caught me by surprise. 'I am impressed, Jim. Out of so many possibilities I saw, you decided to make the ultimate sacrifice.' I didn't say anything. I wanted him to speak. 'You could have decided to go to immediate past, take all the keys, answer all questions of the planets correctly and save yourself from sins. On the contrary, you decided to show him humanity and save his life. Even though there was no certainty of a change in his heart, you took the chance and saved the life of a killer.'

'I didn't save a killer, God. I saved a brother from a killer.'

'I told you that you are special!'

'But I am still going to hell.' I paused. 'A life that will only give me hell.'

'You are forgetting something.' 'What?'

'There's one more portal you can use.' 'What portal? I exhausted all.'

'No, you didn't. You used four. Matt took you to the past when he tortured you, using your portal. You still have one left with you.'

'The Mute Witness. But I don't have a copy with me.' 'You have God with you. I can at least do this for you!'

he pulled out the novel from behind him. 'Take it.'

'What do I do with it?'

'Open page 300 and change your world.'

'I can't do that! It's wrong!' He held my hand and turned the palm upwards. He took his index fingers and started to move it above the lines of my palm. 'Before I go, I will tell you that in life, some things must change while some things must remain the same. Change what you must!' He removed his hand from above my palm. Some lines of my hand had changed and some remained the same.

'What do I have to do?' He kept taking steps backwards. His body was disappearing slowly. 'You would know, Jim, you would know what to do!' He disappeared. His last gift to me was this book and the last portal it had. I opened page 300 and in a second, found myself on the same railway tracks where the boys were going to open the chest. I looked around. The boys had not come here yet.

'If I save myself from getting killed, I will never be born.

But if that's the will of God, so be it!'

After a few minutes, the two boys appeared at the platform.

'I don't see how this is going to be fun. We are supposed to go to school today. Dad will be really angry with us,' Matt's elder brother Damien said to him.

'Don't worry about dad. He never scolds me,' replied Matt.

'But he scolds me and you know that.'

'I said don't worry okay, I'll take care of dad.'

'You always say that and each time it turns out to be an empty promise.'

'This time, I swear that dad won't say anything to you. Now you trust me!' The boy didn't say anything and turned around. In that position he said, 'I will trust you if you swear one more thing.' He turned, 'If we find the treasure, we split it in half.' The other boy seemed reluctant as he made an expression conveying unacceptability. 'Well, okay. What's yours is mine and...'

'...and what's yours in mine too,' the other boy finished. 'But where did you learn the secret of this treasure?'

'Oh! I overheard dad talking to one of his bodyguards. He said, 'I hope my items are well hidden near the signal on the eighth track. Nobody must come to know about it.'

'Dad will kill us if he finds out that we went near his treasure.'

'Don't chicken out now, brother. Come on, I'm going there. It will be fun.'

'I don't like the idea,' Matt grabbed his hand and pulled him to a signal that was not far from the track they were standing at. When they got near the signal, they saw that the Earth was dug up, and there was no treasure.

'Oh bummer, man! Somebody got here first and took it!' Matt said, agitated.

Damien went on thinking and immediately grabbed Matt's hand and said, 'I am your elder brother. If you don't listen to me the next time, I will tell dad!' With that, he pulled Matt away forcibly. I stood away from the two. I saw myself in my past, taking Matt in a positive direction. With a smile on my face, I waited for the boys to disappear and then took the chest back to where it was previously hidden. As I put it down and almost began to put the Earth back over it, a wind started to blow the red sand. My eyes got some sand in them and it forced my eyes to close. I shut them. Feeling that sand was everywhere like it was a sandstorm, I felt dizzy. With my eyes, my senses also shut down.

I woke up slowly. My head was on the table. The fog over my eyes blurred my vision though the book was just inches away from my nose. I lifted myself onto the chair and rubbed my eyes to rid them of obscurity. I was alone in my study. 'How did I get back here?' It was 6:30 AM and I felt that the morning was extremely familiar. How in the world was I alive? My surprise took me back to the table. My seventh novel, Sins of Time, was on the table with a mug of light coffee by it. Everything was unbelievably normal. I got up, but as I turned around, my legs didn't support the weight of my body and I fell to my knees and hands. I tried to remember everything. God, sins, planets, my past life visits. 'Was it a dream?'

Suddenly, I saw Noah bang the door open and come rushing inside, 'Jim you can't keep missing deadlines like this. I can't stall the publisher forever. If this keeps up, your writing days will be history.'

I was shocked to hear the words that she had said the day everything began. 'What happened to you, Jim?' she pulled me to my feet. They were still shivering. My voice lowered to almost a whisper as I told myself, 'Back in time?' I hugged her tight. I was glad that at least she was in my life.

'Ah! Jim, is that you?' I pulled back. 'They've listed you as the most intriguing yet mysterious author of the current generation!'

'You've arranged a session at the Prescott University and want me to finalize the schedule for the afternoon. Right?' I asked. She was flabbergasted.

'How do you know?'

'I just know,' I smiled. 'By the way who's heading the university?'

'Oh! Victoria and Matt Holmes!' Her answer was pleasant news to me. 'Why'd you ask?'

'Nothing specific, just wanted to know the details.' I turned a little sad knowing that Kathryn was still in Los Angeles and that we were separated. I would not have Marshal in my life, either.

'Jim, are you awake?' a voice sounded from the door behind. It opened and in came my life. I couldn't believe that Kathryn had entered. 'My God, look at him Noah. He is finally working on his book!'

Noah turned to Kathryn. I had my mouth open, 'You know I am jealous of you. You're so lucky! He gives you all the time in the world. I wish I had a husband like Jim who also dedicated time to me and my shelter for special kids.'

'You also wished that he wrote and didn't miss the deadline. Hey, is that Sins of Time? I think he's finished it!' She went past me and my eyes were still glued to her. She held the copy in her hand. 'Wow, this is going to break previous records.'

I immediately caught her hand and took the book away from it, placing it on the table. 'Nothing will ever be as important as you are Kathryn,' I hugged her tight and kissed her.

'Jim, what are you doing? Noah's watching!' Her words didn't stop me. Noah turned to leave. 'I will postpone the meeting for you, Jim. I see you are busy. By the way, Jonathan's expecting the copy today so can start editing.'

I turned my back to her. She left the room. Jonathan was alive! I didn't expect things to be this good in this life.

Kathryn pulled me back to her. 'Why did you stop?' We continued loving each other. After our moment, she said, 'There's a guy in LA… What's his name?' she looked down and then back at me. 'Marshal! Yes! That's his name. He has been mailing for a long time now. Seems to me like he's a huge fan!' I looked above her head. 'Take out time to respond to his mail, he will feel nice.'

'Yes, I will.'

'Okay, I have to change. Let me know your program!'

She left me in the room. The happiness was overwhelming. Was all this really happening? I wished it was not a dream. I held my seventh novel in hand. 'Sins of Time,' I read the title. 'I just hope this is all real.'

'It is real if you believe in it!' I turned around. The white sofa had appeared in my room again. 'I was free for a while and thought I would pay you a visit. It's been a long time since I had a nice conversation with someone. Care to join me?'

It was a beautiful morning and the weather was clear. I took my coffee and offered him some. That morning, I had the best coffee of my life.

*****